Them That Go

Becky Mushko

Them That Go is a work of fiction. Characters, names, locations, and events are products of the author's imagination or (in the case of events inspired by a century-old family mystery, the details of which are lost to history) are used fictitiously. While some real places are mentioned, none of the events in the book actually occured in those places. Although a few characters' names were inspired by ancestral names, none of the characters are like their namesakes. Any resemblance to living persons or actual events is purely coincidental.

ISBN: 1523750251
ISBN-13: 978-1523750252

Other books by Becky Mushko:

Ferradiddledumday
Stuck
Patches on the Same Quilt
Miracle of the Concrete Jesus & Other Stories

Kindle E-books only:

The Best 'Un Yet
Over Coffee
Little Meg Reddingoode
Rest in Peace

CONTENTS

Introduction   i

1   Who Am I?   1

2   Early October 1972   5

3   Mid-October   22

4   Decisions   34

5   The Dance   43

6   Discovery   66

7   Halloween, Samhain, & Ghosts   87

8   Setting It Right   98

9   Perchance to Dream   106

10   To Thine Own Self Be True   117

11   Winter Tales   135

12   The Truth Will Out   145

13   Rewards   160

14   Changes   168

15   Summer Days   188

16   Moving On   197

17   Now   203

Acknowledgements   207

"There's always been them that go and them that stay in ever' generation."—Aint Lulie

Caldwell Genealogy

James Elexander Caldwell -------*Mariah Duff ------Jacob Caldwell
(1st husband killed at Cold Harbor)   (2nd husband; 3rd cousin of James)

Duffield   (half-siblings)   Pearl, Cora (married a Byrne)

*Lulie, James , 2 others   (1st half-cousins)   Matthew, Jacob

                Amos----------------(2nd half-cousins)----------------Mary

                        *Annie

INTRODUCTION

For as long as I can remember, I've liked old-timey stories, all things rural, Appalachian lit, fairy tales, folktales, ghost stories, and Shakespeare. A few years ago, I became interested in genealogy and was fascinated how branches of my family moved from one place to another. Some stayed and put down roots; others left for better opportunities. Writing *Them That Go* gave me an opportunity to use these interests.

CHAPTER 1: WHO AM I?

In 1972, I didn't know what a *stereotype* was. As far as I can recollect, nobody in our holler ever used the word. But back then, that's what all the Bosworth County High School kids were. At least the ones I knew.

Stereotypes.

The flower child was Sarenda Lovejoy, probably the only female friend I had at school; she didn't care what the other kids thought. I envied her freedom.

The nerd—the weirdo—was Bert McKeller, another outcast who sat at the same lunch table with Sarenda and me. If computers had existed then, the other kids would have admired him for his knowledge and sought his advice. Instead, they made fun of him.

The rich boy was Alvin Bosworth, whose ancestors had founded the county. His daddy owned the mill, ran the bank, and controlled a good bit of the power in the county. Alvin had his own sports car and took college prep classes.

The jock was Lucas Lawson. Of course he was Bosworth County High's quarterback, and of course he dated the head cheerleader. His heart-melting smile could become a sneer in a heartbeat. His arrogance—his sense of entitlement—was typical of the mountain boys whose daddies had lost their family land and now lived in trailer parks—another cliché. Lucas's good looks, his athletic ability, and his souped-up old truck assured his place at the top of high school hierarchy. Since he was poor, he rode the school bus to save gas money.

The head cheerleader was Loniss Hathaway. She was pretty and her family was well-off, but she wasn't from around here. When Loniss was a sophomore, her daddy had been transferred from out of state to run the mill. Loniss was willing to settle for being Lucas's girlfriend until she went to college and met someone better. But Lucas didn't know that. Why should he? Loniss always wore the latest styles before anyone else did. If smartphones had existed in 1972, Loniss would have been the first to have one.

The Hathaways lived in the biggest house on the hill just inside the town limits, but—even though folks looked up to them—they weren't from around here, so they'd never be fully accepted in the county. Bob Hathaway had been hired by Mr. Bosworth to run the mill, the biggest business in the county. A lot of folks depended on him for their jobs. His wife Dina was in the garden club. Actually, she *was* the garden club; she put the pots of whatever was in season in front of the post office and courthouse—daffodils and tulips in spring, geraniums and petunias in summer, mums in fall, and some sort of evergreen in winter. If Bosworth County High had had a PTA, she'd have been the president. She, of course, wanted the best for her daughter. Women like that always do.

Who was I back then? The quiet mousy one that nobody noticed. I was "The Other," a term I learned years later when I was no longer an Other. But in 1972 I didn't have a word for who I was. All I knew was that I was Annie Caldwell, I lived at the end of a holler, and I wasn't like other kids. I had what Aint Lulie—my great aunt on Daddy's side—called "the gift."

The first time I knew for sure I had the gift, I was five. Mama's milk cow, Old Rhody, had come up to me in the pasture, looked me square in the face, and as good as said, "Annie Caldwell, I want you to know I'm going to lose my calf this time."

When I told Daddy what Old Rhody said, he just laughed at me. The next day, he spent over an hour pulling the calf. I stuffed my fists against my ears so I couldn't hear Rhody bawling. When he finally pulled the calf free, it was dead. He didn't laugh then.

A few months later, when all of our laying hens vanished, one of them sent a picture into my mind to tell me where they were. I told Daddy that Silas Mosby had our chickens hid in his shed. Daddy didn't believe me, but he went to look anyway and came home with our hens.

Mama, who did not have the gift for it skipped her generation and therefore she couldn't understand it, thought I was possessed of the devil. She had Elder Stoutmire from the Church of Divine Holy Light pray over me. Elder Stoutmire—the stereotypical backwoods hellfire and damnation preacher—told her it was likely just a coincidence. "The little gal prob'ly heard folks say what a chicken thief Silas was."

I did not say a word, but let him think what he wanted to think while he beseeched Jesus to drive the demons from my soul. I never again told Mama or Daddy what critters told me.

"Annie, don't waste words on them that will not listen nor understand," Aint Lulie had told me after I'd run to her cabin no sooner had Elder Stoutmire gone. "The first daughter in ever' other generation has always been blest with a gift, though some think it a curse. Been that way for generations in the Caldwells, Duffs, and once in a while in the Byrnes."

Mama had been a Byrne before she married but she had some Caldwell a generation or two back, so I likely got a double dose of the gift. Maybe more, considering the intermarriages of mostly second and third cousins from when this holler was first settled. Aint Lulie could keep track of our tangled lines from way back, but I could never keep straight who was kin to who and in how many ways. But there weren't many of our family left in our holler. What World War II didn't scatter—when boys left Bosworth County and saw a bigger world—or the lack of jobs the last few decades had driven others away, kinfolk had up and left for places where they thought the grass was greener. The ridges of Byrne Mountain were dotted with abandoned cabins that had been empty since before I was born. They hung over us like old ghosts, reminding us of who we are and where we came from. "Always been them that go and them that stay in ever' generation," Aint Lulie has said many a time.

When I started school, I never told my classmates about my gift because it would have set me apart more than I already was. I was the one that nobody played with at recess because I smelled like woodsmoke and didn't know about any TV shows and didn't even own a Barbie. I was the quiet girl who sat in the back row and never caused trouble and only spoke when the teacher asked me a direct question. Mostly, I was invisible. And that was fine, because things were less complicated that way.

"Best not to speak of your gift to them that don't know. Or don't want to know," Aint Lulie once told me.

So I didn't tell anyone. There was nothing to be gained by telling. Most kids at Bosworth County High who even knew of Aint Lulie thought she was a witch because she was gray-headed and missing a few teeth. Because she lived alone at the far end of the holler and never had electricity. Her only modern concession was a well and water pump that my brother Scott had convinced her to let him put in five years earlier because she was getting too old to walk to the spring. In her old age, though, Aint Lulie still gardened. She grew every vegetable she ate and always planted by the signs. She could douse water and cure warts.

Her gift was not like mine, though. She had been born at midnight, and it's well-known through the hills and hollers that a baby born at midnight will have the power to see and talk to ghosts. Dead folks have showed themselves to Aint Lulie—but only close to where they died. Live folks didn't trust her. She was, I suppose, a stereotypical backwoods woman in the eyes of outsiders, though few outsiders ever saw her. But I loved her. In 1972, she was my best friend in the world.

CHAPTER 2: EARLY OCTOBER 1972

From my seat at the back of the bus, I watched Loniss Hathaway disentangle herself from Lucas Lawson's arms, hop into the aisle and shake her pom-poms.

"Who's gonna win, who's gonna win, who's gonna win—hey?" she chanted.

Lucas and his teammates Larry Tiller and Kenny Ketchum hollered, "We're gonna win—hey!"

"Set down, Loniss!" Clovis Wilbur, the bus driver, said. "You know the rules." He pointed to the "no standing while bus is moving" sign near the front door.

Loniss ignored him. She gave her pom-poms another shake and wiggled her butt again.

"Ah, Clovis, give us a break!" Lucas said. "Us Bobcats got a good shot at being regional champions. Let Loniss git us all pumped up."

He winked at Larry and Kenny. They cheered, and Loniss wiggled again. She loved being the center of attention. Especially Lucas's attention. School had been in session for over a month, and already everybody regarded Loniss as the most popular senior. I guess I was the least popular, but that was fine with me.

"What we gonna do in '72?" she chanted. "What we gonna do in '72?"

A couple of her cheerleader friends—Susan Collins and Cheryl McCoy—took up the chant: "We're gonna win in '72! We're gonna win in '72!"

Clovis jerked the bus around a sharp curve and Loniss almost fell, but Lucas reached out his hand and grabbed her butt to steady her. Susan and Cheryl giggled. Even when Loniss was steady, Lucas didn't move his hand. Loniss leaned over and whispered in his ear, and whatever she said made him turn loose. Then she yelled, "Bosworth Bobcats all the way! Hey-hey-hey!"

Lucas's friends guffawed again. Clovis didn't say anything else to Loniss. He was too busy wrestling with the steering wheel as he piloted the bus up the twists and turns of Byrne Mountain Road.

"All the way!" Lucas and his buddies yelled. "All the way! Hey-hey-hey!" They elbowed each other and snickered because "all the way" had another meaning.

I scrunched down and pretended to read my science book. No use letting them see I was watching them—and that I wasn't cheering.

I already knew the Bobcats would lose the game. I knew that Lucas's cousin had bought Lucas a keg and several bottles of liquor for a victory celebration. I knew that Lucas was going to have a pre-game party Friday night. I knew that he and the rest of the team would be in no condition to play on Saturday afternoon. I knew all this because his dog, a Walker hound named Ranger, told me.

Clovis stopped the bus at the biggest house on the crest of the hill. Lucas let go of Loniss and she sashayed down the aisle. The boys hooted and whistled at her all the while she walked up her sidewalk. Clovis shot them an angry look but didn't say anything. But he didn't start the bus again until she'd walked up the three steps onto her front porch. When Kenny and Larry and Lucas got off at the trailer park a half-mile the other side of the hill, Clovis started up before they were more than a few inches away. The bus mirror almost hit Lucas. He shook his fist and yelled something, but I couldn't hear what. A few other kids got off during the next mile or two, and the rest soon after that.

I'm always the last one off. I live in one of the farthest hollers, where nobody lives who ain't blood kin to us and even those don't live all that close. They live deeper into the next holler or up the side of the next mountain, and most of them are old. They get by because they either make a little liquor or their children who didn't stay in the county send them money when they can. I'm the youngest of all of our kin left in these parts. I get by as best I can.

When Clovis finally got to my stop, he turned the bus around in the clearing where what passes for our driveway begins and opened the door for me. "See ya tomorrow, Annie."

Clovis is the only one who ever bids me good-bye. Since I'm the first one on the bus in the morning, he is also the only one who bids me good morning. No one else pays much attention to me.

I waved good-bye and started through the woods toward home. A lot of leaves had fallen in the other night's wind and they crunched under my feet. I think the woods are prettiest in early October. The golds and reds and browns have crept into the leaves, but there's still some green. Like summer is still trying to hang on for as long as it can even though the fall equinox happened over two weeks ago. But it won't be long until a hard frost, and then summer will die as it does every year. Aint Lulie has said for the last few days she can feel in her bones that we'll have a frost before mid-October.

I hardly saw the red fox until he crossed my path, he blended in so. *I mean you no harm—I am only passing through,* he told me. A few birds flew along with me and cooed, *Soon, soon we'll be leaving soon for warmer places. Soon.*

Sometimes I wish I could fly to a warmer place like the birds. Our house has been cold for over two years. The coldness came the day we found out my brother Scott was killed in Vietnam.

When a Bosworth County sheriff's car drove up one Saturday in May of '70, I was sweeping the front porch. I froze no sooner I saw it. Deputy Wiley Shortridge got out and came up the steps. "Annie, could you go get your daddy?" he said. "I got to talk to him."

At first I was afraid he was going to arrest Daddy for something. We don't see police cars in the holler unless they're after somebody—usually for making liquor or growing pot. But I ran in and got Daddy. I knew Mama would listen from behind the screen door because she'd never intrude on the business of men. I went in the yard so as not to bother Wiley and Daddy, but I kept close and took note of the German shepherd in the back seat.

Why do you stare, girl? the dog said. Have you never seen a police dog before? Why are you not afraid? One snap of my teeth and you'd be dead.

I told the dog I meant him no harm. That I only stared because he was such a beautiful dog.

I'm indeed handsome! He sat up straighter. My name is Bruno. I will not

bite you unless my master so orders. Today we bring bad news. I am sorry.
I bade Bruno good-bye and slipped around the side of the house where I wouldn't be seen but could still listen.

Wiley Shortridge handed Daddy the letter. Daddy stared at the envelope for a moment. Slowly he opened it.

"I don't have my glasses," he told Wiley. "You mind reading it to me? I reckon it's about them taxes I owe."

I didn't like standing there and hearing Daddy tell a lie. Truth is, he does not wear glasses on account of he never learned to read. If Wiley Shortridge weren't new to the county, he'd likely have known that. But he'd only been working here about four months.

Wiley took the letter and cleared his throat. "Dear Mr. and Mrs. Caldwell. We regret to inform you," he read, "that your son Scott was involved—" He cleared his throat again and continued reading, "—in a helicopter crash. We are sorry that there was no way we could recover his body."

Mama screamed, but she didn't come outside. She would never let anybody from outside the holler see her grieve. Wiley asked if Mama would be all right. Daddy said he'd take care of things. Wiley got in his car and drove off the way he'd come.

Daddy cussed out loud—something I'd never before heard him do—and pounded his fist against the porch column. I crept back to the porch. I didn't say anything.

"I reckon you heard." He held the crumpled letter in his fist.

I nodded. Then I ran off to tell Aint Lulie what the letter said and to see if she could maybe talk to Scott.

"You know I can't talk to him, Honey," she had said. "He's too far off. I cain't even tell for sure if he's dead or not."

Mama took to bed and cried for three days until the women in her prayer circle brought Elder Stoutmire to pray with her. Daddy started drinking regular.

After a while, Mama started to have hope that Scott might be still alive. "Maybe he got out somehow," she'd say. "If they couldn't find his body, maybe he escaped all that fighting and is hiding out, like he used to hide in the woods when he was little. Maybe he will somehow find his way home."

Over two years passed and not a word from Scott, but she'll still pray for hours for his safe return. Other days, she sits by the window and stares at where our road ends against the mountain and becomes a footpath so narrow you wouldn't know it is there. I would not ever tell Mama I think Scott is dead. She wouldn't listen to me if I did. She wants to believe he is only missing, so I will let her believe that. Hoping Scott is alive gives her something to do.

The three of us go through the motions of living. Mama gets up and fixes breakfast, and I get on the school bus and ride the twelve miles to Bosworth County High School. On the days he doesn't have work at the sawmill, Daddy goes to his shop and pretends to tinker with stuff he means to fix but never does. After Mama feeds the chickens and gathers the eggs, she spends the rest of the day praying and waiting for something that will likely never happen. She comes out again to feed and gather eggs in the early afternoon.

By the time I'm home, the chickens are already cooped for the night. They tell me they don't like going to bed so early. I used to feed them, but Mama said I stayed with them too much, and I ought to be the one to go check on Aint Lulie instead. I figure it's too much for Mama to walk all the way to the cabin and then have to be sociable with Aint Lulie and then do the night chores. But I like visiting Aint Lulie, and I don't mind emptying her slop jar so it's clean for the night or bringing in her stovewood and firewood or pumping water and toting it to the cabin.

At school, though, I try to make myself unnoticeable. Daddy has the dark hair of the Caldwells and Mama has the reddish-blonde of Byrnes, but my hair is halfway between—a dull brown like dried leaves that nobody pays any mind to. In every class, I sit in the far corner of the back row. I never raise my hand. On the bus, I always sit in the back and pretend to study one of my books. I don't speak unless I'm spoken to.

The other kids generally leave me alone. I overhear them talk about parties they've been to and things they've done that their mamas don't know about. They talk about clothes they bought in Bristol or Kingsport or maybe Johnson City, places I have never been. They talk about cars and what they saw on TV and songs they listened to on the radio and who they talked to on the phone. None of what they talk about is part of my world.

My world is the holler and the leaves crunching under my feet. It is the side of Byrne Mountain and its empty cabins hanging over me like a shadow. It is the porch steps that sag in the middle when I walk up them. It is the Warm Morning heater in the front room that someone—Daddy, most likely—has just put coal in and lit today for the first time this fall. It is the smell of woodsmoke from the fireplace and Mama's cookstove that will cling to me all winter and will make some of the town girls say "Phew! What stinks?" if they get too close to me. It is the one bare bulb hanging from the front room ceiling that is so dim that most of our house is in shadows. When Scott hung that bulb, he'd said we ought to have some brightness in the house. Now Scott's shadow hangs over us, too.

* * *

Every day after school, I yell "Hello!" to Mama who is usually in the kitchen if she is not upstairs looking out her window. After I change out of my school clothes, I head deeper into the holler to see how Aint Lulie is doing. When the weather is warm, she will either be sitting on her front porch or else standing in her cabin door. But she is always waiting for me. "Come in, Honey, I swear you're a sight for sore eyes," she will always say.

I always look forward to visiting her. Aint Lulie is the only one in my family who talks to me in full sentences and who is glad to see me.

When the days are long, I help her in the garden and she will give me beans or potatoes or something to take home. When the days are growing short like they are now, we sit by her fireplace after I've done her chores and she tells me old stories. Aint Lulie talks about her grandma who had the gift of second sight and about all the early people of our line who settled this holler in the late 1700s and about the ones that left and the ones who stayed here all their lives and where they are buried facing east on the ridges. I never get tired of hearing about the Caldwells and Byrnes and Duffs who came here after the Revolutionary War when there was land to be had for the asking. Aint Lulie tells me how some toted all their worldly goods—which didn't amount to much—in ox carts. A few rode horses. Most walked. But now they had land of their own, they weren't beholden to any, and that was what counted. "You got land," Aint Lulie says, "you got something."

Aint Lulie is actually my only living great aunt on both Mama's and Daddy's side of the family, but Mama and Daddy never talk much about the old days or who we're kin to. Aint Lulie generally does, and I like hearing her stories. She tells me how our family lines are so tangled that she is a distant cousin to me as well as being my great aunt twice.

"And I'm even kin to myself a couple different ways," she adds.

"You are who you are on account of who your people was, so it's best to know who you come from."

Today, Aint Lulie asked me if I can help her get in wood on Saturday, and I promised her I'd do that. "My bones tell me we gonna have us a hard frost before long. I wanna be ready." She pointed to a half-dozen folded quilts piled on her bed. "I'm trying to figger what one to put over me tonight and the rest of the winter. Mebbe you can help me decide."

I told her I'd be glad to. Of course, she invited me to have supper with her. She usually does.

"Maribelle Lewis's gal stopped by today and give me some butter, fresh milk, and eggs. Won't nothing to do but make up a fresh batch of cornbread. It's nigh about done and it's more'n I can eat. You'd be doing me a favor to eat some. And I'm fixing to fry up some of those last apples we picked."

Of course I accepted. I usually do.

The aroma of baking cornbread filled the cabin and the anticipation of it made my mouth water. Maribelle is a distant cousin on the Duff side who lives with her old maid daughter in the next holler over from us. She still keeps a milk cow and chickens, though I expect the work of keeping them up has fallen to her daughter. Aint Lulie went to school with Maribelle back when the old one-room Duff Schoolhouse still existed, but the two haven't seen each other for years since neither is able to get out much. Maribelle's "gal" is pushing sixty herself, but she comes every two or three weeks to bring supplies and a little local gossip to Aint Lulie, and Aint Lulie always sends back something or other that she's picked or canned to Maribelle. They've done this for years.

While Aint Lulie tended to her cooking, I did the night chores. She didn't need anything taken to the springhouse or fetched from it, so I first took her two empty buckets to the pump and brought back two bucketfuls of water. Next, I brought in an armload of stovewood and then an armload of fireplace logs and refilled her woodbox. Finally I emptied her slop jar in the outhouse and stopped by the pump to rinse it out before bringing it in. I couldn't imagine somebody like Loniss Hathaway fetching water or carrying wood. She likely has no idea what a slop jar is and, if she knew, she likely wouldn't touch it. But I have been doing these chores for years, and all my people before me did them too.

Although Aint Lulie's cabin has plain furnishings, her slop jar is fancy. It is decorated all over with blue flowers and looks like it ought to be used as a flower pot instead of what it is really used for. The lid has a chip in it that's been there as long as I can remember. After I replaced the slop jar in the dogtrot, I asked Aint Lulie how come she had such a fancy one.

She kept her back to me as she stirred the soup. "Oh, that'uz my Aint Pearl's doing. She loved flowers and fancy things. The summer she'uz sixteen, she got a job in the old canning factory that used to be about two'r three miles off. She saved up her money and bought herself some things from the Sears and Roebuck catalogue. One of the first things she ordered was that slop jar and its matching bowl and pitcher. Granny like to had a fit Pearl wasted her money like that." Aint Lulie ladled the soup into two bowls, spooned the fried apples onto plates, and stooped to get the cornbread from the oven.

"We oughn't to talk of slop jars while we eat," she said. "Now you set down. Ain't nothing better'n hot cornbread."

After we finished our supper and she'd put the dishes and spoons to soak in her dishpan, she motioned me to sit by the fire and I did. One by one she brought a quilt from the pile, unfolded it, and laid it over my lap. Then, sitting in her rocking chair beside me, she pointed to different pieces and told me about each one.

"This'n's made outta scraps from clothes you and Scotty wore when y'all was jist chaps. Them pink floweredy patches is from a little dress I made for you no sooner than you'uz born even though it took more'n a year for you to grow into it. All them blue ones is from a couple pair overalls Scotty wore when he'uz toddling about. He'uz bad to wear the knees outten his britches, so he went through clothes real fast." She smiled—remembering, I guess.

"It's real pretty," I said. I couldn't remember wearing a dress with flowers on it. Everything I wore now was plain. I didn't wear dresses much either, since long pants were more practical. For a long time, Mama worried about me dressing like a man—she never in her life had worn long pants and vowed she never would. Finally, though, she decided that pants were less of a sin than the short skirts some girls wore nowadays and had let me order some pants from the Sears catalogue. By her thinking, the pants I wore to school hid my legs better than a short dress would, and I could still wear a decent long dress to church.

I studied the quilt while Aint Lulie told me about the different patches. It was getting harder for me to remember Scott, too. Were his eyes light brown or medium brown? I ought to know that. I remember his hair was the same reddish-blonde as Mama's.

Aint Lulie folded up the quilt, returned it to the pile, and picked up another.

"Now this quilt was one I made for my hope chest when I was about your age. All the gals had a hope chest back in them days. All the pieces are outta goods I made my dresses from. I figgered this quilt to cover me and Sparrell Hobson on our wedding night, but that won't to be." She pursed her lips and folded the quilt back up before I could get a good look at it.

"What happened?"

"He didn't make it back from the war across the water."

I knew she meant World War I. I wanted to ask her about him but decided if she wanted me to know, she would tell me. She didn't say another word about it. She got another quilt.

"Now this'n has always been my favorite." She spread a quilt made of red and brown and gold pieces—the colors of the October woods—on my lap. "I pieced it about twenty year ago when we had us a big snow. Couldn't go nowhere, so I figgered to quilt. No sense in setting around and doing nothing. Time the snow melted, I had me something to show for it."

I ran my finger across the leaf-shaped patches around the edge and felt its softness. "Use this one," I said. I knew I'd like to see its brightness across her bed.

"Well, reckon I might do jist that." She put her other quilts away and spread the leaf-quilt over her bed. It looked even better on the bed than it had on my lap. "Ain't never been used before, so I reckon it's still new. Old saying goes if you sleep under a quilt that's new, your dream will come true."

I asked her what girls had in their hope chests besides quilts. She told me about things stitched and crocheted or embroidered. Nice things for a house. She told me about quilting bees where a bunch of friends stitched all day on a quilt while they gossiped.

"Nowadays, I reckon, gals jist go into a store and buy what they need," she said, "instead of putting all them hours into making a quilt. I don't reckon many have hope chests anymore."

I wondered what she'd done with the things in her hope chest when there was no hope left, but I thought better than to ask her. I figured if she wanted me to know, she'd have told me.

I sat by her fireplace and soaked in its warmth until well after dark. Sometimes we spoke, but mostly we sat in silence and enjoyed each other's company. At home the silence hangs cold and hard like sheets on a clothesline in winter. But the cabin's quiet wrapped us like well-worn quilts and drew us together.

Aint Lulie's cabin is a double-pen with an enclosed dogtrot between the two rooms. The part she mostly lives in was built around 1790 when Absalom Byrne, who'd seen the area a decade earlier when he was in the Revolutionary War, came over the mountains with his new wife and settled down. He'd gotten his land patent a year or two before, girded the trees so they'd die and be ready to cut and build with, and he'd picked out his cabin spot near a spring and sheltered by the mountain. He'd dragged big rocks near to where he'd build his cabin so he'd have foundation stones and chimney stones waiting. That fall he went back to Botetourt County, stockpiled some supplies, married his intended, and by early spring they had started for their new home. He and his wife Elizabeth camped in their wagon until friends and kin could raise his cabin. He had some good bottomland, so he knew he'd prosper.

Aint Lulie has been telling me this story—or similar versions of it—since I was little to set it in my mind so I'd not forget. "There was some Byrnes that stayed home and some that came here," she's told me a couple of times. "And some that left here to go west while others stayed. Same for the Caldwells and Duffs, too. In all families, I reckon, there's them that go and them that stay." But she always ends her story the same way: "The ones that stayed here was fruitful and they multiplied, and that's how come we're here right now."

The other part of the cabin was added a decade later when Absalom's family outgrew the one room and the loft. The dogtrot was added to connect the two halves. Absalom built his cabin to last, and it has. Several generations of Byrnes and Caldwells have lived and died in it. There used to be another building for a kitchen, but it was taken apart when Aint Lulie's papa surprised her mama with a cookstove when Aint Lulie was a girl. He used the logs from the old kitchen to build a barn, and he hauled its chimney stones over to the site he'd picked out to someday build a new house. His mother had warned him that it was bad luck to build a new house with the ruins of an old one.

"I recollect Papa telling Granny that the stones from the kitchen won't the ruins of a house on account nobody ever lived in the kitchen," Aint Lulie once told me. "And Granny telling him right back that she'd spent more time in the kitchen than she reckoned she'd spent in the house, and it'uz a house as far as she was concerned. Papa said he'd be dad-blamed iff'n he wasted good rocks on account of some old saying that likely won't true."

Nothing was ever wasted in the old days. "Waste not, want not," Aint Lulie often says.

The cookstove is still on the opposite side of the fireplace from where we sit and the stovepipe connects it to the chimney. Aint Lulie has banked its fire for the night. After I leave, she will bank the fire in the fireplace and go to bed. She will not let the fire go out. "Not letting a fire go out is a sign of always having everything you need," she says. She is a great believer in signs.

This room where we sit snug near the fire has all Aint Lulie needs. Besides the cookstove and fireplace, there's her bed, a chest, a pie safe, a table with two chairs, a rocking chair, a cupboard, a washstand near the back door, and rows of shelves along one wall where she keeps some of the things she's canned. Two iron skillets and some pans hang from the wall near the stove.

She keeps her clothes and her flour barrel and things she doesn't use everyday in the other room, which also has a bed and dresser. As far as I know, no one has ever slept in that bed during my lifetime. But the bed is ready should it be needed. When I once asked her why she never builds a fire in there, she replied, "It'ud be a waste of good wood with nobody in there to keep warm."

Some things from her garden—potatoes and cabbages and apples and dried herbs—are in the loft where it's cooler. If it gets too cold, she climbs the steep steps and covers them with an old quilt so they won't freeze. She keeps her slop jar in the dogtrot, for privacy I reckon. But she mainly uses it only at night or if it's too cold or rainy for her to go to the outhouse.

The room where she does most of her living has a front door and window that both face the road, which you can't see because of all the trees. In the old days, a pasture and some cleared cropland was there, but there's no longer a need for such. Scott would have cleared the woods and pastured his cows there if he'd lived, but that won't happen now.

Aint Lulie's back door faces her garden spot and the mountain, and there's a narrow path that branches on the right to the outhouse and on the left to the spring. Aint Lulie still uses the spring sometimes even though she has the pump near the house. She's not one to let go of the old ways.

"Aint Lulie, why did you live in this house when your daddy had built the house near the road?" I asked.

"Well," she began, and I knew a story was coming. "Papa built that frame house out of lumber cut from big trees up the mountain. I was about your age—maybe a year older—when it'uz finished. I remember the house-raising. All the neighbors come— folks from the other side of the mountain, and some who won't even kin." Her voice broke off, and I knew she was remembering all those folks again. "Sparrell Hobson was one of 'em. First time I ever laid eyes on him, and I'uz smitten. Said he'd like to come back and court me when I got older. A year later, he come back riding his sorrel mare over the mountain. I saw him regular—ever' two-three weeks except when the weather kept him away. I always could tell jist before he got here by the sound of his mare's hooves on the rocky ground, and I'd be waiting in the yard for him. He'd always say, 'How'd you know I'uz coming?' but I never told him how I'd listen for the mare. He asked Papa for my hand right before he had to go to the war across the water."

"World War I." I could see a mist forming in Aint Lulie's eyes.

"The last time I seen him—when he told me he was set to go— he didn't ride the mare so he kindly caught me by surprise. Now I did live in the house at that time. The room I slept in was the same room you sleep in now. But there won't room in that house for a new husband, so Sparrell and me decided we'd move into this old cabin soon as we married. That'uz all right with Papa, so it looked like everything would work out fine. But it didn't."

Aint Lulie hesitated and rocked for a spell. "He'uz on his way to town that day, and I couldn't look at him hard enough. I watched him walk down the road until he was out of sight. I ought not have done that. Watch somebody leaving 'til they're outta sight, and they'll not come back."

I knew the old saying. Mama had watched Scott until he was out of sight, too, when he kissed her good-bye and left to go in the army. She'd watched him walk down the road and then she watched the road long after she couldn't see him anymore.

"Anyway," Aint Lulie continued, "No sooner he'uz gone, I went ahead and moved into this cabin. I wanted to fix it up and have our home ready for when he got back." She pressed her lips together to hold back the words, but they spilled out anyway. "When I got word, I jist stayed here. By then, I'uz used to living by myself, and I didn't feel like being around other folks nohow. I've made do, I reckon."

"It's late," I said. "I'd better get on home." Then I added the old-timey saying that all the hill and holler folks around here say when they leave, "You better come go with me."

"Cain't," she said, giving the proper response. "You mought as well stay." She didn't look up as I went out the door and into the night's chilly air.

I did not worry about finding my way home in the night although the moon was waning. The path is well worn and the night critters mean me no harm. Even if harm somehow crept in, the critters would let me know. They generally do.

*　*　*

When I went inside, the house was as dark as the woods. Nobody was waiting up for me. I didn't expect them to be. I could hear Daddy snoring upstairs. If Mama was awake, she didn't say anything. Daddy had kept the heater lit, but the overhead light in the front room—the only electric light in the house—wasn't on. Daddy'd never waste electricity by keeping it burning for me. I groped until I found the cord and turned it on. I didn't have any homework to do. I finished most of it in school and the rest on the bus, so I got ready for bed.

I went to the kitchen, pumped some water into the sink, and washed up. Enough light shone in from the front room that I could see what I was doing. I'd already stopped by the outhouse before I came in, so that was taken care of. I usually try to go to the bathroom before I leave school, where there is soft toilet paper and a flush commode. But I always have to go at night, so I ask the spiders to leave me alone, and they do. After I finished washing, I turned off the front room light and went up the stairs to my room. I can find my way in the dark just fine.

For a long time, we had no light in the house at all. Before Scott went away, he planned to have a dairy herd. He had electricity put into the old barn and a line strung from the barn to the house. He cut the poles himself to save money. He'd already started looking at cattle to build his herd when his draft notice came. He decided to put off buying cows until he got back.

"I'll likely have money to buy the best milkers," he'd told Mama and Daddy. "but I mean to have the barn and everything waiting for me when I get home."

When we got the word, Daddy sold the milking machines and the stanchions for half what Scott paid for them. Now he uses the barn for his shop. When he's not working at the sawmill—which is most of the time now—he fixes things for folks. He can make new handles for old rakes and shovels, and sometimes he does a little blacksmith work. I think he goes to his shop mostly so he won't have to watch Mama grieve. And so Mama won't watch him drink.

When I passed Mama and Daddy's room, Mama called out in a loud whisper, "Who's that?"

"It's me," I said. "Annie." I figured she was hoping it might be Scott.

"Oh," she said. "Sleep tight."

When I was little, she always added, "And don't let the bedbugs bite," and I would say, "All right," and we would laugh. But we don't laugh anymore.

In my room, I felt for the box of matches on my nightstand and struck one. I lit my candle so I could see to lay out my clothes for tomorrow. Every night, I undress and hang up my clothes and put on my flannel nightgown and lay out the next day's clothes. I also put on the socks I'll wear to school tomorrow. I always put on my socks at night. My feet stay warmer and I don't have to put my bare feet on the cold floor next morning. I try to arrange things as conveniently as I can. There is no use in making things more complicated than they need to be.

I got an extra quilt from the bottom of my chifferobe. My quilt wasn't pretty like Aint Lulie's. Whatever colors it used to be had long ago faded to a beige-gray. Seems like everything in this house has faded.

The candle cast my shadow over all the walls as I moved around. When I was little, I thought my shadow and Mama's shadow were ghosts.

"We have ghosts in this house," I said once when Mama was putting me to bed.

"There's no such thing as a ghost," she'd said. "It goes agin the Bible."

"Why does Elder Stoutmire say father son and holy ghost?" I asked, but she did not answer. Instead she said, "Say your prayers," and I folded my hands and said, "Now I lay me down to sleep I pray the Lord my soul to keep if I should die before I wake I pray the lord my soul to take." Then I asked her, "Where does he keep it?"

"Huh?" she said. "What?"

"My soul. Where does the lord keep it?" I imagined a big box crammed with souls of children the same age as me. Maybe on a shelf in the clouds.

"In heaven," she said.

"Where will he take it if I die in my sleep?"

"To heaven."

"That doesn't make sense. If it's already there why would he take it where it already is?"

"Don't question God's will," Mama had said.

But eventually she questioned. When Scott didn't come back, she questioned over and over. I knew that Scott's soul wasn't on a shelf on a cloud. It was in a jungle halfway round the world with the rest of him. Or what was left of him. I don't say my prayers at night anymore. Mama prays enough for both of us.

* * *

I climbed into bed and lay awake under the covers and sent my mind out. It didn't take long for it to find the connection I was looking for.

Loniss Hathaway takes a bubble bath in her own bathroom in her warm house. She sticks one leg out of the water and shaves it with long strokes from her silver razor. Then she does the other leg. When she gets out of the tub, she stands naked in front of the mirror and cups her breasts in her hands. She shakes them to one side and then the other like little pom-poms and smiles at her reflection.

"Lean to the left, lean to the right! Go Bobcats! Fight, fight, fight!" she chants. Then she scoops up Precious, her Pekinese who has been lying on the rug, and snuggles the dog against her face.

Loniss didn't know that Precious has been telling me everything she saw tonight—not exactly telling with human words, but with another kind of language mixed with something like thought-pictures between her mind and mine. If I listened just right, I could see Loniss as well as Precious did.

I knew that before Loniss took her bath, she talked to Lucas on her princess phone that was turquoise, the same color as her bedspread. Precious hates the sound of Loniss's voice when she talks baby talk in a high-pitched voice to Lucas. Precious hates Lucas. She should spend her time with me, Precious told me.

I knew that, after supper, Loniss and her mother filled out more college applications. They have been doing that for a week. Mrs. Hathaway wants Loniss to go to Sweetbriar or Hollins. Loniss wants to go to the University of North Carolina, but she'll settle for the University of Tennessee. Mr. Hathaway said they would discuss it later. Then Loniss tried on the new red sequined dress that she and her mother had bought in Knoxville for Loniss to wear to the Harvest Dance in two weeks, and her father took a picture of her standing beside the fireplace with Precious sitting at her feet. Later Loniss and her mother discussed prom dresses and how Loniss would break up with Lucas after the prom, but that was a long way off. Lucas is not good enough for Loniss—everybody already knows that. Loniss is already bored with him. But he is good-looking and a quarterback, so he will do for now. They will make a good-looking couple at the Harvest Dance. And at the prom.

Mr. Hathaway thinks that Loniss should date Alvin Bosworth, whose father owns the mill and the bank, but Loniss said he is a skinny nerd and she'd rather die than date someone who didn't even play any sport she could cheer for. Her mother agreed. The Hathaways only allow Loniss one date a week with Lucas—usually Saturday night after the game. They do not know that sometimes Lucas takes Loniss to his singlewide if his parents are gone, and Loniss does not know a hound curled up under the trailer hears every sound she and Lucas make. Loniss doesn't know that when she is out with Lucas, Precious pees on the carpet in Loniss's room. The carpet is yellow, so Loniss hasn't noticed.

I bade good-bye to Precious and sent my thoughts to Ranger to see what Lucas was up to.

Doggone if i know, Ranger said. *i got my own work to do—i took off and treed myself a coon and I been baying for fifteen-twenty minutes ain't nobody come to shake the coon outten this big poplar.*

Ranger was too busy to talk to me, so I connected to the raccoon.

No problem, he said. *I'll let the stupid hound bay for another hour and then I will slip into the next tree and then the next. I'll be gone before he knows*

I'm not there. Stupid hound.

Through my window, I could see the stars that shone on my house, on Aint Lulie, on Loniss and Lucas, on all critters. I saw the owl—the one who sometimes roosts in our barn—fly past my window. *Sleep,* said the owl, *go to sleep.*

I settled into the darkness, pulled my quilt tighter around my loneliness, and lay myself down to sleep.

CHAPTER 3: MID-OCTOBER

The next morning, I stayed invisible until Miss Brannigan's 3rd period "Landmarks of Literature" class. It's actually just English but with a fancy name. Lately, we've been studying poetry, which a lot of the kids hate. But I don't. I like the sound and rhythm of most poems we read. A lot of the boys pretend to like poetry, though, because they like Miss Brannigan who is young and wears short skirts. She replaced old Mrs. Southwark, who retired last year at age seventy and who had taught at least three generations of Bosworth County students.

"Let's start with 'The Road Not Taken,'" Miss Brannigan said. "What does 'Two roads diverged in a yellow wood' mean?" She looked around. No one raised a hand. Lucas Lawson was reading a note that Loniss had handed him in the hall before class. "Lucas? Maybe you could explain the poem's first line."

Lucas pushed the note up his shirtsleeve and squinted at his lit book. "Oh, that," he said. "Well, what I think the guy who wrote the poem means is, uh, that he's in the woods and he sees two roads."

"Yeah," said Kenny, who has a crush on Miss Brannigan. "Just what the poem says. Two roads are in the woods and this guy looks at them."

Bert McKeller raised his hand. He always waits until a few people give a wrong answer so he can give the right answer and make them look bad. Miss Brannigan called on him.

"It means that the poem's narrator noticed that the roads went in two different directions." He sneered in the direction of the football players. "*Diverged* means 'went in separate directions.'"

A couple of the guys sneered back, but Miss Brannigan smiled at Bert. He continued. "It can also mean that the roads differed. *Diverge* can also mean *differ*.

"Than you, Bert," said Miss Brannigan. "You're exactly right. As usual."

Bert beamed. Lucas made a gagging sound and pretended to vomit. His friends laughed.

Miss Brannigan went through the rest of the poem, line by line. She called on different people and tried to get from them what a line or stanza meant. I was glad she hadn't noticed me.

Finally, she asked, "What does the whole poem mean? It's not really about roads, is it?"

Larry raised his hand. I knew he wanted to get one up on Lucas and Kenny and maybe make Bert look bad. And he had a crush on Miss Brannigan.

"I think it's about deer-hunting," he said. "When you hunt, you have to study the trails. The guy figured that if he went down the trail where nobody much had been, he'd have a better chance of shooting a big buck."

Several boys in the class—including Lucas and Kenny—agreed with him. Then they started talking about hunting season starting in a few weeks. It took Miss Brannigan several minutes to get them back on track. Bert waved his up-stretched hand, but this time she ignored him.

"That's, uh, certainly an interesting interpretation, Larry," she said. "But that's not it."

She looked my way and caught my eye before I could look down. "Annie, what do you think the poem is about?"

"Um, life," I said. "Choices. Choices in life."

"Go on," she said. "You're on the right track. And speak up a bit so everyone can hear you."

"The road represents life," I said. "He's trying to make a choice which way to go in life. And he takes the way not many people chose."

"Right!" said Miss Brannigan.

I heard somebody—Loniss or one of her friends—whisper, "Maybe he chose to be a weirdo like her," but Miss Brannigan acted like she hadn't heard. I looked at the clock. Two more minutes.

Miss Brannigan summed up the poem. "Life is made of choices," she said. "We always have a choice. Sometimes it doesn't seem like it, but we do. Sometimes we might choose to take the road less traveled."

Then the bell rang.

"I choose a fast car for my road," Lucas said on his way out. "And plenty of money. And a good-looking gal beside me." He swung his arm around Loniss, and they walked into the hall together.

I closed my book and notebook. I couldn't help thinking about how wrong Miss Brannigan was. Sometimes life made a choice for you, and you were stuck with it.

I was the last one out of the room. I had no one in particular to meet, and it didn't matter if I was late to 4th period.

"Annie, wait," Miss Brannigan said. "I'm so pleased with your answer."

"Thank you." I didn't know what else to say. I guess I stood there for a few seconds.

"You look like you have a question, Annie. Do you?"

Actually, I did. There was no one to hear but her, so I asked it. "What if life hands you something and you have no choice but to take it? What if you're born with it?"

"Do you mean that life might give you a handicap—like not being able to walk or something?"

"Yeah," I said. "Something like that." It wasn't exactly what I meant, but it was close enough.

"Well," she said, "You can choose how you deal with it. You can sit around and say, 'Oh, poor me!' or you can choose to make the best of it. And, of course, you could choose to ignore your handicap as much as possible."

"Thank you," I said. Maybe if I ignored my gift, I wouldn't be so weird. I hurried toward the gym. Seniors don't have to take physical education, but I help out in the ninth grade class. It's better than having a study hall. I wash the towels and clean up and get out equipment. While the girls are playing volleyball or whatever, I get to take a shower—something I can never do at home.

Mrs. Watson, the PE teacher, smiled when I came in. She didn't mention that I was a couple minutes late. She told me that they wouldn't need any equipment because they were taking physical fitness tests and I could just work on the laundry. In the locker room, I took a load of towels out of the washer and put them in the drier. I picked up an armload of used towels from the hamper and put them in the washer. I loved how the detergent smelled— like lavender—and how warm the room was. I liked the thump-thump sound of the drier and the churning sound of the washer. While the towels washed and dried, I chose a clean towel from a stack and carried it to the showers.

I stood under the warm water and let it rinse me clean. Somebody had left a half-empty bottle of shampoo in the shower stall, so I washed my hair. I must have stayed in the shower for ten minutes. Luckily, no one came in. I dried myself with the warm fluffy towel. Then I found some deodorant. Its owner would never miss the little bit I used.

I choose to be warm and clean, I thought. *I choose to pretend I'm in a warm house with nice smells. I choose to be like everyone else.*

For a moment, I thought maybe I really could.

* * *

All week, I thought about what I would choose to be. On Friday, I walked to the cafeteria warm and clean again, as I'd chosen to be all week. I waited until most of the line had gone through before I got my tray. I don't like for everyone to see my free lunch ticket.

After I got my cheeseburger, french fries, green beans, and milk, I went to my usual seat at the corner table near the trashcans. I always eat lunch with Bert McKeller and Sarenda Lovejoy. They were already there and had started without me.

Bert moved here a few years ago. The other kids hate him because he always has to be right and he always wears a tie. He is the only one besides teachers who wears a tie. Plus he is no good at sports. His father is real old, but his mother is younger. At least that's what Bert once said. I've never seen his parents. From what Bert has also said, they hardly ever go out. The McKellers live in an old house on the western edge of town, so Bert is neither part of the town nor part of the county. Bert doesn't belong anywhere. He sits at the head of the outcast table. Sarenda and I sit on either side of him, facing each other. The chair opposite him is empty. No one ever sits there.

Sarenda's parents are hippies, and I guess she is one, too. Last year, her family moved to a holler on the opposite side of town from mine to get back to nature or something. Sarenda's clothes are even more raggedy than mine, but she doesn't care. She wears brightly colored long skirts, and her hair hangs straight down to her waist. She doesn't wear make-up, but she is prettier than most of the girls who do. When the other kids make fun of her, she just smiles and says, "Peace." Or else she smiles and says nothing. The other kids hate her because they can't make her get upset with their teasing. I don't think Lovejoy is her real last name. Her parents don't go out much either. Sarenda doesn't care what people think, and she doesn't care to be a part of anything. I envy her for that.

So, Bert tries to be right, Sarenda tries to be peaceful, and I try to be invisible. We usually eat in silence, but sometimes Bert gets talkative.

"Who do you think will win the election?" he asked. "Nixon or McGovern."

Sarenda shrugged. I said I didn't care. This set him off.

"How can you not care?" he said, loud enough for a few of the other kids to turn and glare at him. "This is history we're talking about! Our future!"

Sarenda shrugged again. This time I shrugged, too. I took a big bite of cheeseburger so my mouth would be too full to talk. The other kids turned away from us and went back to talking about their lives and what they saw on TV and other important stuff.

"You know what?" Bert punctuated the air with a forkful of green beans. "This is the problem. Too many people just don't care." He poked the green beans into his mouth and then banged the fork against his plate.

Sarenda smiled and flashed him the peace symbol while he was chewing. I took another bite of cheeseburger. He swallowed, gave up, and changed the subject.

"So," he said, "Are either of you going to the Harvest Dance?"

We shook our heads. I concentrated on sticking my fork into my own green beans. I wasn't about to wave them around.

"Why not?" Bert's voice was a little louder than it needed to be.

"I don't do school dances," Sarenda said. "I might dance with the wind on the hill under the stars, but dancing in a sweat-filled gymnasium? No way! Too many bad vibes."

Sarenda and Bert looked at me, waiting for my answer.

"My parents don't approve of dancing," I said. What I didn't say was even if they did approve, I still wouldn't want to go.

"I don't think I'll go either," Bert said. "I was just wondering."

We didn't ask him why he wasn't going. We already knew that no girl would likely go with him even if he had the nerve to ask.

"Tell you what, Bert, " Sarenda said. "I'll dance for you now. How's that?"

"Yeah, sure," Bert said, like he didn't really mean it.

She picked up her tray and waltzed with it around the cafeteria, her hair and skirt swirling out from her body. Other kids stopped eating and talking to look. I heard someone call her a crazy pothead. While everyone watched Sarenda, I dumped my leftovers in the trash and took my tray to the dirty dish window. Nobody even looked my way. After Sarenda had danced around the edge of the whole cafeteria, she gave a deep curtsy. No one applauded, but a couple of guys whistled.

After lunch, the football players were excused from fifth and sixth periods for football practice. Only half my fifth period government class was there, so we watched a movie. It was nice to sit in the dark while the projector flickered, and I didn't have to worry about Mr. Wardell asking me a question.

Sixth period home ec was all girls, so nobody was missing. All the sewing machines were occupied. I hunched over my Singer and worked on putting the zipper in my skirt. Mrs. Carlton passed by twice and nodded approvingly each time. I always paid attention to details, so I never had the mismatched seams or puckered stitches that the others had. Mrs. Carlton only stopped to help when she saw problems. She never stopped for me.

After sixth period, I went outside to get on the bus, but it wasn't there. Likely Clovis hadn't finished the afternoon milking in time. Since the football players were still at practice, only a handful of us stood and waited. One was Loniss. I could tell she didn't like waiting. She finally sat on the wall and kept looking at her watch. I could see her from where I leaned against one of the maple trees along the school driveway.

After the other buses had gone, I saw Alvin Bosworth drive out of the parking lot in his red MG with the top down. He pulled up in front of Loniss and gunned the MG's engine. At first she didn't look at him. He said something I couldn't hear over the roar of the engine, and I saw her say something back to him. He got out and opened the passenger side door. She got off the wall, brushed off her skirt, and got into his car. When he closed the door, she smiled at him. Or maybe she was just smiling because she got to ride in a cute little convertible and she didn't have to wait. I saw her glance back in the direction of the football field as Alvin drove by it. I knew that Lucas would have been too busy to see her.

Five minutes later, Clovis showed up. He was full of apologies why he was late. "One of the cows had some trouble," he said. "Had to wait for the vet." Even though we were all seated, he didn't take off. "Where's Loniss?" he asked.

"She got a ride," Janie Tackett said, and she and her seatmate giggled. Janie would like to be one of Loniss's friends, but she isn't a cheerleader and she has pimples and greasy hair. In elementary school, when other kids would ask what was stinking, Janie was the one who would always point to me and say, "That girl smells just like an old fireplace." She never once called me by name. I was glad when she failed fifth grade and we didn't have to be in the same class anymore. She still wrinkles her nose when she passes by me, though.

"Well, okay, then," Clovis said, and pulled the bus into the road. He sounded kind of disappointed. A couple of the kids asked him about the old-fashioned milk can he had on the seat behind him.

"Oh, that," he said. "I got a bunch of them things. I was hoping to sell that'un to one a'them antique dealers comes to town ever so often. But he won't there today."

On the ride home, I connected with one of his cows. *No trouble here*, Number 63 said. *We're all fine. Didn't see Clovis. His daddy milked us. Wish he'd feed us more.*

Later, just before we got to my stop, Precious popped into my head. *Where is she?* Precious said. *She should have been home. I saw the bus. I waited. She didn't get off the bus. I'm waiting! Where is she? Why didn't she come home? Doesn't she still love me? I'm waiting?*

I could feel Precious jumping up and down by the front door. I told the frantic little dog not to worry, but I don't think she believed me.

"See you Monday, Annie," Clovis said when he stopped to let me off. "You have a good weekend."

"You, too," I said. "I hope your cow does better."

Liar! I wanted to yell at him. *Liar! Your cows are fine.* But I didn't say another word.

Soon I was on the path to Aint Lulie's. Walking through the

woods made me think of that poem again. But two roads didn't diverge in these woods. A packed-dirt driveway went from the bus stop to the front of my house. Then it became a narrow path to Aint Lulie's cabin. There were no choices. No divergence.

Along the path, a few birds called to me and a possum muttered, but I chose not to answer them. *I'll see if I can make choices*, I thought. I tried to close my mind to things that wanted to come in.

Before I could see her cabin, I smelled Aint Lulie's woodsmoke. I could follow the path blindfolded just by the smell. I don't think woodsmoke stinks at all. It smells wonderful and warm and welcoming.

Inside, by the light from the fireplace, I saw the leaf-quilt spread on her bed.

"Set down," she said, "and make yourself to home. Soup's about done."

I pulled a chair up to the table, and she put a bowl of soup and some fresh bread in front of me. While we ate, we talked. She asked me about school, and I told her my skirt was nearly finished. Then I changed the subject.

"Aint Lulie," I said, "has anybody in our family ever given up our gift?"

She looked at me like I was addled. "Why'd a body want to do that?"

"To be normal," I said. "To be just like everyone else."

She leaned over the oilcloth table covering and looked me square in the eye. "There ain't no normal. Ain't no one person ever been jist like another. Even twins is different, for all that they might look alike."

"But seems like my gift is a burden to me," I said. "It sets me apart."

"I recollect I felt the same way about mine at first," she said. "T'uz about five, the same age you was when you talked to them chickens, when I first found out what my gift was. Papa had took me along with him to the mill where he wanted some of his wheat ground up into flour. It'uz the first time he took jist me and not the others, so I thought I was something. I set up on the wagon seat jist as proud. When we come to the mill, a couple wagons was ahead of us. I got tired waiting so I hopped down and went to look around, and I seen a gal peeping around the big tree that leaned over the millpond. I ain't never before seen her, so I didn't know who she was. She had long dark hair and looked to be a year or so older'n me. I recollect she had on the purtiest blue dress. She hollered to me to come play hide-and-seek with her, that she'd found a real good place where nobody had been able find her. I told her I'd have to ask my papa, and she said that she'd wait. So I went back to the wagon where Papa had been talking with some other fellers. 'Papa, they's a dark-haired gal in a blue dress wants me to come play with her,' I said. 'Is it all right for me to do that?'

"All the men got real quiet. The one said, 'A dark-haired gal in a blue dress?' Another said, 'Where might she be?' So I pointed over to where she was and said, 'She's right yonder, peeping out from around that big tree.'

"Papa got off the wagon and took a'holt of me by the shoulders. 'Lulie,' he said, 'ain't no gal there,' and the other men was looking at me real wide-eyed. 'You go see,' I told him. 'She said she found a real good hiding place.' Well, the men drapped what they was doing, and all of 'em but Papa raced toward that tree. Papa kept holding me back.

"I watched the men go to the other side of the tree and look down into the pond, and then one ran back to the mill and got some sacks and ran back to the tree. He laid the sacks on the ground. One man helt onto another'n while he scooted down the tree root where it went into the pond and reached under the water. He pulled something out and laid it on the sacks. I got a glimpse of blue and wanted to go see, but Papa kept a'holt of me. They wrapped the sacks around it, and carried it to the mill-house. When they passed by me, they gave me the oddest looks. Papa said we was going home and would get our wheat ground another day.

"On the way home, he told me the men had been saying a little gal had turned up missing a couple days earlier and couldn't nobody find where she went. And that little gal had dark hair and was wearing a blue dress. 'I don't know how you knowed what you did,' he said, 'but I reckon you got the gift that Ma talks about.'"

Aint Lulie hadn't answered my question, so I tried again. "But has anybody ever given up the gift?"

She reached across the table and took my hand. "Not any I know of," she said. "At times the gift might be a heavy burden to bear, but it'uz give to us for a reason. It ain't for us to refuse." She turned my hand so it was palm up and studied it in the firelight.

"What do you see?" I asked.

She shrugged and, for a split second, she frowned. "Nothing you don't already know. Plus I ain't all that good at hand-reading. My Granny Mariah on the Duff side, she could take one look and tell you more about yourself than you'd ever learn in your lifetime. Them Duffs was good at seeing the future."

I could tell that she didn't want to talk about what she saw in my hand. So I changed the subject again. "Aint Lulie, do you think everybody gets choices? I mean, can they choose who they want to be or do?"

"Well, in some things, I reckon. Others, not." She picked up my empty bowl and carried it to her dishpan. "You can choose what you put on to wear everyday, but you can only choose from what you got and what the weather is." She washed and dried my bowl and set it on the shelf. "Say you had a garden that'uz too dry. You couldn't choose for it to rain. Best you could do is choose to tote water from the creek. Or, if you'uz foolish, you could choose to let it dry up." She washed and dried the spoons while she thought for a bit. "And you can always choose if you want to stay or go. For generations, our people has done jist that. Some stayed put while others moved on." She wiped out her cast iron pan, rinsed it, dried it off, and hung it from its peg. The pan was over a hundred years old.

I could tell that she was about to veer off into telling me about the Caldwells that had stayed in Botetourt County and the ones that had come here and the ones that had gone farther west, but she still hadn't given me the answer I wanted. I asked her outright. "But could I choose to give up my gift?"

"I don't know how you'd do that, Honey."

"I mean I could choose to ignore it. Just not talk nor listen to animals anymore. If I play like it's not there, it won't be there, will it?"

She sat in her rocker and laughed. "You can 'play like' all you want, but playing like don't make it so. You had best be who you'uz meant to be."

I was quiet for a while. The only sounds were the ticking of her mantle clock and the creaking of her rocker. And the soft crackle and hiss of the fire.

"Who was I meant to be?" I finally said.

"That I cannot tell you," she said. "Everbody has to find out theirself. But you was put on this earth for a purpose, and you had best make do with the gifts you got. Pretending something ain't there don't mean it ain't there."

I nodded. Not to agree with her, but just to let her know that I heard what she said. There was no way I'd ever make her understand that I just wanted to be a regular person.

"One thing I'll tell you, though," she said, " is that there's things 'round us that most folks don't see or hear. If only we look, we can see 'em. If only we listen, we can hear 'em. And maybe it was meant for you and me to do that."

The fire was burning low. She eased out of her rocker and put another log on the dog-irons. Flames licked up from the embers, and soon the burning log brightened the whole room. She settled back into her rocker. I listened to it creak while she rocked back and forth. I wanted to stay where it was warm and bright, but it was late and I figured I'd better start for home.

"I'd best be going," I said. "I'll come back tomorrow and help you get some more wood in." Then I added, "You better come go with me."

"Cain't," she answered, commencing the expected reply: "You mought as well stay."

"Cain't." I stepped into the darkness.

I hurried along the dark path, taking care not to answer any creature that called out to me. The wind blew at my thin jacket, and I walked faster along the one path I had always known.

By the time I reached home, clouds hid the sliver of moon and I felt my way through the darkness and onto the porch.

Later, I huddled under my quilt and stopped my ears against the owl's hoot as he flew by and tuned out the pleadings of a small dog in the biggest house on a hill. For a while, I thought about choices and what Aint Lulie had said. Then I decided to listen to the unhappy little dog. I opened my mind and let Precious in.

Where have you been? I've called and called you! My mistress came home late. There was yelling and much unhappiness. She went to her room and slammed her door and left me in the hall. I don't know what to do.

Start from the beginning, I told Precious. Tell me what happened when Loniss got home.

Precious poured out the story. Loniss had called her mother to tell her she'd be late. Two hours later, Alvin brought her home. He'd sped up the driveway in his little red car. Precious didn't like how the engine sounded. Both Loniss's parents had seen from the window, and Precious herself was able to see by standing on the sofa. *Small dogs must take drastic measures.* Her mother was angry Loniss was so late, but her father was delighted that she was finally dating the richest boy in town.

"I'm not dating him!" Loniss had yelled. "I was tired of waiting for the bus. I wanted to see what riding in his MG felt like. He drove toward Gate City. We stopped to get a bite to eat. That's where I called you from. It wasn't a real date!"

"I'm sure it wasn't," her mother had said. "But think how this looks. Everyone knows you go with Lucas—well, at least you will until after the prom. It just doesn't seem proper to break off so sudden."

"Now, Dina" her father had said, "This is what we've wanted. Finally she has a boyfriend worthy of her."

"He's NOT my boyfriend!" Loniss yelled. "If I had my own car, I could have driven myself home!"

"We've talked about this before," her mother said. "You'll get your car when you graduate."

Loniss had stormed off to her room and slammed the door.

What will I do? Precious said. *I always sleep with her. She has closed me out.*

I told Precious to pee outside Loniss's door and then go sleep on the sofa. By the time I tuned her out, Precious was already squatting.

CHAPTER 4: DECISIONS

On Saturday, I helped Aint Lulie tote wood to her cabin on an old wooden slide that the two of us pulled by a ravelly rope. It was the same slide that oxen had pulled when she was a girl, though it would have been loaded much heavier back then.

"It did the job then, it does the job now," Aint Lulie always says whenever we use it. "No use in gitting rid of something jist on account it's old."

I knew it was easier to get the wood in now instead of waiting until the snow fell or the wind blew strong. All morning, I dragged the slide back and forth to the woods where the last ice storm's deadfall was dry enough to make good stovewood. Sometimes I had to cut one of the larger logs with a handsaw, but I mostly found enough smaller pieces Aint Lulie could use.

Though the morning had been frosty, by mid-day the weather was warm. I was sweating by the time I dumped the second load next to her porch.

"Best be prepared," Aint Lulie said. "Make hay while the sun shines."

"And get wood when you can get it," I said, as we started back to the woods.

Finally we dumped the last load near her porch. I stood the bigger logs on end so I could split them down the middle. From the shed I got the old go-devil to split the up-ended logs into stovewood.

"Make sure you spit into your hands before you commence to

chop," she said. "It makes for good luck."

After spitting into my hands, I swung the old go-devil up and down so many times I lost count. Before long, I'd split enough kindling so she'd be well fixed for the next couple weeks. I left a good-sized pile on her porch and another in her woodshed with half the pile split into stove-size pieces. The bigger logs would go into her fireplace when the weather got colder.

"We're blessed to have so much deadfall," she said. "Good things come outta that bad storm." She brought me inside and rubbed some of her salve onto my hands.

"Smells good, don't it?" Aint Lulie said. I didn't realize she was talking about the salve until she said, "It's got comfrey and plantain in it."

I nodded. My hands felt better already.

I thought about Loniss Hathaway and knew she had never split nor carried wood. I knew her hands were not callused like mine, and her face wasn't red from doing heavy work. She wore makeup on her face and pink polish on her fingernails. While I'd been splitting kindling, she'd put her cheerleading uniform on, her parents had driven her to school where she'd gotten on the bus with the team and the other cheerleaders, and they'd gone to the game in the next county.

I wondered how much the Bobcats would lose by and if Lucas would take it out on Loniss. I wondered if Lucas would find out she'd gone for a ride with Alvin. I wondered if I should ask Precious what was going on.

I decided to contact Ranger instead of Precious. He was asleep under the trailer but he woke right up when I went into his mind.

. . . wouldn't take me for a run they drank the bad-smelling stuff and smoked cigarettes that won't cigarettes smelled too sweet and wobbled around and rolled on the ground and laughed and i made myself scarce for they weren't theirselves and drank more until they slept the deep sleep and i went to the woods and ran. . . .

I thanked Ranger and let him go back to sleep. Then I remembered that I was going to choose to give up the gift for a while. I snapped my mind shut and spent the rest of the day keeping it closed up tight while I helped Aint Lulie with her chores.

I left at nearly dusk and on my way home I picked some twigs from a sassafras tree to use as toothbrushes. I thought of Loniss again. She'd have a real toothbrush and probably minty-tasting toothpaste. She'd likely never chewed a sassafras twig and used the brush-like end to clean her teeth. But that's what I'd always done.

When I got home, Mama had supper on the table. "Church tomorrow," she said. "Plan to go."

After she'd said the blessing, we ate in silence the way we generally do.

After supper, I went to bed and slept sound until I heard Mama call, "Breakfast ready!" Did I sleep so sound because I kept my mind closed to any critters or because I was so tired from hauling and chopping wood? I don't know.

I put on my ugly long dress and went with Mama to church. It was easier to just go than try to explain why I didn't want to. I figured if I could close my mind to the critters, I could close it to Elder Stoutmire. Mama asked Daddy if he wanted to go, like she always does. He said he had things to do, like he always does, but he'd drive us and come get us after. The three of us rode in silence up the mountain to the church.

After Daddy dropped us off and Mama had wandered over to where the women in her prayer circle gathered, I heard a couple men talking about yesterday's football game and how sorry they thought Lucas Lawson was.

"Dropped the damn ball!" one said. "Had a clear run to the goal but the little bastard dropped the ball!"

"Cost me $50," said another man. "Figgered my bet was a sure thing. Oughta take it outta his worthless hide."

"Sorriest game I ever seen," a third man said.

I couldn't hear everything they said, but I learned the Bosworth Bobcats lost by twenty-one points and it was likely Lucas's fault. Mama and I went in and took our usual places on our usual pew. Elder Stoutmire made a few announcements—the ladies circle would meet on Monday, the church needed some donations of firewood to get through the winter, a few shut-ins needed praying for. Then he launched into a sermon about hell's fiery furnace that awaited all sinners.

Throughout Elder Stoutmire's hour-long sermon, I sat ramrod straight on the hard pew and ignored him. During the altar call, Mama looked my way a time or two, but I resisted. I know it embarrassed her that I was way over twelve and not saved. Even when the congregation sang "Just As I Am" and Elder Stoutmire stalked up and down the aisle and confronted sinners with the horrors of hell, I sat straight. When he came to me, I met his gaze instead of turning away. He backed away as if he knew I'd resist and sought out another sinner who was an easier mark.

So, I thought, *this is what it's like to be noticed.*

On the way home, I tried to talk to my parents but got no real answers to what chores did Daddy do all morning, was that a new hat Mrs. Groves was wearing, and did they think we'd get frost tonight. My parents were so set in their ways of not saying much that I didn't expect much from them. But what could I expect from me?

* * *

On Monday, I said "Good morning!" to Clovis before he spoke to me. I noticed on the seat behind him, he had an old milk can tied up so it wouldn't tip over. Likely this was another he'd try to sell in town. On the ride to school, I didn't slump down in my seat like I usually did, but the other kids never looked my way. They were quieter than usual, I guess because of the football game. Nobody spoke to Lucas. Loniss never got on the bus, so I guess her daddy had driven her to school. Or maybe Alvin had picked her up. I could have asked Precious, but I decided not to.

I was the last one off the bus, but I walked into the school like I was someone special. I didn't slump and I kept my head high. The other kids still ignored me, but now they had to be deliberate about it. When I looked into their faces, they were the ones who turned away. Even Janie Tackett only halfway wrinkled her nose before turning her back. When I walked down the hall, kids stepped aside to let me through.

In first period math class, I raised my hand. Mr. Thomas had to check his seating chart before he called me by name. He'd never called on me before. I gave the correct answer to his question about quadratic equations. A few kids turned to look at me. I looked back and smiled. They looked away quick.

In all my morning classes, I was the first one to answer the teacher's questions. Only Miss Brannigan said she was glad to see me participating more. "You made a good contribution to today's class," she told me as I was leaving.

English class had been a lot quieter than usual, though. Lucas and his buddies didn't joke and cut up. Loniss didn't flirt with him. When the bell rang, Loniss pushed ahead and almost ran out of class. Lucas didn't even try to catch up with her. He kept his eyes down and didn't talk to anybody.

In PE, after I started the laundry and took my shower, I noticed a lipstick someone had thrown into the trashcan. I fished it out. It was nearly new. Probably the owner decided she didn't like the color or, more likely, her friends didn't like it. I slipped it in my pocket.

At lunch, when Bert started talking politics, I told him that I didn't like Nixon—in fact, I blamed him for my brother's death—but McGovern didn't have a chance because folks thought he was too radical, so that was that. I'd heard a couple of men talking about it after church and they'd used the word *radical*. I wasn't for sure what it meant, but it sounded good.

Bert gaped at me. You'd think he'd seen a ghost. "My gosh, Annie, I didn't know you were interested in—"

"I gave you my opinion, and that's that. I don't want to talk about politics anymore," I announced. "Bert, if you start, I'll sit at another table."

"Me, too," Sarenda said. "Politics is so boring."

"What is this, women's lib or something?" Bert asked. "Isn't women's lib political?"

Sarenda and I looked at each other. We shook our heads.

"No," I said. "Women can choose how they act. They can even choose if they want to be liberated, whatever that means." *And I can choose how I'll be*, I thought. I felt liberated.

I stood tall the rest of the day. I wasn't the last one in line or out the door. I even said "hi" to a few kids who looked like they needed someone to speak to them. It felt weird. Not bad weird, just weird.

In government class, we discussed the up-coming election. Mr. Wardell, after asking all the boys who pretty much said what they'd heard from their daddies, said, "Now we'll get the ladies' opinions."

When he asked me, I said pretty much what I had said to Bert at lunch.

"That's, uh, interesting," Mr. Wardell said. "Very interesting." Everyone knew he was a democrat. The McGovern button on his vest pretty much announced it.

In home ec, I stopped Mrs. Carlton when she walked past me. "I've almost finished my skirt," I said. "I just need to hem it."

"Uh, yes," she said. She seemed confused that anyone—especially me—would just say something without asking for help.

"Are you having problems with that?"

"No," I said. "But I was wondering if I could make a quilt next. Nobody else is close to finishing their skirts, so I figured I could work on a quilt by myself until everyone else is done."

Mrs. Carlton nodded but didn't say anything. I reckon she wasn't used to anyone asking to do extra work. She sure wasn't used to me talking, much less asking for something.

"Would it be all right if I picked out some scraps from the scrap bags?"

"Well, sure. I guess," Mrs. Carlton said. "Help yourself."

Every time we cut out a pattern, we tossed the leftover material into a bag. Mrs. Carlton would put the bag into the home ec closet. When one bag filled up, she'd start another. I don't know what she ever did with all the material. Threw it away at the end of the year, maybe. There were already six or seven full bags in the closet.

Anyhow, I finished hemming my skirt and showed it to Mrs. Carlton. She looked it over, noticed that my seams were straight, my zipper didn't pucker, and the hem was even. She didn't say anything about my skirt being so much longer than anyone else's. Mama wouldn't like it if I came home with a short skirt.

After Mrs. Carlton put my A in her gradebook, I went to the closet and pulled material that I thought I could use from the bags. I was looking for bright colors. A few of the other girls looked up from their sewing machines, and I heard somebody—Loniss's cheerleader friend Susan, I think—say "rag picker" and a few others laughed.

Mrs. Carlton pretended she didn't hear, but a few minutes before the bell rang, she gave me a paper bag and asked if I'd like to take some scraps home to cut out.

I stuffed my bag full and put my folded-up skirt on top. I was the first one out when the bell rang. I was the first one on the bus, too. I noticed the old milkcan was on the seat behind Clovis, so I guess he hadn't been able to sell it. But now it was turned on its side, not tied upright. I still sat in the back and my bag sat beside me. But I didn't keep my head buried in my book. I looked out the window mostly. Sometimes I watched the others.

I couldn't watch Loniss, though. She wasn't on the bus. Clovis waited about five minutes before he pulled away. She hadn't been on the bus this morning either. Her daddy had brought her in late. When I was in first period, I'd looked out the window and saw Mr.

Hathaway pull up in front of the school and let Loniss out of his Buick. Maybe he'd picked her up after school, too. Maybe she didn't want to be around Lucas. Something must have happened between Loniss and Lucas, but I decided I wouldn't talk to Precious. If they'd broken up, the little dog would at least be happy.

Lucas and his buddies were quiet on the way home, too. I guess they were still mad about losing. A couple of Loniss's friends whispered to each other, their heads close. They didn't flirt with the boys like they sometimes do. Janie Tackett leaned forward to hear what they were saying, and they shut up. So nobody on the bus said much of anything. And, of course, nobody said anything to me until Clovis let me off and told me good-by.

I dragged my bag into the house. Beside the coat rack sat another bag. I looked in. Half a dozen white blouses—obviously used and starting to yellow—were in it. Mama had brought them home from church for me, I reckoned. She got most of my clothes from the church exchange. Women bring in what's been outgrown and exchange it for somebody else's out-grown clothes. Whatever isn't taken by summer goes in the ladies' prayer circle rummage sale.

The bag of clothes meant that somebody had taken Mama to church today—likely one of the prayer circle women. If somebody doesn't go to prayer circle for a few weeks, the other women come after her, like buzzards circling a carcass.

Mama came out of the kitchen. She was still wearing her good dress, so I guess she'd just got home. She pointed to the bag and almost smiled. "New clothes. Yours."

I already hated those blouses. I hated that I'd have to wear someone else's discards. But I'd never in a million years tell her so.

She pointed to my bag and looked puzzled.

"I've got some scrap material," I said. "The home ec teacher gave me the leftovers so I could make a quilt. And I finished my skirt." I pulled it out of the bag and held it up so she could see it was long enough to be decent."

"Pretty," Mama said. "Real nice." She brushed past me and went upstairs.

"I'm going to Aint Lulie's," I said, but I doubt she heard me. Anyway, she knew where I'd be. Where else did I ever go in the evenings?

I folded my skirt and put it on top of the blouses. Then I took both bags with me. The only sounds I heard on the path were the rustling leaves. No critters were around. Likely some of them were denning up for the winter, and a lot of the birds had flown south already.

Soon as I finished Aint Lulie's chores, I spread out my scraps on her bed and told her what I wanted to do. She picked through the pieces and admired some of the colors. "You want to do a special pattern, or jist a crazy quilt?" she asked.

I hadn't thought about a pattern. All I'd thought was quilt. "I'm not sure," I said.

Well," she said, "if you ain't sure, we'll jist make us a crazy quilt. It's easier'n most anything." She fetched a pair of scissors from her workbasket. "Now you smooth out all these scraps and cut some squares and rectangles. Size don't much matter."

"Oh," I said, "I finished my skirt. Want to see it?"

Of course she did. I pulled it out of the bag, and she fingered the hem and turned it inside out to study the seams. After she'd studied on it a while, she pronounced it a fine skirt. She pointed to the bag. "What else you got in there?"

"Some old blouses Mama brought home from church. They weren't fit for their owner to wear any more, I guess. And they've turned yellow." I knew if I wore them to school, Loniss's friends would make fun of me. But I didn't dare tell Aint Lulie that. I dumped them out of the bag so she could see.

She held them one by one in front of the window. Even in the fading light she could see their dinginess. "I reckon I might be able to fix 'em," she said, "iff'n you trust me with 'em a couple days."

"I don't reckon I have anything to lose." I started cutting the squares.

While I snipped away, Aint Lulie stood at the stove and stirred the pot. The smell of her stew made my mouth water.

By the time her stew was ready, I'd cut a bunch of squares and rectangles. After we'd eaten and cleared the table, we arranged the pieces different ways to get an idea what the quilt might look like. She got some pins from a little wooden box on the shelf, and we pinned some pieces together. I put the pinned pieces back in my bag to take to school and promised I'd bring her pins back. I knew she'd had them all her life, and they were likely her mother's, too. Aint Lulie never wasted anything.

I walked back in the light of the full moon and kept my mind closed in case any critters lurked in the woods. I didn't have to listen to them. It was my choice, my decision.

CHAPTER 5: THE DANCE

Next day, both on the bus and at school, I acted pretty much the same as I did the day before. I smiled at the few people who smiled at me, answered a few questions in class, and ate lunch with Bert and Sarenda. If they noticed I was chattier than usual, they didn't mention it.

Loniss hadn't been on the bus again. But she was there in English class where she took a seat on the opposite side of the room from where Lucas sat. She took Bert's front row seat, so he had to find another when he came in. I saw Lucas pass Loniss a note when Miss Brannigan was writing on the board, but Loniss tossed it in the trash can without reading it. She was out the door and down the hall as soon as the bell rang, so Lucas never got a chance to talk to her.

In the cafeteria she sat with Susan and Cheryl and some other cheerleaders, but she kept her back to Lucas. I saw Lucas watching her from time to time. Then he'd laugh with his buddies—a little louder than necessary, like he was trying to attract attention to himself. Loniss never once looked his way.

"What's with Loniss and Lucas?" Sarenda asked. "Did they break up?"

"She took my seat," Bert said. "Just sat in it like she owned the place. Miss Brannigan didn't even say a word to her."

"How would I know what's going on?" I said. "They don't tell me their business. Maybe they did break up." I took a big bite of macaroni and cheese so my mouth would be too full to say anything else for a while.

"So who's she going to the dance with?" Sarenda asked.

I shrugged. I could have asked Precious, but I remembered I'd made up my mind not to talk to animals anymore. Plus, Sarenda and Bert would have asked how I knew, and they would have thought I was crazy if I said a little dog told me. I liked being normal.

"You know," Bert said, "the three of us should go. To the dance, I mean."

Sarenda and I stopped eating and stared at him.

"I don't dance," I said. "And I don't have a dress to wear." I took a forkful of meatloaf and chewed slowly. I was afraid Bert would ask me why I didn't dance. Then I realized I had already told him the other day.

"You know what I think about school dances?" Sarenda picked at her salad. "A bunch of kids playing dress-up and pretending to be someone they're not. Boring. B-o-r-r-r-i-n-g!" She stabbed a carrot with her fork.

"OK, maybe we won't actually go to the dance," Bert said. "We could just get together and sit on the hill behind the gym. We could see through the window from up there. Kind of like we're studying the dance. Like we're scientists doing research."

"Sit on the hill in the moonlight. I could go for that," Sarenda said. "Supposed to be nearly a full moon on the twenty-second."

"How would we get here? I can't walk all the way from home." I concentrated on pushing my the macaroni and cheese around on my plate so I wouldn't have to look at Bert.

"I could drive," he said. "I'm pretty sure my parents will let me have the car. They never use it on weekends. I could pick both of you up."

For a few minutes we debated the idea of watching the dance. After a while, the idea didn't seem so bad. I knew Mama would never let me go to a dance, though, but I didn't tell Bert or Sarenda. Maybe I could think of something.

In home ec class, Mrs. Carlton provided that something. She stopped by my sewing machine and watched me stitch together the quilt pieces I'd pinned. "That's going to be just beautiful, Annie," she said. "I'm so glad you've decided to make a quilt." Instead of moving on, she just stood there.

I didn't know what to say and concentrated on stitching. When

I came to the end of a row, I finally spoke. "My great-aunt helped me cut the pieces. She knows all about quilts."

I thought Mrs. Carlton would go on to the next sewing machine, but she didn't.

"There's something I'd like to ask you, Annie," she said. "Would you like to earn a little money?"

"How?" I didn't look up. I concentrated on removing the pins and sticking them onto a scrap of paper so I wouldn't lose them. "I don't think my parents would let me have a job."

"Oh, it's not a real job," she said. "More like helping me for just one night. I have to prepare and serve the refreshments for the Harvest Dance. My niece usually helps, but she has to be out of town on the twenty-first. I need someone to help set me up and serve for about two hours. You wouldn't have to help for the whole dance—just until most of the food is eaten. Then help me clear the tables and all."

"I don't know. I don't have anything to wear."

"I'll pay you twenty dollars," she said. "And your new skirt will be just fine. Wear a nice blouse, and I'll provide an apron and hat."

"Could I let you know tomorrow?" I could use the twenty dollars. Surely Mama would understand about earning money. Problem was, I didn't have a nice blouse.

"Well, yes, I guess that will be fine." She went on to the next sewing machine where Mary Rose Lennert had caught the fabric in the zipper-foot. Mary Rose looked like she was about to cry.

I watched Mrs. Carlton move around the room. I wondered why she didn't ask anyone else. Why me? She was probably sure that I wouldn't have a date. And she must have figured from the way I dressed that I likely needed the money.

After school, Loniss didn't get on the bus. Susan told Clovis that Loniss said not to wait for her. I saw Lucas crane his neck around as if he might be looking for her. As the bus pulled away, I caught a glimpse of Loniss walking to the parking lot with Alvin Bosworth.

On the ride home, I thought about Mrs. Carlton's offer. The more I thought, the more I wanted to do it. No sooner was I off the bus, I made a quick visit to Aint Lulie and returned her pins and told her about the job offer. I told her that I thought I could get a ride. Aint Lulie thought working at the dance was a good idea.

"It don't hurt none for you to git out and be social. And the money is sure easy enough. But best not tell your mama about the dance. Jist tell her you can git paid to help a teacher."

"Mrs. Carlton said I could wear my new skirt with a nice blouse, but I don't have a nice blouse."

"Well, I reckon you do now." Aint Lulie went to her back-porch clothesline and pulled off the blouses that she'd dyed. She held up one that was a beautiful shade of gold. "This'n oughta do. I cut some broomsedge to make the dye, and it turned out real good. Once I starch this blouse up good and iron it, it'll look good as new. And I found some lace in my old hope chest. I could stitch some onto the collar to kindly dress it up a bit if you want."

"Sure," I said. "That'd be nice." I had never before worn lace that I could remember.

I almost skipped through the woods on my way home. The owl hooted, but I paid it no mind. The quarter moon shone bright and turned the dry leaves silver and the path gold. I tried to plan how I would ask Mama about helping out at the dance. I even said aloud, "How can I ask Mama?"

"Whoo-Whooo-Whoo?" the owl called out.

For moment, I forgot my promise and connected with the owl. *Ask your daddy*, the owl said. *That's whoooo.*

Asking Daddy hadn't occurred to me before. If he said yes, Mama wouldn't go against his word. She believed a wife should be obedient unto her husband.

"That's a good idea," I told the owl.

Owls are known to be wise, the owl replied, and flapped away into the night.

I saw the light on in the barn, so I figured now might be a good time to talk to Daddy. I wasn't sure if I ought to knock or what. I peeked in the window. Daddy sat in a straight chair that leaned against the wall. He looked like he was asleep. A beer bottle sat on the floor beside the chair.

I crept to the door and knocked even though it was open. I couldn't hear anything. I knocked again, louder. "Daddy?" I said.

"Huh?" I heard him say. "Whazzat?"

"It's me. Annie." I didn't go in. I'd wait for him to invite me.

"Something the matter?" he said. "Your ma all right?"

"She's okay, I guess. I just wanted to ask you something."

I heard the chair scrape. "Well, come on in."

I threaded my way through his junk until I came to the open

space where he sat. The beer bottle was gone. For a minute neither of us said anything.

"Set yourself down." He pointed to a stool. "You was gonna ask me something?"

"Yeah. I was wondering if it might be all right if I helped a teacher. She'll give me twenty dollars for a couple hours work."

Daddy whistled. "Twenty dollars? That's more'n I made in a month when I's your age. And I was doing heavy work. Farm work." He shook his head like he might not believe me. "What kinda work this teacher want you to do?"

"Mrs. Carlton—she's the home ec teacher—wants me to help her set up and serve food at the Harvest Dance Saturday night."

"How you gonna git there?"

"Well, I might be able to hitch a ride with some kids I know." I watched a frown spread over his face. I thought fast before he could say no. "Or maybe you could drive me."

He nodded. "Might be able to. But you know your ma don't hold with dancing?"

"I won't be dancing. I'll be working."

"That's so," he said. "I reckon you want me to talk to your ma."

"If you don't mind. She might understand better if you explained it to her."

He nodded. This was the longest conversation I'd had with Daddy since Scott was killed. It felt strange, but a good kind of strange.

"Well," he said, "you better git on to the house. I'll be up directly. I'll see what I can do."

I threaded my way back outside. It was almost full dark. There was no telling how long Daddy would stay out.

Mama must have already been asleep when I went inside. She didn't say anything. I went to bed and thought about hope chests. Anybody could use a chest full of hope. I know I could.

When she put my breakfast on the table the next morning, she didn't say anything. I guess Daddy hadn't got a chance to tell her. He was still asleep.

* * *

At lunch I told Bert and Sarenda that I'd be working at the dance. I told Bert that I didn't know if I would need a ride or not. "I'll have to let you know," I said.

"I was hoping you'd be up on the hill with us," Bert said.

"Studying everything, you know."

"Maybe you and Sarenda could study everyone from inside. You wouldn't have to dance or anything. Just sit there and talk and watch or something."

"I don't know," Sarenda said. "It seems so . . . so. . . ." She shrugged. I guess she didn't know how it seemed.

"Sarenda, that just might work," Bert said. "Besides, it might rain or be cold. After Annie finishes working, maybe we could still go out sit on the hill and watch. If it isn't raining or too cold, that is."

So, that's how my friends decided to go to the dance.

During sixth period, I told Mrs. Carlton that if she still wanted me to help her, I could do it.

"That's wonderful, Annie," she said. "I don't know how I could do everything by myself."

Then I worked on my quilt. None of the other girls was even close to finishing her skirt. I liked making a quilt better than I thought I would. I liked figuring out how the pieces would fit and what colors looked good together. Mrs. Carlton stopped by twice and complimented me on it. A few of the other girls even glanced over to see what I was doing. Nobody called me rag-picker. Class time flew by and the bell rang. I had to hurry to get everything packed up.

Loniss wasn't on the bus again. Cheryl and Susan gossiped together as if they didn't even miss her. Janie Tackett had moved to the seat across the aisle from Lucas, who sat alone now, but he didn't look her way. Larry and Kenny still sat behind him, but the three didn't say much. Nobody said much anymore. Even Clovis had stopped asking where Loniss was.

The team had one more football game before the season ended, but I guess it didn't count since they were out of the running for the district championship. Nobody on the bus mentioned it—at least not that I could hear.

* * *

At home, Mama was waiting in the front room. I could see the worry in her eyes. "Your daddy done told me," she said.

"About me working for the home ec teacher?" I asked.

She nodded. "Work is all right. But don't dance," she said, shaking her head. "Sinful."

"I'm not dancing. I'll be busy with the food. Besides, I don't even know how to dance. Even if I did, no one would ask me to."

"Well, all right." She stared at me like she wanted to say something else. But then she went upstairs.

She must have been thinking about it all day. When she wasn't thinking about Scott, that is.

* * *

As the dance drew closer, more and more kids talked about it at school. Well, the girls did. Those with dates already lined up talked about their dresses. Those without dates talked about which boys might not have dates yet and how could they get those boys to ask them. The Harvest Dance was the highlight of the fall. Halloween wasn't much celebrated in Bosworth County. Some of the churches were against it, houses were too far apart for trick-or-treating, and anyone pulling pranks or destroying anything was likely to get shot. So the dance was the big social event. But I'd never cared much for social events before. Probably because I'd never gone to any.

In 4th period, when I was folding the towels, I heard a couple of the girls gossiping about why Loniss and Lucas broke up.

"I heard Janie Tackett tell Lucas she saw Loniss kissing Alvin Bosworth in the parking lot," one girl said.

"Odds are good Janie was lying," said another girl. "She's had her eye on Lucas for I don't know how long."

"Well, I heard that Lucas confronted Loniss about it, and they had a big fight because she thought he didn't trust her," said the first girl.

I kept folding towels and didn't look their way. But I wasn't surprised that Janie Tackett might be involved.

On Saturday, I helped Aint Lulie get in more wood. "The signs point to colder weather," she said. "Likely we'll get a frost tonight." Even though the day was clear with not a cloud in the sky, the air seemed cooler by afternoon and I did not sweat from all the wood-hauling. "Clear days that soon get colder make Old Man Winter soon get bolder," Aint Lulie said as she built up the fire. "And it looks to be a clear night, too. 'Stars bright means a cold night,' Granny used to say. And 'Clear moon, frost soon.' Best put an extra kiver on the bed tonight."

I told her I'd do that.

When I'd walked home from Aint Lulie's, I'd noticed how quiet the woods were. A lot of the birds were gone now, headed to a warmer place than this. For a moment, I thought about contacting some of the birds that still lingered but thought better of it. But, as I lay in bed and waited for sleep, a little dog spoke to me from high on a hill in town: *I have made a nest under the covers, and I'll keep warm tonight.* And a hound at the trailer park broke in: *by the light of the moon, i'll tree me a coon.*

Before I got into bed, I pulled an old quilt out of the chest and put it on top of my regular quilt so I'd have an extra layer of warmth. I burrowed beneath my covers like some of the critters were likely doing in the leaves tonight. From my window, I could see the stars sparkle so clear and the quarter moon's bright light.

* * *

On Sunday morning, my room was so cold I didn't want to get out of bed. I looked out my frost-dotted window to see the grass glistening with misty white. When I went downstairs, Daddy was building up a fire in the Warm Morning heater, and Mama's cookstove took some of the chill out of the kitchen. The ride to church was cold since Daddy's truck had no heat, and I kept my coat tight around me.

Before preaching started, not many lingered outside to talk about the last game where the team lost again. It was an away game, so I guess most folks didn't want to spend the money to drive wherever it was played. It was too cold to stand outside, and there was a fire in the stove inside, so the church filled earlier than usual. Elder Stoutmire again asked for more donations of wood, mentioned some folks who needed extra prayer, and launched into his sermon by railing against temptation and sin. He used the upcoming dance as an example of an opportunity for young folks to be lured into sin and cautioned them to not be led into temptation. A lot of the older folks nodded and mumbled, "Amen." Some of the girls I knew for sure were going to the dance looked down lest Elder Stoutmire single them out. A few boys looked down, too, but first they cast sidelong glances to the girls. But I looked straight ahead, and the preacher's words blew past me like an ill wind.

On Monday, those same kids who looked down at church were talking about the dance and what fun it was going to be.

The week sped by. Mr. Wardell talked more and more about the upcoming election and tried to get us as excited about it as he was, Miss Brannigan continued the study of poems, and I continued to work on my quilt, which was taking shape nicely. A few girls would stop by my sewing machine to see how it was coming along. One or two mentioned their grandmas used to quilt. It was odd having girls who never used to speak to me suddenly tell me things. I almost felt like a regular person.

On the day of the dance, as soon as I got home from helping Aint Lulie, I carried water inside and filled the tub. Luckily the day had been warm—real Indian summer—so it wasn't cold in the house and I didn't have to build a fire. The day before, I'd taken a long shower at school and washed my hair, so I figured my hair would be all right.

When I'd helped Aint Lulie that morning with her yardwork, I'd kept a hat on so nothing would get in my hair and it would stay clean. She'd lent me a pair of her work gloves so I could pull the dead plants from her garden and not mess up my hands. Before I left, she handed me my skirt and the blouse she'd fixed with the lace on it.

"You have a real good time," she said. "Don't break too many boys' hearts."

"Not much chance of that," I told her. She ought to know that I'm not pretty enough to attract the boys.

"Wait a minute," she said. She picked some lemon balm from her herb patch beside the porch. "Rub this on you before you go. It'll make you smell pretty. Good thing the frost ain't nipped it yet."

I thanked her. "You better come go with me," I added.

"Cain't. You mought as well stay," she said as she stepped inside. She turned her back to me before I could answer "cain't." On the way home, I took care not to let my skirt or blouse catch on the branches.

Daddy was waiting on the front porch when I got there. The skin on his face was red and smooth like he'd shaved. "What time you reckon we ort to go?" he said.

"It starts at seven. I need to be there by five-thirty to help Mrs. Carlton get everything ready," I said.

"Well, I 'spect we better start about five, then." He snuffed out his cigarette, tossed the butt over the rail, and headed toward his shop before I could say anything else.

I took my skirt and blouse upstairs and hung them up before I started hauling water into the kitchen. Mama, who'd been stirring some soup on the stove, moved the pot to the back burner and left to give me some privacy. I heard her going up the steps, so I figured she'd spend the time looking out the upstairs window and waiting. Or maybe praying for my soul. The soup simmered without her.

After I'd scrubbed off all the morning's sweat and grime, I put on my robe and dipped my bathwater into buckets that I emptied onto what was left of Mama's sage plant near the kitchen door. I hung the tub back on its nail on the porch and fixed myself a bowl of soup. After I ate, I went straight upstairs to get ready.

While I rubbed the lemon balm on my skin, I heard Mama go back downstairs. Soon I heard Daddy come in. I guessed he ate earlier than usual so he wouldn't get hungry while he drove me to school. Meanwhile, I cleaned my best church shoes as good as I could and hoped nobody would notice how old and worn they were. Then I brushed my hair and pinned it up. I slipped the lipstick I'd found into my coat pocket along with a couple of quarters and a handkerchief. I didn't see any sense in carrying a pocketbook. I didn't have much to put in it anyway.

At quarter to five, I came downstairs. Daddy was waiting in the front room. He looked at his watch. "Reckon we'd best git started," he said. "Won't hurt to be early."

Mama came in from the kitchen. "Real purty," she said. I didn't know if she meant my clothes or me. She wiped her hands on her apron and gave me a sort of wave as I followed Daddy out the door.

He'd spread a towel over the passenger side of the truck seat. "No use to ruin them good clothes," he said.

Before long, we were on our way. In my mind, I could hear Precious digging at my thoughts. *Not now*, I told her. I wanted to say, *Not ever again*. I kept my eyes on the road ahead as Daddy and I headed to town.

It was turning dark when he let me off at the door and said he'd be back in two or three hours and for me to wait by the door for him. I watched him drive over to the far side of the lot where the woods began, and there he parked his truck. Likely he wasn't going anywhere. I hoped nobody would notice him.

Mrs. Carlton opened the door for me and I followed her to the home ec room where she handed me a white apron and cap. I put on my lipstick, hung up my coat, and we got busy moving plates of cookies and bowls of punch to the gym. I lost count of how many trips we made. I wondered how the kids would ever be able to eat so much. The gym looked so pretty with the colored crepe paper streamers that the pep club had put up the day before. In each basketball goal was a big bucket of flowers. The bleachers had been pushed against the wall and the janitor had set up tables in front. Mrs. Carlton handed me a stack of gold tablecloths, and before long we had each table covered. The gym hardly looked like a gym at all.

At six-thirty, Mr. Darley the principal arrived and told us how good everything looked.

"Make sure you keep an eye on the punchbowl," he said. "No telling if some boy will get the idea to spike it."

"We've got everything covered," Mrs. Carlton said and gave me a wink.

A few teachers who'd signed up to chaperone came in, and Mrs. Carlton went to talk to them. The DJ arrived and set up his record player and speakers. Some members of the school band who were going to play a couple of numbers set up in the opposite corner. I straightened a few tablecloths even though they looked fine. I just felt like I needed something to do.

At ten minutes to seven, Mrs. Carlton and I took our places behind the serving table. Through the closed door I could hear sounds of cars pulling into the lot and excited voices near the door.

At five minutes to seven, Deputy Wiley Shortridge and Bruno came through the door and headed toward Mr. Darley. I was glad Bruno didn't look my way.

"Some guy in an old truck at the end of the lot," I heard Wiley say. "You want me to run him off?"

Before Mr. Darley could answer, I spoke up. "That's my daddy," I said. "He's just waiting for me to finish work. He didn't—didn't want to be in the way."

"Oh, well, I guess that's all right," Mr. Darley said. "But wouldn't you like to invite him in? We could always use another chaperone."

I thought about Daddy and his grimy overalls and what the other kids would say. "He said he'd prefer to wait in the truck." It was only a little lie, but Bruno glared at me. *Liar*, he growled.

Bruno and Wiley strolled around the gym, checking things out I guess. As they passed the table, Wiley snaked out his hand and grabbed a couple of cookies.

"Everything looks OK," he said to Mr. Darley. "Me and Bruno will go keep an eye on things outside."

At exactly seven, Mr. Darley opened the doors and the kids streamed in. I looked for Bert and Sarenda but didn't see them in the crowd. I watched the boys looking awkward in their suits and girls showing off their fancy dresses. A few weren't dressed any fancier than I was, which kind of surprised me. I watched the popular fancier-dressed girls look around for tables where they could see and be seen.

Loniss Hathaway came in with Alvin Bosworth. Her hair was all piled up on top of her head with little ringlets hanging down, and she wore the prettiest red dress I'd ever seen. Part of it was covered with red sequins that glittered like stars. She wore earrings and a matching ring made from some kind of white stones that sparkled whenever the light caught them. When she waved at her friends, reflections from her ring sent bits of light dancing around the room. I was reminded of the "Richard Corey" poem that Miss Brannigan had us read because Loniss was rich and "glittered when she walked." I'd never seen anyone so pretty, and I had to remind myself not to stare. But lots of others stared too.

Alvin had on what I figured must be a tuxedo. His hand grasped Loniss's elbow, and he steered her over to a table in the middle of the front row. I watched the other girls, who'd never been popular and didn't dress fancy, sit at the back tables where they wouldn't be seen and where maybe nobody would notice that they didn't have dates or sparkly dresses or fine jewelry. I watched them look enviously at Loniss. And I watched Lucas Lawson, sitting at a back table with his buddies Larry and Kenny, stare at Loniss, too. I guess none of them brought dates either.

When the tables were filled, Mr. Darley picked up the microphone and welcomed everyone and said he hoped they'd have a good time and would drive home safely afterwards. Nobody paid much attention to him, so he signaled the band to start playing. A bunch of the boys got up to get punch and cookies for their girlfriends. Seemed like nobody wanted to be the first to dance. I got so busy ladling punch that I lost sight of Loniss. I lost sight of anyone who wasn't right in front of me.

Soon the band stopped playing and the musicians put up their instruments and went to join their dates. The DJ took over and announced some songs he'd be playing. I'd never heard of most of them, but when the music started, a few kids got up and danced. Alvin and Loniss were among them. Lucas and his buddies glared at them. Lucas took a little bottle from his coat pocket, swigged from it, and passed it to Kenny who took a sip and passed it to Larry. It must have given Lucas courage because he swaggered over to Janie Tackett and invited her to dance. From the look on her face, you'd have thought she'd been crowned queen. Two other girls sitting at her table giggled.

About that time, Sarenda made her entrance. She wore something like a ballet dancer would wear, only longer. Her outfit sparkled and glittered, but not as much as Loniss's, and she danced by herself to the center of the gym and spun around a few times. Most of the kids stopped dancing and formed a big circle around her. On her head was a sparkly crown, and she carried a wand with a star on the end.

"I'm your fairy godmother," she announced as she danced around the circle, "and I have the power to make dreams come true."

Some kids laughed at her or made remarks—"stupid hippie," "must be high," stuff like that. She waved her wand at some and yelled curses at them.

"A pox on thee!" she shouted at Janie Tackett, who'd made some kind of remark to Sarenda that I couldn't hear. "May your pimples increase in size!" Janie fled back to her table and left Lucas standing.

"May trouble plague your days!" Sarenda shouted at him. Twirling around, she waved her wand in Alvin and Loniss's general direction. "May the high and mighty be brought low!" she yelled. "You know who I mean!" She twirled around faster and faster. "And may all of you get what you so richly deserve!"

Mr. Darley hurried toward Sarenda, grabbed her arm, and escorted her to the side where Bert waited. That part of the gym was too dark for me to see what was going on. Likely Bert was having second thoughts about bringing her inside.

I stood behind my table and watched the kids venture back on the floor to dance again. Sarenda didn't join them. After a few minutes, Mrs. Carlton sent me back to the home ec room for more cookies and punch. When I trundled the metal serving cart across the gym floor, I thought everyone would stare at me, but no one bothered. Maybe the music was too loud for anyone to hear the rattling cart. Maybe they were still thinking about Sarenda. I looked for her and Bert but didn't see them. Maybe they'd gone out to sit on the hilltop after all, or maybe Bert had convinced her to move to one of the tables further back in the dark.

Coming back through the hall, I saw Wiley and Bruno. "Cookies look good," Wiley said.

"Would you like one?" I said, and he scooped up three. While he stuffed them in his mouth, I handed a cookie to Bruno who snapped it up.

Thank you, said Bruno. Wiley said nothing. He and Bruno headed toward the gym. I guess there was no reason for him to stay outside.

By the time I got back to the gym where I set out the cookies and refilled the punchbowl, Mr. Darley was standing in a circle of light in the middle of the floor. Behind him, on the platform next to the DJ's table, were two chairs covered in gold-colored cloth. Each chair had a crown on it. Nearby was a boy from the yearbook staff with his camera ready.

"Now it's time to crown the king and queen of the Harvest Dance," Mr. Darley announced. He cleared his throat and his secretary Miss Filsten came forward with two envelopes. "We'll crown the queen first," he said, slowly opening one envelope. "And the winner is—Loniss Hathaway!"

There was some polite clapping, but nobody was really surprised. Loniss usually won things like this. She came forward, Miss Filsten put the crown on her head, and the yearbook boy snapped her picture. I watched Alvin edge closer. Likely he figured he'd be crowned king.

"Now for the king," Mr. Darley said, opening the envelope even slower than he did the first time. "The king of the 1972 Bosworth County Harvest Dance is—Lucas Lawson!"

Not many clapped for Lucas when he came forward. Then I remembered. The voting had been weeks ago—before Loniss dumped Lucas.

Mr. Darley took the crown from Miss Filsten and put it on Lucas's head. Lucas and Loniss stood side by side, but with some distance between them. When the yearbook boy came up to take a picture, he had to ask them to move closer together. Neither one smiled for the camera. The crowd gathered around them, so I couldn't see what happened next. But I could hear it.

The DJ started a slow dance record—I think he said the song was called "Let's Stay Together"—and Mr. Darley announced, "Now the king and queen will lead everyone in a dance."

I heard Lucas say loud enough for everyone to hear, "Looks like you gotta dance with me after all, Loniss!" and I heard Loniss say even louder, "I'd rather die first!" She pushed her way out of the crowd, past my table, and out the door. She wasn't wearing her crown when she left. Alvin was close behind her, though.

Lucas stood alone and laughed. He pitched his crown to Mr. Darley and went back his buddies. Mr. Darley announced for everyone to go ahead and dance. A few couples moved back onto the dance floor, and then a few more. Before long most couples were dancing. Lucas must have slipped out somehow because no one saw him after that.

While I was taking the empty punchbowl and cookie plates back to the home ec room, I saw Alvin coming back. I guess to get Loniss's coat or something. He was frowning and didn't look my way.

Before I could watch what he did next, Mrs. Carleton handed me an envelope and told me what a big help I'd been. "You can go ahead and leave if you want, or else go join your friends," she said. "I can do the clean-up myself."

After I thanked her, I walked toward the dark area to see if I could find Bert and Sarenda, but I didn't see them. All I saw were some couples making out. I hurried outside and stood in the light by the door. *So that's what a dance is*, I thought. I looked around to see if Bert and Sarenda might be outside, but the trees blocked the full moon on the hillside, so I couldn't tell if they were there or not. I didn't see Alvin's MG or Lucas's truck.

It wasn't long until I heard Daddy's truck start up and saw his headlights come on. In less than a minute, he'd pulled up to the gym door and I got in. I could smell liquor in the truck but I didn't see any bottle. Under the seat, I reckoned.

"That teacher pay you?" he asked before we were even out of the parking lot. I nodded. "If you want," he said, "I could put the money away and keep it safe for you."

I knew if he got his hands on my money, he'd drink it up before the week was out. "I need it to buy some warm clothes for winter," I told him. That was a lie. I'd make do this winter with what I had.

He turned onto the road and changed the subject. "Ya know,

when I was younger, I was quite the dancer. Went to every dance they had around here. I was first on the floor and last one off."

"Why don't you dance anymore?" I asked.

"I met your mama," he said. Then he was quiet.

We drove off into the dark and up the mountain. I hoped he could keep the truck on the road until we got home.

* * *

Sunday morning was chilly and cloudy with a hint of winter in the air. Mama didn't say a word about the dance. Did she think even talking about a dance—especially on Sunday—might be sinful? I was tired from staying on my feet so long and being up way past my regular bedtime. I didn't want to go to church but Mama didn't give me any choice.

After breakfast, Daddy drove us to church, dropped us off at the edge of the graveled area, and drove off. Mama might have been able to get him to give up dancing, but he wouldn't give her his Sunday mornings. At least he hadn't since Scott died.

Elder Stoutmire hadn't yet opened the door, and folks waiting to get inside seemed quieter than usual. The men weren't laughing or talking or complaining. Mostly they whispered and looked serious. I stayed close to Mama as we walked toward the door. We were nearly on the porch when one of the women stopped her and whispered, "Oh, Miz Caldwell, did you hear about that gal from the high school being missing?"

Mama shook her head. "Who?" she asked.

"The mill manager's gal," the woman said. "Might be she's run off. Or could be somebody took her."

Another woman agreed. "She'll fetch a pretty penny in ransom money if somebody done took her."

What little information there was about Loniss's disappearance circled around the group. Someone was kin to the dispatcher for the state police and had already heard about the call the Hathaways made at first daylight.

So. Maybe Loniss didn't go home last night. I sent my thoughts to Precious.

She came home, the dog told me. *They all said good night and thought she was going to bed, but then somebody knocked on the door, so soft only a dog's keen ears could hear. But Loniss saw the lights from her window, and closed me in her room when she went downstairs. She still had on her dress. I heard the door open and then close. She didn't come back. I couldn't see how she got away. I scratched and scratched on the door but nobody came until Mom found me this morning when Loniss didn't come down to breakfast. There was yelling, but not at me. Before long, a car making a squealing noise came. I didn't like the sound and howled.*

Maybe somebody did kidnap Loniss. But who?

Mama hustled me into the church, and we took our usual seats. A fire was going in the church stove, but it hadn't yet taken the chill out. Likely Elder Stoutmire had started it an hour or so earlier. Through the window, I could see a large pile of split wood that someone had dropped off. It hadn't been there the week before. Part of it was already stacked. I wondered why whoever brought it hadn't stacked the whole pile.

Before Elder Stoutmire launched into his sermon, he asked the congregation to join him in praying for the little lost gal. He'd likely never met Loniss—her folks wouldn't attend a church like this one. He wouldn't approve of the dress she wore last night or her dancing. But at least he didn't mention the dance and instead beseeched God to look after the lost sheep and guide her safely home to the fold. What else could he do? Then he thanked whoever had donated and stacked most of the split firewood for the church. He asked for help stacking the rest of it and mentioned more firewood donations were still needed to get the church through the winter. Nobody spoke up to volunteer though. Most folks had their own winter work to do.

While Elder Stoutmire droned on, I wondered if Loniss had run off with Alvin Bosworth. Maybe they'd gone across the state line to get married. Every so often a high school girl did something like that, usually to escape a bad home situation or else to get married before the baby she was carrying started to show. But Loniss had a good home and parents who gave her everything. And I figured she was too careful to get herself in a family way.

After preaching, Daddy was waiting to pick us up. All Mama said was "Mill manager's gal is missing. I knowed nothing good would come from all that dancing."

"I seen her," Daddy said. "I seen her leave the dance early. She looked real mad. Then that banker's boy come out and handed her coat to her, and she got in his little car. Lucas come out then hisself, and him and that rich boy threw a few punches at each other. They musta seen Shortridge coming toward 'em on account they broke off fighting and left."

"Reckon you ought to tell the law?" Mama said.

"Wiley Shortridge saw as much as me. Maybe more. He follered 'em a little ways and then come back."

Then the longest Sunday morning conversation we'd had in a couple of years ended, and we rode the rest of the way in familiar silence. But I heard the sound of a bottle roll and clink under Daddy's seat. If Mama heard it, she didn't let on.

After dinner, I ran to Aint Lulie to tell her the news. I was hoping she might have gotten a sign or something, but she hadn't. "Well, it's a full moon tonight," she said. "The Hunter's Moon. There's some folks believe that a full moon causes madness, and you oughtn't sleep in the light of it. But I don't reckon that had anything to do with that gal being gone."

I stayed with Aint Lulie the rest of the afternoon, telling her about what the dance was like and what all I saw. She told me about the dances and play parties she used to go to in people's houses. "They'd roll up the rug if there was one and move all the furniture to the side. Somebody generally had a fiddle, and we'd all dance 'til we couldn't dance no more. Lotta folks danced the clog, and I reckon I'uz one of 'em when I'uz about your age."

Soup simmered on the stove, and Aint Lulie insisted I eat some with her before I went home. It was dark when we finished. As I picked up my coat from off her bed, I remembered what she'd said the other day about dreaming under a new quilt. "Did you have any dreams the night you slept under your new quilt?" I asked her.

"I might've, but I cain't recollect real good," she said. "Something about somebody's bad fortune leading to another's good fortune. Didn't make a whole lot of sense to me, tell you the truth." She cleared the table while I buttoned up my coat.

"The full moon ought to light you home pretty good," she said just before we said our usual good-byes.

And it did. I could hear sounds of animals on the move amid the dry leaves, but I spoke to none of them. I couldn't help but wonder, though, how a bad fortune could lead to a good fortune.

* * *

On Monday morning, Clovis asked me first thing if I'd heard about Loniss.

"Elder Stoutmire said she was missing and had us pray," I told him. I didn't mention that Daddy saw Alvin and Lucas fighting.

He didn't ask the others that got on after me. I guess he figured they'd tell without being asked, but none of them did. Not many on the bus talked about Loniss being gone. Lucas wasn't on the bus either, and his friends Kenny and Larry were awfully quiet. Loniss's friends Susan and Cheryl tried to get a prayer circle going for Loniss on the bus, but only a few participated. Janie and few of the other girls whispered back and forth. Clovis didn't say another word. I didn't either.

At school, though, it seemed like everybody was talking about Loniss and Lucas not being there. Alvin had a black eye and some bruises on his face, but he wasn't saying much. Kids speculated on what might have happened. Somebody said the state police had questioned him first thing, and his daddy had gotten a lawyer who told him not to say anything, and a rumor spread through school that Alvin might be involved. Another rumor spread that maybe Loniss and Lucas had gotten back together and run off to get married. At any rate, no one had seen Loniss or Lucas since the night of the dance. If they did, they were keeping quiet about it.

Teachers tried to hold class like always, but nobody paid much attention. While Mr. Wardell tried as usual to get everybody excited about next week's election, I turned my mind toward Ranger.

He didn't come home last night, Ranger told me. *i don't know where he's at. i howled this mornin until the woman come out to feed me she was complainin that her sorry son won't there to look after me or do his mornin' chores. i didn't see the man, but sometimes he goes off for days too. "Like father, like son," the woman said. she dumped some scraps in my pan and then untied me so I could run free.*

At lunch, Bert and Sarenda speculated on what might have happened.

"I'm pretty sure that Loniss has been kidnapped," Bert said, "and it's just a matter of time before the Hathaways get a ransom note."

"More like Loniss is hiding out to get attention," Sarenda said, "and I'll bet you that maybe Lucas is helping her."

When they asked me what I thought, I said I didn't know. And I really didn't, even though a bad feeling had slithered across me like a snake. I didn't tell them I'd talked to Lucas's hound or Loniss's little dog.

By mid-afternoon, Wiley Shortridge was taking kids out of class and asking them what they saw at the dance. When my turn came—during home ec—I told him I was too busy serving refreshments to have seen much. That I'd seen Loniss get mad and leave, that Alvin had gone after her, and that Lucas had left, too. Apparently that was what everybody else had seen. He didn't have much to go on.

As the week wore on, the speculations continued. On Tuesday, the state police came and talked to a lot of the kids Wiley Shortridge had talked to, and a search team with a bloodhound scoured the woods behind the school. From the school's back windows, we could watch them going back and forth through the woods. Both the state police and the search team came up empty-handed. *They ain't here*, the bloodhound told me. *Never have been in these woods. Only trace is in the parking lot and in the building. My time is wasted here.* The state police didn't bother talking to me.

In home ec, I finished stitching together my quilt top, and Mrs. Carlson held it up to show the other girls and told them how quilts had been a Appalachian tradition for a couple hundred years and how women used to get together to have quiltings. "Of course, that was before we had sewing machines," she said. "Now, Annie needs a bottom for the quilt and some batting to put between. Whether her quilt will be a lightweight quilt or a heavy one depends on how thick the batting is. After the top, batting, and bottom are pinned together, the actual quilting begins."

Then she explained how the quilting would be done. Afterward, a few told me my quilt top was real pretty.

Tuesday evening, I told Aint Lulie about all the goings-on. "Seems to me that gal is where she or somebody don't want nobody to find her. And they ain't found that Lawson boy?"

"Nobody's seen him," I told her. "It's all a big mystery." Then I went about my chores while Aint Lulie fixed us something to eat.

On Wednesday, kids talked about how they saw the Hathaways on TV the night before, and how they begged for someone to tell them anything that might help. The Hathaways told on TV how Loniss had come in from the dance and seemed upset and didn't want to talk much. Mrs. Hathaway told about calling Loniss down for Sunday morning breakfast and how, when Loniss and her dog didn't come downstairs, she went to her room and couldn't find her. Her bed hadn't been slept in. Her dog was upset. The kids picked apart the details like buzzards cleaning up a carcass, but I said nothing.

At lunch Bert wanted to pick apart the details again. "Seems like somebody ought to have seen her by now," he said. "If she's alive, that is."

"I don't want to hear another word about her," Sarenda said. "No good comes from talking about it. We'll know when we know." I sided with Sarenda.

In home ec, I worked on the bottom for my quilt. I decided to make it of long strips of solid-color material about six inches wide sewed together. I was lucky to find a lot of red and blue and yellow material in the rag bags. Some of the girls watched while I cut the strips.

"I could iron what you've already cut," Cheryl offered. "That way you'd finish quicker."

I took her up on her offer. Seems like the girls were almost as interested in the mystery of how my quilt would look as they were about the mystery of Loniss's disappearance. Or maybe it just took their minds off what could have happened to their friend.

Meanwhile the leaves continued to fall, and the days and nights grew cooler. As soon as I got home from school, I still went to Aint Lulie's to see about her and her chores. When I came back into the cabin's warmth after emptying and cleaning Aint Lulie's slop jar, I thought of her Aint Pearl who had ordered it so long ago and how little I'd ever heard her spoken of.

"Why won't anybody ever talk about your Aint Pearl?" I asked. "Mama won't even allow her name to be mentioned."

"It's a long story," Aint Lulie said, "and a right sad one." She took some leftover biscuits from a bowl on the table and put them into the warming oven. "I'll tell it to you after we get us something to eat. Maribelle's gal stopped by today and give me some blackberry jelly. It'll go good with these biscuits."

After we eaten the last biscuit, I threw a couple more logs in the fireplace. We pulled our chairs close to the fire. I could hear the crackle of the flames inside and a light wind starting to blow outside. Lights and shadows danced around the cabin. Aint Lulie started her story.

"Aint Pearl's full name was Annie Pearl. You're named for her. That'uz your daddy's doing, and your mama didn't care for it but wouldn't go agin him. But to get to the story, Pearl was Papa's youngest sister. Actually, she was his half-sister, for Papa's daddy was Granny's first husband, James Elexander Caldwell. He didn't make it back from Cold Harbor, but his third cousin Jacob

Caldwell did. Won't long til Jacob married James Elexander's widow. He was a good bit older'n her, but she needed a husband and he'uz willing. Marrying him is why Mariah Duff Caldwell is your great-great-grandma twice, and your daddy is a second half-cousin or something like that to your mama. There's more kinship in the mix, too. If I ain't mistaken, Mariah and James Elexander was second or third cousins on the Caldwell side and possibly third or fourth cousins on the Duff side. Now there's some folks around here has married first cousins, but none of our direct line ever married closer than second. Still, if you was to want to marry somebody ain't kin to you, you gotta go off somewheres far. That's what my papa done when he married my mama, Sarah Dempsey. She lived over the mountain."

I was getting confused by how tangled up our family lines were. And she still hadn't gotten back to what happened to Pearl. "You were going to tell me how Pearl died," I reminded her.

"I'm gitting to it," she said. "But that path kindly has some twists and turns. Now Jacob and Mariah had two girls, your Great-great-aunt Pearl and your Great-grandma Cora."

Already I was having trouble keeping track of who I was kin to and how many different ways, but I did my best to follow what she was saying.

"Pearl was only nine years older than me, so we was more like sisters ourselves. She'uz born late in her mama's life. Her daddy Jacob, who was a good fifteen years older than her mama, died when Pearl was four or five. Papa—recollect he was James Elexander's boy Duffield?—well, he took over this house then. He was new-married but still living at home. A lot of men brung their brides home so their mamas could teach 'em to cook things the husband liked. Cora—recollect, she'uz your great-grandma?—was Papa's half-sister and Pearl's full sister. Cora was maybe ten or eleven at the time. So when Papa married my mama, she moved into this cabin where her mother-in-law and two sisters-in-law were already living. That'uz how folks did in the old days. Whole bunch under one roof. Papa and Mama lived on this side of the house, and my grandma and my aunts lived on the other. The women shared the kitchen. That old kitchen'uz still in use then. You keeping up with me?"

I nodded. But this wasn't getting to the secret of Pearl's death. There was no use in hurrying Aint Lulie, though.

"Anyhow, won't long 'til I come along, and four years later come my first brother—who is your granddaddy James Caldwell—and then a few years later come brother Elex and finally my little sister Amma. We all lived like one big family. The house'uz getting a mite crowded, but Papa won't ready to build the new place yet. Since I'uz the oldest, I went to live on the other side and slept in the loft with Pearl and Cora. My little brothers slept in the loft on this side, and my baby sister slept in this room with Mama and Daddy."

Aint Lulie kept going on about how they lived when she was little. I guess it pleased her to remember how things used to be. But it was getting late, and I still didn't know why no one would speak of Pearl. And Aint Lulie was taking her sweet time getting to it. Outside the wind howled louder and made a sighing sound in the chimney. I dreaded having to walk home in the wind and the dark.

Aint Lulie yawned. "I reckon this story'll take a mite longer that I first thought it would. Mebbe we ought to quit here for the night."

I was tired too, so I agreed. Making my way home in the dark, I thought about all those who came before me. I was glad that the path I traveled homeward was straight and not twisty like the family line that resulted in me. And I was glad I was going home, even if my home was cold and silent and not bright and warm like Loniss's.

When I came out of the woods, I looked up at the moon and wondered if Loniss was maybe looking up at the same moon tonight.

CHAPTER 6: DISCOVERY

As the week wore on, folks talked about Loniss less and less. Nobody had heard anything new, and no news was good news. Aint Lulie finally told me more about her Aint Pearl, though. On Thursday we got a bit of sleet that had started as a cold rain, so Aint Lulie's fire felt good and her stew and biscuits tasted even better.

"Don't like the way the sleet comes in fits and starts." Aint Lulie peeked out the window at the darkness setting in. "Kindly like a lap baby fighting off sleep. It don't bode well."

I wasn't sure if I should ask again about Aint Pearl, but I really wanted to know. But after a while, Aint Lulie sat down in her rocker and began to talk of Pearl again.

"Pearl fancied flowers and pretty things. She'uz always bringing bunches of daisies and Queen Anne's lace and other wildflowers into the house, even though Granny declared they'uz weeds and not fitten for house decorations. Sometimes she'd bring in bunches of pokeberries because she liked the color so much. Pearl'uz the one who planted that Madame Hardy rose by the house corner. Somebody she knew give her a slip of it. In mid-April, when the lilac bushes 'round the old kitchen would bloom, she'd bring in armloads of lilacs and this place would smell so good." Aint Lulie smiled at the good memories.

"And her hats! I don't believe she had a hat that didn't have flowers on it. She wore her hair pinned up on top of her head with her hat perched up on top. She looked like a fine lady, too fine for the likes of around here. Granny would tell her she ought not be putting on such airs.

"T'uz about ten when we all went to a box supper at church. That'uz where gals old enough to go courting would fix up a supper and single men would bid on it. So Cora and Pearl both fixed boxes. A railroad man visiting some'a his Byrne kinfolks in town came with 'em to the church and bid the highest on Cora's box and got to eat it with her. I reckon they'uz smitten with each other right off. He visited ever time he got a chance, and four or five months later they run off and got married. He worked outta Bristol, so she had to go off all that way with him. She'd left a note pinned to her pillow, so we all knowed what she'uz doing, but still it took two weeks for us to get a letter from her saying she'uz all right and not to worry. 'Well, I ain't surprised,' I recollect Granny saying. 'I once saw in her hand that she'd find happiness far away.'

"That'uz when I held out my hand to Granny. 'What do you see in my hand?' I asked her. She studied on it for a bit. 'You will be strong and live long. Happiness will come later than sooner. But you will be wise and see what others don't,' she told me. It didn't make a lot of sense to me back then, but I never forgot her words. I've studied over 'em a time and a time."

"But what about Pearl?" I asked. "Did she find a beau?"

"Pearl found herself a beau indeed. Otha Tompkins, who won't from around here, come to work in timbering out the far side of the mountain. He'uz at the church and bid on her box, so the two et supper together. A week or two later he come calling, and he'd stop to see her ever so often. He even give her a picture of hisself, and she set it up on her dresser. He'uz seven years older'n her, and Papa didn't think much of that a'tall. I reckon he was afraid she'd run off, too, and she won't quite old enough. Whenever Otha come courting, Papa tried his best to keep his eye on Pearl. But whenever Papa had work to do and couldn't watch 'em, he bade me stay close and said he'd switch me good if I didn't mind him. I reckon Otha got tired of somebody else always being around, and he took to hiring a buggy and taking Pearl for rides. Papa laid down the law to Pearl that she won't allowed to go less'n I went along. Otha always made me sit in the boot—that's a little space in back, kindly like a wagon bed only a good bit smaller—and told me not to look forward. But I still could still hear kissing sounds, so I knowed what they'uz doing. Sometimes they'd whisper and laugh and carry on. I didn't care much for Otha, but I liked going on buggy rides, though, even though it'uz a rough ride in the boot."

"Did your grandma ever say if she saw anything in Pearl's hand?"

"I saw her study Pearl's hand once when she'uz picking a splinter out. She frowned and looked away when she saw me watching. I asked her later if she saw anything besides the splinter."

"What did she say?"

"Said it looked to her like Pearl wouldn't run off like Cora did. But she said I won't to tell her. Turns out, Pearl did go off for a while, but we knowed where she was headed. Cora had got in the family way and sent for Pearl to come to Bristol and stay until after the baby come." Aint Lulie smiled. "That baby'uz your Great Uncle Matthew."

I tossed another log onto the fire and watched the sparks fly up. From what I could tell, it sounded like the wind had died down. And I hoped Aint Lulie was getting close to the end of her story.

"Otha didn't want her to go all that far off, but Pearl declared her sister needed her help and she couldn't very well refuse. It'uz October then—'bout this time a' year—and he give her an opal ring. Said it was to remember him by 'til she come back. They'uz setting on the porch, and I'uz around the corner where they couldn't see me, but I could hear what they said. 'I'll never forget you, Otha,' Pearl said. I reckon they kissed a spell, for they'uz quiet for a minute or two. 'Well, I gotta be on my way,' he said. I heard hoofbeats as his horse trotted off, so I come onto the porch with Pearl and we watched him go down the road. He never looked back. Pearl had her hand hid in the fold of her skirt.

"When we'd gone inside, I said, 'I wanna see your ring.' 'What ring?' Granny up and said, 'Why'd he give you a ring?' I didn't like the look on Granny's face. 'It's jist a keepsake,' Pearl said. Granny snatched Pearl's hand away from her skirt and studied on that ring. A dark look passed over Granny's face. 'You oughtn't have that on your hand. It brings bad luck to wear an opal if it ain't your birthstone.' Pearl laughed. 'That's jist an old saying,' she said. 'A ring don't bring luck good or bad.'

"But Pearl took the ring up to the loft and put it in her dresser drawer. That night, after she brushed her hair in front of the mirror and then brushed mine, she took the ring from outta the drawer and slipped it on. That ring sparkled in the moonlight like it had a life a' its own. 'Don't you dare tell, Ma,' she whispered. And I didn't. I reckon I ort to have, but I didn't."

"Why not?" I asked.

"Granny always blamed that ring for Pearl dying."

The sleet was pinging hard against the cabin roof, and Aint Lulie said I'd best go before it got worse. We said our farewells in the old way, and I fairly ran down the path in the dark. I was chilled to the bone when I got inside. Even after I was in bed with quilts piled on me, I shivered for a long time before sleep overtook me.

* * *

School was late because of the icy roads. I'd figured it would be, so I stayed in the front room until I heard the bus coming. Then, with my coat clutched tight around me, I ran down the drive while Clovis waited. A lot of kids didn't even come to school. I guess they figured school would be called off. And I heard some of the roads were even more treacherous than mine.

The first two classes were cancelled, so English was my first class. Miss Brannigan read us a short poem called "Fire and Ice" that was about how the world might be destroyed. It was by the same man who'd written the poem about the road diverging. Nobody much felt like discussing it, though. She read us another, "Stopping by Woods on a Snowy Evening." Some of the boys laughed when she got to the word "queer" in the second stanza. One sentence stuck in my mind: "But I have promises to keep, and miles to go before I sleep."

In home ec, I finished the bottom of my quilt. I was folding it up and wondering how I would get any batts for the filling when Mrs. Carlson stopped by and told me she'd found a couple bags of batting at home and, if I could use them, she'd let me have them.

"How much would I owe you for them?" I asked.

"Not a cent!" she said. "I bought them years ago and never got around to using them. They're just taking up space. I guess they were waiting for someone who could use them."

By the time class was over, the roads were clear. I couldn't wait to tell Aint Lulie about my good fortune, even though it was likely that Mrs. Carlson was just giving me charity.

Since not many were on the bus and Clovis didn't have to make as many stops, we made pretty good time. The kids were starting to talk a little more again, as if the whole Loniss and Lucas thing never happened. Larry took to sitting behind Susan and Cheryl, so Janie Tackett moved into the empty seat beside Kenny. He didn't look thrilled, but he didn't ask her to move either. I guess she figured he was the next best thing to Lucas. And the talk turned back to who watched what on TV, who'd already gotten new winter clothes, and what there was to do on weekends now that the weather was getting colder.

"Hey, Clovis!" yelled Larry. "I hear tell you got yourself a brand new Ford Ranger F-150. Izzat true?"

"Yep," said Clovis. "A blue one."

"Pretty good for a bus driver's salary," Kenny said. "Or maybe the milk business has improved."

"Mebbe it has." Clovis pulled up to the trailer park and let Kenny and Larry off.

* * *

That evening Aint Lulie announced, "Maribelle's gal stopped by this afternoon to see how I'uz doing. She'uz glad to see the ice hadn't caused me no problems. She brung me some fresh-made peach crisp, and I figgered I'd save it 'til you got here. I reckon I'll put it in the warming oven now."

I hurried to get my chores done. While the smell of peach crisp filled the cabin, she continued her story about Pearl. "I missed Pearl something awful while she'uz gone helping Aint Cora. I reckon Otha missed her too. After she'd been gone a couple weeks, he took off work and went to Bristol to spend the day, and they had their picture made together. She sent us their picture and Granny put it up on the mantelpiece. A man and woman don't have their picture made together without they'uz getting mighty serious.

"But something happened, and we couldn't figure out what or why. Otha never was one to write, so could be they kindly lost touch. Could be they fell out about something. Pearl never would say much about it. Christmas came and went, and she never heard the first word from him.

"In mid-January, Granny'uz down at the store in town when she heard that right after Christmas that Otha got married to a gal who lived two ridges over. Granny won't back from town ten minutes 'til she took that picture off'n the mantelpiece.

"I reckon it like to about broke Pearl's heart when she found out. Granny had wrote the news to Cora, and I reckon Cora was the one to tell Pearl. It'uz late January before Cora decided she could manage the baby by herself, and Pearl come on back home. Daddy hitched up the black gelding to the buggy and went to get her at the station, but he didn't ask me if I wanted to go with him."

Aint Lulie rocked for a minute, thinking. Well," she said, "I reckon that peach crisp is ready to eat." She got up and spooned some into two bowls and handed me one. While we ate, she continued her story.

"Pearl didn't seem like herself—more like the husk of who she used to be. Awful quiet for somebody who used to be so talky. I reckon she'uz still a mite upset about Otha getting married. I wanted her to tell me all about Bristol and what all there was to see and do there, but she said she won't feeling like talking about it jist yet. I reckon Bristol didn't agree much with her. Even though she had fleshened up some while she'd been gone, she was sickly in the mornings. Mama said Pearl was likely having female trouble.

"It won't but a few days after she come back that I heard her and Granny talking real low to each other. I'd been sent to the spring to fetch water, and I reckon I got back sooner than they expected me to. I'uz about to open the door and go in, but I stayed out in the cold so I could listen. There was enough space around the door that both wind and words went right through it. I heard Granny tell Pearl if she wanted to git reg'lar—'git reg'lar' was Granny's exact words—she'd have to take herself a dose of laudanum and jump from the high end of the porch a couple of times. Something told me I'd better not let them catch me listening, so I stayed outside until I heard one of them walking toward the door. Then I clunked my bucket against the doorstep so they knowed I'uz about to come in.

"I guess she done it the next morning while I'd rode off to the post office on the gelding. Mama'd decided to order Pearl something called Cardui that was supposed to be good for women, and I carried her order off to mail. Time I got back, Pearl had took to bed. Granny said I ought not to bother Pearl but to let her sleep. The only times she got up for the next few days was to go to the outhouse. When she didn't feel up to going out, she used her slop jar, and it fell to me to keep it emptied. One day I dropped the lid, and that's how it got that chipped place in it. Pearl didn't say nothing about it, though.

"In time Pearl got better, but she won't like she used to be. She didn't care about going to church or to any get-togethers folks'uz having. She mostly kept to herself and stayed upstairs. Granny said Pearl was run down and it would take a while to build her strength back up."

Aint Lulie stood up and stretched and took my empty bowl. "I'm real tired for some reason tonight," she said. "I'm gonna have to run you off early. Reckon I need to rest up so we can get my garden cleared off tomorrow."

We said our good-byes, and I started down the path. I felt like I still had miles to go before I'd sleep. But at least tomorrow was Saturday, so I'd be able to sleep a little later.

* * *

Saturday was cool and cloudy. Mama had baked biscuits for breakfast, so mid-morning I carried some to Aint Lulie. I found her sitting in her rocking chair with a quilt wrapped around her. I reckoned she hadn't added many logs to the fire which had burned lower than she usually let it.

"I'm feeling a mite puny this morning," she said. "Feeling my age, I reckon. Seems like the cold goes right through me now. Didn't used to." She perked up some when she saw the biscuits.

I got the fire built up and made up her bed. It was the first time I could remember her bed not being made in the morning. Aint Lulie wanted to "set a spell" before we went out, so we ate the biscuits while the cabin warmed up. To pass the time while we were setting, she picked up her story about Pearl where she'd left off.

"Seemed like Pearl was getting a mite better as spring wore on," she began. "Looked like the earth greening up and the flowers a'blooming cheered her up some, and she got her strength back and started working in the garden. She even talked about going back to work at the canning factory when it started up in summer. But she still kept close to home, except on some Sundays now and then when she felt like going to church. No sooner services was done, though, she'd go and set in the buggy until everbody else was ready to leave.

"One Saturday long about mid-June, Pearl got up early and worked in the garden. I recollect she hoed the weeds outta the rows of beans and sweet corn that had started coming up good, picked some peas for dinner and pulled some lettuce. She set the peas and lettuce on the table and went back out to pick some daisies. A few poke plants had berries, so she picked some a'them, too, along with some lily-of-the-valley and snakeroot. Those white flowers with the purplish-red poke stems and berries made a right pretty bouquet. When she brung 'em in the house and was putting 'em in a jar of water, Ma took her to task about it. 'The chaps'll git into them pokeberries and make a mess!' she said. Then Granny said, 'Them berries and snakeroot could make a chap real sick if they was to eat 'em. You best take 'em outta here.' Pearl allowed she'd take her bouquet upstairs where the chaps couldn't get it."

I'd heard Aint Lulie use the word *chaps* to mean *children* before. I guess she meant her little brothers and sister. If so, my granddaddy was likely one of the chaps. But I wasn't about to interrupt her to find out.

"Anyways, 'bout mid-morning, Granny decided she needed some saleratus and coffee and sugar from the store and told Pearl to go saddle the black gelding and ride to town and fetch 'em. Pearl took off her apron, put on her good bonnet, and stuffed the money Granny gave her into her reticule."

"A reticule?" I asked.

"That'uz a little drawstring handbag ladies carried. They could loop the cords around their wrists and it would be outta the way for them to hold the reins. After Pearl had rode off, Granny told me 'Your ma and me thought it'd do her good to get out some. She's pined for that no-good Tompkins boy long enough.' But Pearl'uz back in less'n two hours, and it looked to me like she'd been crying. She set the sack with Granny's goods on the table and went straight up to the loft. 'Looks like she's got a bee in her bonnet about something,' Granny said to Ma. Pearl had left the gelding sweaty and still saddled outside the back door, so it fell to me to do the unsaddling and currying.

"Time I was back from putting the gelding out to pasture, Granny had got dinner ready and was calling everbody to come eat. Pearl come on down from the loft real quiet-like and ate right along with the rest of us. I recollect it was a real good dinner. Ma had shelled out and cooked those peas, and Granny had baked some of her light rolls. After everbody finished eating and my brothers went out to play and Papa went back to cutting hay up in the top field, the womenfolk commenced to cleaning up.

"While they'uz washing dishes, Ma happened to ask Pearl if she seen anybody at the store. Pearl answered, 'Indeed I did! I saw that no-good Otha and his wife coming outta the store as I was going in. She'uz all plumped out like she'uz about to have a baby any minute. Didn't even have the common decency to stay home in her condition! No sooner they saw me, they turned their backs and walked off.' We didn't know what to say. Pearl throwed down her dishrag and hurried up to the loft where she flung herself on her bed. After a while I climbed up to see how she'uz getting on, but her face was agin the wall and it sounded like she'uz crying. I spoke her name, but she didn't look my way or say ary a thing. I went on back downstairs."

Aint Lulie stood up and stretched. "I got some soup I need to put on the stove. Why don't you see to the chores while I git the soup started."

She fetched a Mason jar from the dogtrot while I brought in some more wood and a few buckets of water. While her soup simmered, she made a trip to the outhouse and I split a little stovewood. When we'd finished our chores and I'd added another log to the fire, she sat down in her rocker and sighed. I felt like she was getting to the worst part.

"A couple hours later, we heard Pearl retching something awful. Ma was busy tending to my baby sister, so Granny was the one climbed up to see to Pearl. She hollered down to me to get some wet rags on account Pearl was feverish. I done what she told me and run to the loft with 'em. Pearl looked awful bad, but she asked me if I could help her to the outhouse. It was all I could do to get her down the steps and out the door. She stayed in the outhouse for a good twenty minutes or more. While I waited to help her back, Granny called from the house. She said she reckoned we ought to have Pearl downstairs until she got better. 'T'uz too old to be climbing up that loft,' she said. 'No telling how many times Pearl's gonna need tending.'

"I helped Granny pull the trundle bed outten from under her big bed. Ma wanted to come in to help, but Granny stopped her and said if Pearl had something catching, best thing would be not to risk having the chaps catch it. Granny had me fetch Pearl's bedclothes from upstairs and set 'em outside for washing later. Granny won't gonna take no chances.

"When Pearl come outta the outhouse, we helped her into bed. I went back up to the loft and fetched Pearl's nightgown and her slop jar. It was might nigh full, so I carried it out and emptied it.

She thrashed around and moaned most of the afternoon. Granny brought in a basin for her to retch into, and Granny and me took turns sitting with her. Every hour or so, we had to hold the basin for her or else help her to the slop jar. I emptied that slop jar a couple more times before nightfall. When I was in there alone with her, Pearl asked me to fetch her reticule from the loft and I done it, though I didn't know why she had need of it. I figgered if it give her comfort to have it, she ort to have it. She tucked it under her pillow and dropped off to sleep."

Aint Lulie eased out of her rocker and went to the stove to see to her soup. It must have been ready because she spooned it into two bowls and set them on the table. "We'd best eat it while it's hot," she said. "Nothing like hot soup on a cold day. Then we can go out and commence to cleaning off that garden."

She didn't say anything more about Pearl while we ate. After we'd finished and she'd put the bowls and spoons in the dishpan, we bundled up and went out back. I got a couple of rakes, a hoe, and a corn knife from the shed. Even though the sun had broken through the clouds, there was still a nip in the air. Aint Lulie carried a basket in case we found something that might be useful. "Granny always said that anything still good had to come out of the garden by Samhaim, else it had to be left."

"Samhain?" I asked.

"Last day of October is Samhain eve. Folks call it Halloween nowadays. But Granny always follered the old ways." She looked over her garden with a critical eye. "Don't reckon we'll find much still worth eating, though. Likely them frosts we had took it all."

Aint Lulie still followed a lot of the old ways, too. I grubbed around with the hoe in what was left of the potato patch and found a couple of potatoes that still looked all right. Aint Lulie put them in the basket. "Waste not, want not," she said. Then she pulled up the dried remains of her tomato plants. She'd eaten the last tomato weeks ago. "I reckon we'll git us a frost agin tonight," she said. "I feel it in my bones. 'The nights git longer, the cold gits stronger,' Granny used to say."

"That reminds me," I said. "Daylight Savings Time ends early tomorrow morning, so dark will come earlier tomorrow night because of it. Don't forget to set your clock back an hour."

"Never did set my clock ahead last spring," Aint Lulie said. "I cain't figger why they want to mess with the time like that.

Leastways we're gitting back in the regular way now."

"One of the teachers said it was so folks could work longer," I said.

"Now that don't make no sense a'tall." Aint Lulie shook her head. "It's like cutting off the bottom of a quilt and sewing what you cut off onto the top so you can pull the covers up higher when all you gotta do is pull your legs up closer agin your body. Working sunup to sundown's the natural way. Ain't no good comes from messing with the natural way a'things."

I had to admit she was right. I concentrated on cutting down the last of the cornstalks. Then we pulled out the dead bean vines, raked the garden clean, and went back inside to warm up.

Once she'd hung up her bonnet and shawl, Aint Lulie sat back down. I got the fire going good again and sat down, too. The fire's warmth wrapped around me, and the coldness left my bones. I wasn't sure if Aint Lulie would tell anymore about Pearl, but she picked right up where she'd left off.

"Pearl won't able to eat any supper, and Mama kept the chaps quiet as she could so as not to disturb her. I reckon everbody figgered whatever ailed Pearl would soon run its course. Granny said for me to go on up to the loft and get some sleep, and she'd see to Pearl during the night. Sleep didn't come to me easy. I could see the lamplight glowing down below, and ever so often I'd hear Pearl heaving. Sometimes she'd cry about how bad her belly hurt. Long 'bout midnight—I knowed what time on account I heard the clock chime—I heard a awful commotion. Granny called out to Papa, 'Duffie, you got to go fetch the doctor now! Pearl's having a fit!' I pulled on my clothes and ran with Papa down to the barn. I held the lantern while he saddled the gelding. Then he galloped off into the night. I recollect it'uz a clear night with lots of stars and the moon was waning gibbous, so at least he had enough light to see by.

"I went back in and set with Pearl while Granny emptied the basin. Moonlight shining in on her made Pearl look unusual pale. Ever so often, she would twitch or jerk, and her opal ring would shine bits of moonlight around the room. That ring hadn't been on her finger before I went to bed. It must've been in her reticule, and could be that'uz why Pearl wanted so bad for me to fetch it. I'd of took the ring off and hid it before Granny saw it, but Pearl's fingers had swoll up so bad. The ring stayed put, so I pulled the sheet up over her hands to keep Granny from taking note of it. I smoothed the wrinkles outten the sheet, and Pearl looked like she was sleeping peaceful. Won't long 'til Granny come back, and we both set with her. Neither of us spoke a word, but Granny kept her head down like she was praying. I reckon I did the same. Ever so often Pearl would moan or groan or thrash around, but she seemed quieter than she'd been a few hours earlier. Her breathing got slower and slower.

"Dr. Baker got there right before four in the morning, and Dr. Lane and Papa came in jist before daybreak, about the time the rooster commenced crowing. Them two doctors asked for more light, so Granny brought in the lamp from the other room and Papa lit the lantern again. The doctors worked on Pearl a good while, but she had another fit. It was awful to hear and see, but it didn't last too long. Then she quieted down for a spell and her breath come heavy and raspy. When the clock struck eight, she slipped away and was gone.

"The doctors told us how sorry they was, but there jist won't much they could do.

"Papa rode out to tell the nearest neighbors, who'd tell the ones on the other side of 'em, who'd tell the next, and so on. We didn't go to church that day, but everybody who did got the news no sooner than they set foot on the church grounds.

"In betwixt crying, Mama and Granny and I spent the morning washing and dressing Pearl in her best clothes and fixing her hair real nice. Papa started work on her coffin. He had some fine walnut boards in the barn loft and figgered they'd do jist fine. I don't recollect any of us ate breakfast, but Mama fixed a little something for the chaps. They'd stayed in the loft on account they were skeered by all the commotion, so Mama took a plate up to 'em.

"When Granny finally noticed the ring, she won't none too happy. 'That ring's what done it,' she said. 'I tried to warn her, but she paid me no mind. But I swan I never took note of that ring on her finger when she first took sick.'

"The ring stayed on Pearl's finger, and she'uz buried with it.

"By that afternoon, we had her laid out as nice as could be. If you didn't know, you'd figger she was jist sleeping. Folks kept coming to pay their respects. Women brought food—Lord! You never saw so much food. And men helped Papa finish the coffin and dig the grave up on the hill.

By nightfall, they'uz done and we laid Pearl in her coffin. We'uz gonna take turns setting up with her, but none of us could sleep, so we all set up. Next day, before we closed the lid, I tucked a few of her roses that'uz blooming into her hand."

Aint Lulie got up and took her Bible off the shelf where she always kept it. "I still got the piece that was wrote up in the paper about her." She thumbed through her Bible until she found what she was seeking. She handed me a yellowed slip of paper, and I leaned closer to the fire to have enough light to read it.

The sudden death of Miss Annie Pearl Caldwell, younger daughter of the late Jacob Caldwell, occurred early last Sunday morning and was a great shock to the Byrne Mountain community.

Miss Caldwell was apparently in the best of health, but on last Saturday afternoon she suffered an attack of cholera morbus, and suffered greatly from that time until the end came early Sunday morning. Doctors Baker and Lane were both summoned Sunday morning, but Miss Caldwell's time had come.

Miss Caldwell was twenty years of age, and had been a member of Byrne Mountain Church for several years.

Her remains were interred in the Byrne-Caldwell-Duff Cemetery on her family farm last Monday evening, and a very large crowd of family and friends were in attendance.

Mourning her passing are her mother, Mrs. Jacob Caldwell; her half-brother, Mr. Duffield Caldwell; a sister Mrs. Andrew Byrne; and several in-laws, nieces, and nephews. The stricken family have the deepest sympathy of the entire community in their dark hour of trouble.

The deceased was a bright, cheerful girl who was liked by all who knew her. Although she is gone from us, her memory remains.

I handed the clipping back to Aint Lulie, and she put it back into her Bible. "Well," she said, that'uz what happened here. Right'n the next room. It'uz a sad, sad time.

"She come back to visit me the night after she'uz buried. I was jist laying down in bed when she floated in front of me and smiled. She laid her finger across her lips like she'uz telling me to keep quiet about what I knew. Then she'uz gone."

Neither of us spoke for a while. Finally Aint Lulie asked me if I'd get a few more buckets of water so she could heat them up to wash with. She added some wood to the stove and got out her two kettles to boil the water, while I took the buckets out to fill. By the time I got back and emptied the buckets into the kettles, she had her washbasin on the table ready to fill when the water was warm enough.

Long shadows were stretching across the yard, and I figured I ought to head home. I knew Aint Lulie would eat the rest of the soup for her supper and would be fine until the next day. Likely Daddy would look in on her if he didn't have to work. Sometimes he did that.

On my way home, I studied about Pearl's death. If the doctors had declared what the cause was—and it was even printed in the paper—why were folks so hush-hush about the whole thing? Why hadn't I ever heard of cholera morbus anyhow? Was there something Aint Lulie wasn't telling me? There'd be no point in asking Mama or Daddy, for they surely wouldn't talk about it.

* * *

Something else I didn't know was that, while Aint Lulie and I had been cleaning off the garden, the police found Lucas Lawson and locked him up in the county jail. But Mama and Daddy and I didn't find out anything about it until Sunday morning.

"Something big must be going on," Daddy said when he drove into the church lot. "Lookit all them folks talking." He let Mama and me out and pulled over to the edge of the woods where he'd usually wait for us. A couple other men were parked there, and one went over to Daddy's truck.

The whole churchyard was buzzing with the news that Lucas had been discovered holed up drunk in an old abandoned cabin up the side of one of the mountains. What had given him away was the smoke coming from the chimney. The man who owned the land had been rabbit hunting on the next ridge and saw it. He was afraid somebody might be making liquor on his property so, soon as he got home, he called the law and they went to investigate.

The details differed from who'd heard what from who else, but the fact was that Lucas was the last person to see Loniss, and Lucas was now in the Bosworth County jail. By the time Elder Stoutmire finally got to the church and unlocked the door to let everybody inside, the news had spread through the whole crowd.

When I put together what everybody was saying, I decided what must have happened was this: Lucas and Alvin had fought after the dance, and Loniss went home with Alvin. Lucas had followed them but stayed out of sight for several minutes after Alvin had left. Then he knocked on the door real soft, and Loniss heard him and came out. She must have agreed to sit in his truck and to listen to what he wanted to tell her. But Lucas had driven off, and they'd ended up a mile or two away where they'd argued. She got out of his truck in the dark, and he tried to follow her. That's when somebody hit him from behind, or so he said. If somebody did hit Lucas and knock him out, whoever hit him must have put him back in his truck. He came to about dawn and looked around for Loniss and couldn't find her.

Here's where the accounts differed: Some folks said Lucas figured he'd be in big trouble. Others allowed as how he'd been beat up pretty bad and didn't want to face anybody for a while. Some folks said he had some food stashed in the cabin. Others said he'd stopped by home and stocked up on supplies. But everybody agreed that he was hiding out.

Elder Stoutmire prayed long and hard that the little gal would be found safe and that Lucas would confess all he knew to both God and the police. Then he thanked whoever it was who had donated even more wood and had stacked it so nice. The lord would surely bless whoever did it, and now the church had more than enough to last the winter.

On the way home, Mama and Daddy didn't say much about Lucas. "The lord knows where that gal is," was all Mama would say. "I reckon at least one other'n knows," Daddy said. "And it ain't likely whoever he is'll speak up 'til he's made to."

After we'd had eaten our dinner, I put some pork chops, mashed potatoes, and green beans on a plate to take to Aint Lulie in case she hadn't felt up to fixing anything for herself. But she declared she'd already et and would save what I brought for her supper.

She listened while I told her what I knew. "If they found the boy but not the gal, it ain't likely she'uz still among the living," she said. "But I hope to goodness I'uz wrong."

All that afternoon, while I stayed and helped Aint Lulie, neither of us spoke again about young girls who had died or who might be dead. But while I wondered about Loniss, I also still wondered about Pearl and the disease that killed her. I made up my mind to find out more about cholera morbus.

* * *

On Monday morning, Clovis didn't say a word about Lucas being arrested; neither did Kenny or Larry. The girls on the bus gossiped some, but in whispers so I couldn't hear what they were saying. It was pretty plain, though, that Lucas and Loniss hadn't run off and gotten married as some had hoped.

Classes were pretty quiet, too. Teachers got on with the lessons, and that was that. I guess Miss Brannigan didn't much feel like teaching because she took our class to the library and told us to check out a book we might like. Because I'd liked some short stories by Jesse Stuart that we read back in September, I decided to look for something else he'd written. I found one pretty quick— *The Thread that Runs So True*, about his early years working in Kentucky schools. I'd heard something about it before, and thought it might be nice to read some of his old time accounts of country school-teaching to Aint Lulie.

While I was in the library, I wondered if I could look up anything on cholera morbus. At first, I didn't have much luck, so I had to ask Miss Spencer, the librarian. She peered over her bifocals at me and declared she couldn't imagine why I'd want to know anything about it, so I lied and told her I might do a report on old-time disorders. She mentioned that her mother had a friend who died of it long ago, but she'd never heard it mentioned in the last half-century or so. "Times change," she said. "But there might be something about it in one of the old medical books." She pointed to a shelf down in the corner of the reference section.

The shelf was so dusty, it looked like no one had gotten a book from it for a long time. I sat on the floor so I could see the books better. I thumbed through a few, and in a really old book called *The Eclectic Practice of Medicine* by somebody named Ellingwood, I learned that cholera morbus often took place in hot weather and "is caused by the absorption of toxins elaborated by bacterial activity within the gastrointestinal tract. The ingestion of decomposing food, unripe fruit, raw vegetables and large quantities of ice water and alcoholic beverages in seasons of great heat are predisposing factors." That sounded like a fancy way of saying that something you ate didn't agree with you. Since Pearl died in June, it's possible that the weather might have been very hot, but Aint Lulie didn't say. But Pearl likely ate the same things as the others, and no one else got sick.

I looked through another book, *Poisons*, by Robert Amory and a bunch of other writers. From this book's description, I decided cholera morbus was what we call the stomach flu today because its main symptoms were vomiting and diarrhea.

But something else Amory wrote caught my attention. He mentioned that cholera morbus was sometimes confused with poisoning because the symptoms were similar. But cholera morbus was rarely fatal, and—if it was—death generally came several days later. In poisoning, death usually takes place within a day.

Pearl died less than twenty-four hours after getting sick. *Did she—? But how?*

When the bell rang, I put the books back on the shelf and headed for the locker room where I hoped I could take a hot shower and maybe wash away what I was thinking.

At lunch, Bert wanted to talk about Lucas being found, but I told him I was tired of hearing about it all morning and not to say another word until he had heard something that not everybody else had already repeated numerous times today. Sarenda said that she found the same old news boring as well as depressing, and he'd have to sit by himself if he brought it up again. Bert tried to talk about the election, but we shut him up on that too. Finally the three of us ate in silence.

In government class, all Mr. Wardell could talk about was the election and what was at stake. He asked who'd been watching news about it on TV, and only a few raised their hands. "Why not?" he asked. "Why aren't all of you watching?"

I don't think he wanted an answer like the one I gave him: "Not everybody here has a TV set."

"Oh," he said. "Oh." Like the idea had never before occurred to him.

Then Bert added, "And some of those who do can't get good reception in the hollers."

One of the football players mumbled, "And them that has TVs might not be interested," but I don't think Mr. Wardell heard him. At any rate, now Mr. Wardell knew that not everyone was as privileged as he was.

"What we want to talk about," said Susan Collins, "is another current event. Everybody wants to know what happened to Loniss."

Several others muttered agreement with her. Mr. Wardell asked if anyone had anything to say about it, and the kids took turns rehashing what everybody already knew while Mr. Wardell listened.

The biggest news came from Larry Tiller, whose trailer was close to the Lawson's. "My daddy said they set bond at $10,000 for Lucas," he said, "but ain't no way Mr. Lawson could come up with that much money. That's why Lucas is still in jail. He didn't do nothing. So why is he in jail?"

Mr. Wardell looked stumped for an answer. Then he was saved by the bell.

In home ec, Mrs. Carlton pushed a couple of tables together to make one big table so I'd have room to put my quilt together. She helped me lay out my quilt with the backing on the bottom, the batting in between, and the top, of course, on top. Several of the other girls stopped what they were working on and came over to watch. Mrs. Carlton showed us how to pin the pieces together. She did a little bit and then gave the box of pins to me.

"That's gonna take a while," Cheryl McCoy said. "Maybe some of us could help."

"I think that's a good idea," Mrs. Carlton said. "It'll surely save time. But it's Annie's quilt, so it's up to her."

I thought for a minute. The quilt had been my idea, and Cheryl had been one of those who made fun of me when I started. But I thought about what Aint Lulie had said about quilting bees when she was young. "My great-aunt told me about how girls got together in the old days and quilted," I said. "It'll be fine if anyone wants to help me."

Cheryl and a couple others gathered around the table, and Mrs. Carlton gave each a handful of pins. This was the first time I could remember that other girls actually wanted to work with me. Nobody said much. We were too busy concentrating on getting the quilt pinned to talk, so no gossip was exchanged like in Aint Lulie's day. By the time the bell rang, we were done. Mrs. Carlton helped me roll up the quilt so it would be ready to stitch tomorrow.

On the bus, I started reading *The Thread That Runs So True*. I was pretty well into it by the time Clovis reached my stop. Jesse Stuart started teaching school when he was my age. I couldn't imagine doing that. I wondered how it would have been to go to a country school like the one where he had first taught. A lot of the book was about problems he had with different people and different factions in the county where he worked, but some of it was about his experiences with his students in rural schools. Maybe if I read some of those parts, Aint Lulie would tell me about her school days. Or about other things that happened when she was young. Or maybe more about Pearl.

That evening I told Aint Lulie how the girls were helping me with my quilt, and she thought that was real nice of them. I guess it was. They hadn't treated me like an outcast, but more like a regular person. I showed Aint Lulie the book I had gotten. She squinted at it and read out the title.

"They's a song by that name," she said, "that we used to sing at play-parties. Lessee if I can recollect it." She rocked for a minute and then sang in a high-pitched voice, "The needle's eye, it doth supply, the thread that runs so true, many a beau have I let go because I wanted you. That'uz the girls' part. The boys sang this'n." She dropped her voice to a lower pitch. "The needle's eye, it doth supply the thread that runs so true, many a lass have I let pass because I wanted you. They's more, but I cain't recollect. I do recollect Sparrell Hobson and me singing it, though.

"When I'uz a gal used to we had a lot of play parties this time of year. All the crops'uz in and the real bad weather was still a ways off. We had us some good times back then."

By the firelight, I read her the chapter where Jesse Stuart started teaching at the country school and how his students ran out at recess to play "the thread that runs so true" tug-of-war and how he had to fight one boy who was a lot bigger than he was.

"That'uz real good," she said when I closed the book. "Kindly put me in mind of old times. Schoolteachers had a hard row to hoe. But I recollect we didn't have many fights at our school. Maybe on account so many of us was kin to each other."

I saw my opening. "Speaking of old times and kin, I think there's something about the way Pearl died that you didn't tell me. Why nobody talks about it."

Aint Lulie inhaled sharply, then exhaled. Her hands clenched onto the arms of her rocker, and she sat up a little straighter. "What makes you think that?"

"There were a couple old books in the library that talked about cholera morbus. How most folks didn't die of it but got better in a few days."

"That so?" she said.

"And in one book it told how cholera morbus had the same symptoms as poisoning. Only folks who had cholera morbus usually recovered in a few days, but folks who were poisoned died within a day." Aint Lulie didn't say a word. She just stared into the fire. I swallowed hard and added, "Like Pearl."

"You'uz always sharp as a tack," she said. "I reckoned you might figger it out. So I reckon I ort to tell you the rest of it. But you got to promise me that you won't let on to your mama about what I'm gonna tell you."

I promised. Aint Lulie slumped back in her rocker and rocked a bit. The creaking of the rocker against the old oak floor sounded louder than usual. Or maybe it was my imagination. She rocked back and forth a few more times before she began.

"The day after Pearl had been laid to rest, we'uz cleaning up. It being Monday, Granny was getting ready to do the wash, and she told me to bring down any of Pearl's things that needed washing. And to sweep up the loft room and all. Well, I got together my sheets and petticoats, and aprons and such that needed cleaning, and a few clothes that Pearl had wore the week before. Granny already had Pearl's sheets that had got soiled when Pearl was first so sick, and she'd already put 'em in a pot to soak.

"After I took all the things to Granny, I come back and commenced to sweeping. I pulled Pearl's bed away from the wall and found the picture that Otha had give her—the one of him by hisself. Somebody—Pearl herself, I reckon—had took a pin and scratched across his neck like she was trying to cut his throat. I didn't fault her none for that on account he done her wrong by marrying that other gal.

When I'd got all around her bed swept up, I happen to remember Pearl's bouquet that she'd put together on Saturday. It struck me odd that it won't on the table between our beds where she'd put it. I figgered maybe Granny had moved it so she'd had more room to help Pearl. Well, when I moved my own bed to sweep under it, I found the jar on the floor under my own bed. It'uz pushed way back, like it was meant to be hid. When I got it out and looked at it, I knowed for certain Pearl didn't die a natural death.

"The daisies was still there, but the poke berries was gone and what'uz left of the stems had been gnawed down to nubs. Same for the snakeroot and the lily-of-the valley. I knowed no mouse or other varmint coulda et 'em.

"I found a couple empty bottles under my bed, too. A phial like laudanum come in and a Cardui bottle. Granny kept remedies like that in a chest where the chaps couldn't reach 'em. And them bottles was full last I saw 'em."

"Pearl poisoned herself, didn't she?" I asked.

Aint Lulie sighed deeply—like a great weight had been lifted from her—and nodded. "I reckon it'uz bad enough to be jilted by Otha Tompkins, but to see his wife so close to having his baby and him turn away and not even give her the time a' day—well, I reckon it'uz more'n Pearl could stand."

"But why doesn't anybody speak of it now?"

"On account of the shame. Taking your own life is a great sin. It means you'll not git into the kingdom of heaven."

Then I understood. Of course Mama wouldn't want it known that someone she was kin to was burning in hell.

"I reckon you'll keep the secret, too." The way Aint Lulie said it was more like an order than an opinion.

I nodded. The secret would stay with me.

CHAPTER 7: HALLOWEEN, SAMHAIN, & GHOSTS

Next day, kids were a little more talkative on the bus and at school. But it was Halloween and that gave a lot of them something other to talk about than Lucas and Loniss. Of course, everybody was too old for trick or treating now, but a lot of the kids remembered when they did. They remembered scary stuff from when they were little. But they didn't want to think about the scary stuff now. They didn't want to think about Loniss maybe being dead. They didn't want to think about Lucas maybe being the one who killed her. It was easier to not mention them at all. Just like not mentioning Aint Pearl, I thought. The bad parts of life were better when no one spoke of them.

In English class, Miss Brannigan surprised us when she said, "Ghosts have played an important part in literature. Since it's Halloween, it's appropriate that we'll start reading one of the classics of literature where a ghost was instrumental in getting the story started."

Mamie Harper raised her hand. "If you'll excuse me, ma'am, I don't think my mama and daddy would want me to study that. They don't believe in ghosts."

Mamie's family goes to the Church of the Straight and Narrow, which is even stricter than the Divine Church of Holy Light. She wears dark skirts that nearly drag the ground and a permanent sour expression on her face, like she's bitten into a persimmon that hasn't yet been touched by frost. She never hesitates to correct someone whose ideas might differ from hers. The kids who don't make fun of her tend to ignore her.

Miss Brannigan told Mamie she didn't have to believe in ghosts to study and understand the story.

"My daddy vowed he seen a ghost once," Kenny Ketchum said. "One night when he was out coon hunting."

"Was it when he was drinking?" Larry Tiller asked, and some of the boys laughed.

Kenny ignored Larry's comment. "He said the hounds treed something, but then they ran off instead of barking at whatever it was. Daddy looked up in the tree and seen something kinda misty white up there. He didn't stick around. Time he got to his truck, his hounds was already there."

Somebody said Kenny was just making it up, and several kids got into a dispute about whether ghosts were real or not. Before long most of the kids were voicing their opinions. Mamie kept quiet. So did I.

Susan Collins' hand shot up, and Miss Brannigan called on her. "A cousin of mine told me that a college near Bristol is haunted by a girl named Vera who hanged herself when her love affair with one of the teachers went wrong. That was way back in the 1800s."

A few others muttered that they'd heard that one, too.

Cheryl wasn't about to be outdone by her friend. "I heard about another girl in Kingsport a long time ago who drowned herself on account her sweetheart had been drowned in the Holston River," she said. "The story goes that her ghost wears a white dress and keeps looking for him."

Bert looked bored. He and I—and Mamie—were probably the only ones not involved in the discussion. Then he raised his hand. "A few years ago, my family went to Big Stone Gap to see *Trail of the Lonesome Pine*." He looked condescendingly at Larry and Kenny. "That's a play based on a book by John Fox, who's been dead for awhile. We'd heard that the house where John Fox once lived was haunted by spirits who sometimes walked around the property. We drove by after the play was over, and we didn't see a thing."

Nobody responded to Bert's comment. A few more kids jumped in about ghost stories they'd heard. Mamie put her hands over her ears.

Finally Miss Brannigan interrupted. "Class," she said, "I'm glad you're having such a—*spirited*—discussion. What we're going to study for the next few weeks is *Hamlet* by William Shakespeare. And Mamie, the ghost only appears in the first few scenes. You may keep your book closed during those."

Bert brightened up a little when he heard we'd be reading a classic. At least I saw him smile. Most of the kids groaned. They knew from studying *Romeo and Juliet* a few years ago that Shakespeare was hard to understand as well as boring. Of course, that was back when old Mrs. Southwark was still teaching, and she had a way of making everything boring. But Bert knew he'd be able to answer questions about literature when nobody else could. He was happiest when he knew more than anybody else.

Miss Brannigan walked up and down the aisles handing out the paperback books. "At least go into this play with an open mind. Shakespeare raises some important issues, some that still might be important today."

Kenny and Larry and a few other guys turned to look when she went past. She was wearing a fairly short skirt for a teacher. When she came to the empty desks where Loniss and Lucas had sat, she paused for a second, but I don't think anyone but me noticed.

When everyone had a book, she told us that the play took place a long time ago in a place called Elsinore, which was in Denmark. She called on a few boys to read the first scene, where Hamlet's friends see the ghost of Hamlet's father. Mamie kept her book closed and her head bowed, but everyone else followed along. In the second scene, Bert volunteered to read the part of Hamlet. In the third scene Bert read Polonius, who is kind of long-winded so it suited him. We were finishing the third scene—where Laertes is getting ready to go on a trip and is giving advice to his sister Ophelia and their father Polonius is giving advice to Laertes— when the bell rang. As we left, we stacked the books on Miss Brannigan's desk.

At lunch, Bert and Sarenda and I discussed what we'd read so far. Sarenda was in the class after ours, but Miss Brannigan covered the same things in both classes. Sarenda believed in ghosts and Bert didn't, but they both liked reading the play even though Sarenda thought it took too long to get to the main part of the story.

"What if Loniss is a ghost now?" Sarenda said. "If she's alive, somebody should have seen her by now. But if she's dead, maybe her ghost is right here watching us. Maybe her ghost could tell somebody what happened if they knew how to ask."

"Let's not talk about that," I said. "Besides, not all dead people are ghosts." I didn't like where the conversation was going.

* * *

In home ec, Mrs. Carlton and I unrolled my pinned-up quilt. "Now you could sew the layers on the machine, but it'll be really awkward to sew around all those pins. The best thing to do is to baste it by hand and then machine-stitch it. Or, you could do it the old way, and sew everything by hand until you put the edging on."

"I think I'd like to do it the old way," I said.

"That'll take a lot of work and a lot of extra time," she said, "but your quilt will be more authentic."

Cheryl McCoy spoke up. "If you don't mind, I could help you stitch. I was telling my grandma last night about how you were making a quilt like your great-aunt used to do, and she told me a lot of old stories about how she and her friends used to get together and quilt when she was my age."

Did this mean Cheryl was my friend? "Sure," I said. "Like in the old days." Then Mary Rose Lennert and Ellen Goins, who had just finished their skirts, volunteered.

While the others still worked on their skirts, Mrs. Carlton told us four that it was important that we all use the same number of stitches per inch. "Six is the least you should use," she said, "but eight would look much better and make for a tighter quilt."

"How do we measure stitches?" Cheryl asked the question before I even thought about it. "It seems like we'd be picking up the tape measure right often."

"How to measure is right in your hand," Mrs. Carlton said. She held up her index finger and crooked it. "See? The space between the first and second knuckle is approximately an inch."

We compared our fingers with each other and then with a tape measure. Seemed like Mrs. Carlton was right. Around the room, others stopped what they were doing to look at their index fingers.

Before long the four of us were stitching away. We didn't talk much because we all had to concentrate so hard on what we were doing. But we talked a little.

"I remember when my mom would sew my Halloween costumes when I was little," Mary Rose said. "Usually she made something easy to sew. Like one year I was a ghost."

I was afraid the conversation would drift to ghosts, but Cheryl said, "One year Mama made me a ballerina outfit."

"I reckon it's easier just to buy costumes now," I said. I didn't want to have to say I'd never in my life had a costume.

The others agreed that it probably was.

Every so often, Mrs. Carlton would stop by and check what we were doing. When class was almost over, she showed us how to mark our stopping place with our needles and a slip of paper.

* * *

That evening, I took Aint Lulie a sack of supplies that Mama and Daddy had gotten her in town. While she fixed soup and I put her groceries away, I told her about how some of the girls were helping me sew by hand and how they'd been talking about the ways they dressed up for Halloween when they were younger.

"Did you celebrate Halloween?" I asked.

"Not as sich," she said. "To a good many of us, it'uz Samhain Eve. According to Granny, that'uz when the veil between the world of the living and the world of the dead is thinnest. That's when spirits could walk the earth if they'd a mind to. Granny would tell us some scary stories back then. I can recollect bits and pieces, but I wish I could recollect all've 'em now."

She ladled out our soup and we ate by firelight. After we'd gotten our night work done up, we sat closer to the fire, and I read her some more from *The Thread That Runs So True*.

When I stepped into the dark and started toward home, I wondered what it was like to be a little kid out trick-or-treating. I wondered what costumes Loniss must have worn. I couldn't imagine her as a ghost. She was likely a princess or a queen, I figured. She must have worn something fancy and sparkly and not homemade.

* * *

The first day of November was gray and drizzly. At school nobody had heard any more news about Loniss, except that her parents were on TV again and were offering a big reward for information leading to her safe return. Lucas was still in jail. Nothing was new.

Miss Brannigan summarized what had happened so far in *Hamlet* and asked what we thought of the characters. Not many had opinions except Bert. We read scene four, where Hamlet sees the ghost, and scene five where Hamlet finds out what the ghost wants. Even though Bert wanted to be Hamlet again, Miss

Brannigan asked me to read the part instead. Bert read the part of the ghost. When I got to the part that said, "The time is out of joint: O cursed spite, That ever I was born to set it right!" it gave me shivers. Mamie, who'd sat with head bowed and book closed during the reading, gave me a hateful look.

After we finished Act I, Miss Brannigan asked why Hamlet said, "Never make known what you have seen tonight." Several kids said that if you went around saying you saw a ghost and that ghost told you something, other folks would think you were crazy. Several others said that if you told you were planning to get revenge on somebody, it might get back to that person and ruin your plans. Others said that sometimes it was just a good idea to keep your mouth shut. I kept my mouth shut.

* * *

At lunch, we didn't talk about *Hamlet*. Instead, Bert speculated on the reward the Hathaways were offering. He couldn't figure why the investigators hadn't come up with some leads yet. But Sarenda told him that if anyone knew something they'd have come forward before this, so that shut him up. In government class, Mr. Wardell toned down talking about Nixon and McGovern and instead explained how the electoral college worked, though he did mention the election was less than a week away. In home ec, I kept working on my quilt and the other girls kept helping me.

"I was telling my grandma about helping you with your quilt," Cheryl said. "Grandma said when she was my age, she'd already made a couple of quilts, and she was glad I was learning how. So, I was thinking, Annie, would you help me make one after we finish yours?"

That was the first time any classmate had ever called me by name or asked me for help. "Sure," I said. "I'd be glad to help." The feeling of being glad took me by surprise. Then Cheryl started talking about what colors she wanted to be in her quilt.

Mary Rose, who was always real quiet but not as quiet as me, spoke up. "My sister is going to have a baby in the spring. I'd like to make a little quilt for the baby. Would y'all help me with it?"

We agreed that we would. We thought that would be a great baby gift. Ellen Goins, the other girl who was helping us, said she'd like to make a baby quilt for her little sister, too. Soon we were chatting away about what colors we'd use and how our quilts would look and how big a baby quilt ought to be.

Mrs. Carlson stopped by the table, and we told her what we wanted to do and asked if it was all right with her. "You know," she said, "I'd planned for the class to make placemats and napkins next, but if you all really want to make quilts, I guess that would be all right." A few other girls chimed in and said they'd rather make quilts, too. Before long, the whole class wanted to try making quilts. "Well, then," Mrs. Carlson said, "that's just what we'll do."

When class ended, we had maybe a third of my quilt's top, batting, and bottom stitched together. It was starting to look like a real quilt.

On the bus, Cheryl's cheerleader friend Susan Collins was sitting with Larry. Cheryl, who'd taken a seat about midway back on the bus, asked me as I was passing by if I'd like to sit with her. I hesitated, wondering if I was ready to be more sociable. I decided I was. Cheryl slid over and made room for me. It felt odd not to sit by myself in the back.

* * *

With the days getting shorter, it was nearly dark before I got to Aint Lulie's cabin. Seemed like the light drizzle that had been falling on and off all day made the dark come sooner. She wasn't at the door waiting for me and, for a moment, I feared the worst. But maybe she just didn't want to let in the cold and damp. I tried the door, and it swung open. Aint Lulie was slumped in her rocker by the fire, which had burned so low it was nearly gone. She had never before let a fire burn so low. A chill hung in the room. Her eyes were closed.

"Aint Lulie, what's the matter?" I touched her shoulder, and her eyes jerked open. "Are you sick?"

"No, child, I was jist dozing." Then she saw how low the fire had gotten. "Law, I've done near let my fire go out."

"I'll get some wood." I hurried to the woodpile. When I returned, she was standing up. I built up the fire in the fireplace and started a fire in her stove. I brought in another armload of split wood, so she wouldn't have to tote it herself. Shivering, I stood near the fireplace to dry and warm myself.

"Pearl paid me a visit late last night and kept me up late. I meant to jist cat-nap a little this afternoon, but I purely lost track of the time," she said. "I meant to have us something fixed to eat time you got here." She hustled to the dogtrot to fetch some vegetables she'd canned back in the summer.

"Aint Lulie," I said when she returned and was opening the jars, "I think you might have been dreaming. Your aunt has been dead for a long time."

"Indeed she has, but recollect she died in this very house." Aint Lulie poured green beans into one pot and corn into another. "So I can talk to her if I got a mind to. This'uz the first time she come to visit since right after she died, and she only done that to bid me farewell, not to stay a spell and visit. She kindly took me by surprise last night. But it'uz Samhain Eve, and that'uz when the dead can walk the earth if they take a notion to. Plus rain's been falling and a breeze'uz blowing earlier. Everbody knows spirits can ride wind and water."

I didn't know that. This whole thing was getting a little creepy, even though I knew Aint Lulie's gift did let her talk to the dead. Aint Lulie decided some fried apples would taste good on a cold night, so she got a jar from the shelf and put a couple of pats of butter in her big skillet before pouring the apples in. "Good thing about this chilly weather is that the butter don't melt in the house," Aint Lulie said. "Saves a trip to the springhouse to fetch it and take it back." She stirred some sugar into the apples and butter.

While she was busy at the stove, I did my usual chores. I sort of wanted to know why Pearl had visited Aint Lulie. If she had indeed visited. If Aint Lulie hadn't just dreamed it. I wondered if Pearl's ghost, like the ghost of Hamlet's father, had any messages for Aint Lulie. Maybe Pearl had unfinished business to take care of.

After my work was done, I asked, "Did Pearl say anything?"

"Oh, this and that. Said she knowed she'd been talked of lately and was glad she'uz still being thought of. Said right after she done what she done, she'uz sorry she done it. But she's doing all right where she's at, and a lot of kinfolk keep her company. Said she'd jist been missing her little dollbaby."

"Dollbaby?" I asked. "Did she have a favorite doll?"

"She meant me. She called me her dollbaby when I'uz little. She used to tote me around and dress me up and fuss over me. It'uz right good to see her again. She told me I ort to get out some. Be around other folks. Maybe go to church ever now and then."

"I know Mama would be glad if you went to church with us."

"I'll think on it," she said. "Now why don't you read me another'n of them schoolteacher stories while I finish up cooking."

And that's what I did. In fact, I read a couple. When I was

done, I said, "I'll have to take the book back with me tonight. Miss Brannigan said our class is going to the library tomorrow."

"Well, I thank you for reading to me," she said, while she dished out our supper. "My eyes is getting so cloudy, I cain't rightly read to myself much anymore."

After we ate, we sat close to the fire. I was hoping she'd tell a little more about Pearl's visit, but she had other stories on her mind.

"Them stories you been reading me puts me in mind of when I was a gal and all the stories the old folks'd tell around the fire. I use'ta know a lot of old stories when I'uz a chap, but most I done forgot. But I recollect a fairy story that a schoolteacher read out of a book to us at Duff Schoolhouse, though. She'd read to us on a Friday if we'd been good all week. It'uz a fairy story about a horse race."

"Can you tell it to me?" I figured she wasn't going to say anymore about Pearl.

"Well," she said, "I reckon I might could give it a try." She rocked back and forth a couple of times. "Back in the old days in Ireland, seemed like the fairies was uncommon fond of horses and most was good riders. A lotta young men liked to show off in them days, kindly like they still do, and sometimes they'd end up racing agin the fairies and their horses. 'Course not many could outride them fairies. They got magic on their side. I recollect their king, name of Finvarra, rode a big black horse with flames of fire blowing outta its nose.

"Anyway, it happened that a young man from Galway was headed to a big race and happened to ride by a hill where the high-ranking fairies and their king liked to git together. Won't long 'til that young man'uz joined by a stranger riding on a big black horse. The stranger asked the man for the time of day, and the man told him. They rode side by side for a piece, and I reckon the man'uz glad to have company, him being in a strange part of the county and all. They talked about this and that, and the man was kindly surprised that the stranger knowed he'uz going to be racing his horse.

"'Now for them races tomorrow,' said the stranger, 'if you desire victory, I know a man what never loses a race no matter the horse he rides. I can have him meet up with you afore the race commences.'

"The young man thanked the stranger, and they parted ways. Early next morning, the young man was saddling up his horse when a right odd-looking little feller come along and proclaimed he was fixing to ride the young man's horse. Well, no sooner the young man had tightened the girth, did the little feller hop on the horse's back and take off jist as fast as fast can be.

"The young man kindly got addled and didn't quite know what'uz happening until somebody handed him a big gold cup on account his horse had won. He looked around for the little feller that rode, but he'uz nowheres to be seen. But the stranger on the big black horse rode up, and he told the young man to foller him home and git hisself something to eat. The young man thought that would be all right, so he went with the stranger. They rode for a ways and a ways until they come upon a big house all lit up, and a lotta servants was running to and fro to git things ready.

"Now, that young man come from a right good family hisself and they always had plenty, but the stranger had way more'n him. Never before had the young man seen sich food nor sich fancy plates and cups. There'uz lots of other folks there, but the young man knowed nary a one've 'em. Nonetheless, they spoke to him liked they'd knowed him all their life. After they'd all et, music commenced playing and folks went into a big room to dance. They tried to draw the young man into the dance, but he'd got a mite suspecting. For one thing, he saw his own brother dancing on the far side of the room. But a few years back, that brother had drownded in the river. Then he looked around real good, and it struck him that all them folks he seen was dead folks that he'd either oncet knowed or else knowed of. All of 'em had a real pale look, but their eyes was bright as candle-flames. He knowed something won't right.

"He'uz backing away and about to run off for home, when the prettiest young gal come up to him and clamped onto his wrist with her pale hand. 'You cain't leave without you dance with me,' she said. 'You loved me oncet. And I loved you. Recollect?'

"He looked down at the hand that held his wrist, and seen on her finger a ring he had give to his sweetheart who had died the year before. 'Dance with me agin,' the gal said. 'Like you used to.'

"He looked her full in the face and seen she was indeed his dead sweetheart, and where her hand circled his wrist it burnt him like fire, even after he'd done broke away from her and went to find the stranger whose house it was. He found him and said, 'I got to go from here. Everbody here is dead.'

"The stranger offered him another drink, but the young man knowed better than to take it. The stranger kept on insisting, and finally the young man took the bottle. When he'd drunk it all down, the music come to a stop and all the dancers vanished into thin air. The young man hisself passed out into a deep sleep. He slept 'til next afternoon when he woke up in his own bed with his daddy hovering over him, real worried. After he'd come to his senses, he found his horse in its stall and the gold cup beside the stable door. He finally threw the cup in the river on account he didn't want no truck with magic. He never agin went near where them fairies met, and he never agin saw that stranger.

"Only thing though, for all his life a red mark circled his wrist, and it was said that his dead sweetheart sometimes come to him in dreams. He never did marry, so I reckon you cain't say he lived happy ever after."

Aint Lulie smiled. "Not long after the teacher read us that story, our ambling mare birthed a black colt. I wanted Papa to name the colt Finvarra after the fairy king in the teacher's book, but Papa said that was too much of a name for a little colt and we'd meet halfway and call him Finn. Finn was the black gelding that Pearl rode to the store the day she took sick, and the one Papa rode to get the doctor. Finn was a good horse."

I thought that was the end of the story, but Aint Lulie had a little more. "Pearl always liked Finn, too. She said she still rides him whenever she gits a chance. Said he still gaits as good as when he was alive."

On my way home, I clutched the book under my coat to keep it dry, and I thought about ghosts and the story Aint Lulie had told me. I knew I'd never make known some of the things I'd heard tonight.

CHAPTER 8: SETTING IT RIGHT

In English class the next day, I was hoping we could spend the whole time in the library. But Miss Brannigan had other ideas. "We'll only go to the library for a few minutes," she said, "and before we go, we'll discuss what we've already read in *Hamlet*. Does anyone have any ideas to share?" No one answered. "Well, what do you think of the story line so far?" she asked. "Do you buy into what's happening?"

Kenny, who was always trying to get in good with Miss Brannigan, said, "It's right hard to make sense of in places, but not as bad as I thought it would be. It's pretty good that Hamlet decided to get revenge for his daddy's death." Several boys nodded their agreement. "Even if a ghost was the one to get things started."

Mamie Harper's hand shot up. "I don't think Shakespeare needed to put that ghost in a'tall," Mamie said. "A servant or somebody could've told Hamlet about his uncle killing his daddy without bringing a ghost into it. Ain't no need of ghosts."

"That's an interesting point," Miss Brannigan said. "Does anyone else find it hard to believe that a ghost could report a murder?" There was some mumbling throughout the class. Apparently no one wanted to take a stand. I certainly didn't.

Finally Lizzie Cleveland, who sits in the back row on the other side of the room from me, spoke up. "I know of a case where a woman was killed by her husband a long time ago and her ghost got him sent to prison. My aunt told me about it once. She lives in

West Virginia up near where it happened."

"Can you tell us more about it?" Miss Brannigan seemed interested

"If y'all are gonna talk about ghosts again, may I be excused to go on to the library?" Mamie asked.

"Yes, Mamie," Miss Brannigan said. "I think that would be a good idea."

After Mamie left, Miss Brannigan asked Lizzie to report what she knew. Lizzie was never one to talk up much in class, so it was kind of a surprise that she had something to say.

"Well, Mama and me visited Aunt Sarah two summers ago, and along the road we'd passed a sign about the Greenbrier ghost. We didn't stop to read it, but you don't normally see many road signs about ghosts, so that night we asked Aunt Sarah if she knew anything about it. She said near about everybody around there knew the story, so she'd tell us."

"What did she tell?" Miss Brannigan asked.

"Well, Aunt Sarah said back in the 1890s a woman named Zona married a good-looking stranger who come to town. He worked as a blacksmith, so he was real strong. But he was real mean, too, and Zona's mama didn't much like him. One winter day, the blacksmith sent a boy to his house for some reason or other, and the boy found Zona dead at the foot of the steps. The boy run back and told everybody, and the doctor was fetched to see about Zona. But the blacksmith got there before the doctor and was carrying on something awful about his wife being dead. He'd even took her and put her to bed and had her all cleaned up and dressed, even though other womenfolk are supposed to do that for a woman, not the husband."

Several girls nodded. Likely they had witnessed some home burials. A lot of folks in the county can't afford a funeral home and have to make do the old way.

"Anyhow, the doctor didn't get to examine her real good, what with the blacksmith carrying on and crying and hanging onto her. When somebody rode out to fetch Zona's mama, she said that no doubt that devil had done killed her daughter hisself."

Nobody was saying a word while Lizzie told this. It wasn't like some of the boys to be so quiet.

"Well," Lizzie continued, "next day, they carried Zona in her coffin out to her parents' farm to get buried. The blacksmith stuck pretty tight to that coffin even during the wake. He put a pillow on one side of her head and a rolled up sheet on the other, which struck her family as odd, but he said it seemed like to him it made Zona more comfortable, so they didn't mess with what he was doing. He tied a scarf around her neck, too, and said it was her favorite so she ought to be buried with it.

"Right before they closed up the coffin, Zona's mama slipped that sheet out of the coffin. After Zona was buried and folks had left, Zona's mama washed the sheet but couldn't get a stain out of it no matter how hard she tried. She took it as a sign that Zona didn't die no natural death.

"Meanwhile, she started to pray that her daughter would come to her and tell what happened. She prayed and prayed every night for nigh onto a month until Zona's ghost appeared and said her husband had got mad and killed her. He beat her some and choked her and broke her neck.

"Zona's mama went to a lawyer who listened to what she said and got the doctor and some deputies to look into what had gone on. They dug up Zona and examined her real good this time." Lizzie paused to take a breath. This was the longest I—and likely everyone else—had ever heard her talk.

"What did they find out?" Susan Collins asked.

"Found out that her neck was indeed broke and her windpipe was mashed and her neck was bruised up like somebody had got a'holt of it, so they arrested the blacksmith, and he was tried for murder and sent to prison. Turns out he'd been married twice before and his second wife had died mysterious too.

"At least that's the story my aunt told me," Lizzie said. "I thought it's kind of like in *Hamlet*. A ghost appears and tells about a murder."

"It kind of is," Miss Brannigan said. "It kind of is. Now, we'd better get on to the library while we still have time."

"But I have something to say about *Hamlet*," Bert said. "You all are forgetting the war angle. Remember that, as the play begins, Denmark is at war."

But no one responded. Some of us had already been touched by war, and we didn't want to think about it. We lined up and went to the library. Mamie was already there.

This time I found a book about different quilt patterns. Some looked easy and some looked real hard. I figured it wouldn't hurt to know how to make some of them.

At lunch Bert was in a snit. "No one wants to discuss serious stuff," he said. "Hamlet has a lot of implications, like the war Denmark is in with Norway. That's a parallel to what's happening in Vietnam. All anybody wants to talk about is ghosts!"

I didn't tell him that that Vietnam hung over my family like a ghost, but I thought about it.

"Peace out, Bert," Sarenda said. "We hear enough about Vietnam on the news. I'd rather hear about ghosts." She leaned over the table and looked him in the eye. "There are more things in heaven and earth, Bertram, than are dreamt of in your philosophy."

"Very funny," he said. "Ha, ha."

Then I told her about the ghost story that Lizzie had told our class. "I think I've heard of that one," she said. "At least it sounds familiar."

In home ec, as the four of us stitched away on my quilt, we continued our discussion of what we'd make next. I showed the others the book I'd gotten from the library, and we talked about what patterns we liked and whether they'd be easy or hard.

That night, I showed the book to Aint Lulie, too. She pointed to different patterns and recollected those she had worked on long ago. She thought I ought to do a log cabin pattern next. She said that it was fairly easy and made up nice.

Things were looking up at school. I was starting to be a regular person that other regular people talked to. If I missed my gift, it wasn't by much.

* * *

Miss Brannigan had just started reviewing what happened so far in *Hamlet* before we started Act II when Mr. Darley came in. Usually whenever the principal appears in class, someone's in big trouble. The boys looked around at each other, but nobody looked guilty. Miss Brannigan stopped the review and said, "Hello, Mr. Darley. Do you need to see someone?"

"I need to speak with you, if you don't mind stepping out into the hall for a moment. It seems some parents are here with a, uh, concern."

She told us to go ahead and silently read the first scene of Act II. Luckily, she didn't quite close the door all the way so we could hear what went on. From where I was sitting, I could get a glimpse of the hall and see that Mamie and her parents were with Mr.

Darley. Cheryl mouthed to me, "Who's out there?" and I mouthed back, "Mamie and the Harpers." Word spread through the class who it was. We were all super-quiet so we could hear most of what was being said.

"Miss Brannigan," Mr. Darley began, "The Harpers are concerned that you are, uh, teaching impressionable students about the, uh, occult."

"I beg your pardon?" she said. "I don't understand."

"Ghosts!" Mr. Harper said. "You're teaching 'em to believe in ghosts. That ain't your place to do that!"

"Mamie says you've been discussing ghosts in class," Mr. Darley said. "Have you?"

"The play we're reading has a ghost in it." Miss Brannigan stood up a little straighter and I think she looked Mr. Harper square in the eye. "The play is a made-up story. The students are free to believe what they want."

"Cain't you jest skip over them parts with ghosts and things kids ort not know about?" Mr. Harper was leaning toward her with a mean look on his face. It looked like he was used to getting his way.

"The ghost plays a pivotal part in the story," Miss Brannigan said. "The play wouldn't make sense without the ghost revealing certain information."

"But still, you're gitting them kids to believe in things that ain't true—things that'll cause 'em to stray from the path of righteousness. Things that'll make the devil happy!" Mr. Harper was getting so loud that everyone could hear what he was saying. A couple of the boys were clenching their fists.

"I'm doing no such thing!" she fired back.

"What's the play?" Mr. Darley asked Miss Brannigan.

"*Hamlet*. It's on the state-mandated curriculum for the senior Landmarks of Literature class."

"I see," Mr. Darley said. "That does create a dilemma."

Bert jumped out of his seat and strode to the door. "She's not teaching us ghosts!" he said. "She's teaching us literature! And she's doing a good job of it, too!"

There was a chorus of *yeah*s from all the boys and most of the girls. Larry and Kenny jumped out of their seats and stood beside Bert.

"Beg your pardon, Mr. Darley," said Bert, "but you really ought to ask the class about what's going on and what we're learning."

"Why don't y'all come on in?" asked Larry. "Then we can all talk about it."

Miss Brannigan came in, followed by Mr. Darley, followed by the Harpers. Mamie sat down in her usual place. Her face looked even more sour than usual. Miss Brannigan asked Kenny and Larry to get seats for the Harpers. The only available ones were Loniss's and Lucas's seats, so the two boys pulled them to the front. Then they and Bert took their own seats. Mr. and Mrs. Harper sat down facing the class. Both were dressed head to toe in black. They looked like giant crows. Mr. Darley and Miss Brannigan stood facing us.

Bert was enjoying the attention, and he wasn't about to quit. "We were just reviewing Act I," Bert said. "Now the play starts way back in the old days in Denmark when a war was about to get started with Norway. So folks are a little nervous."

Kenny took it from there. "Some guys guarding the castle thought they saw the king who was dead and buried, so they reported it, but the ones they reported it to didn't believe it. Meanwhile, the dead king's brother Claudius is now king and he's married the dead king's widow, and he gives a big speech at a fancy party. He notices that Hamlet is still in mourning and tells him that it makes him seem like a sissy and he ought to stay home instead of going back off to school."

I noticed Mrs. Harper had a sour look just like Mamie's.

Mr. Harper spoke up. "I don't think this is a'tall fitting—"

Larry cut him off. "Anyway, it gets to Hamlet that his dead daddy has been seen. Hamlet goes and looks for him, and his daddy tells Hamlet he's been murdered by the brother who married Hamlet's mother."

Bert couldn't stand it that they'd skipped a part and interrupted Larry. "But before that, Laertes—who is going off to school in France—gives some advice to his sister Ophelia that Hamlet might not love her as much as she thinks."

Susan joined the conversation. "Their daddy Polonius comes in, and he gives advice to both of them. He doesn't think much of Hamlet either, and he tells Ophelia she's not to see him again."

Kenny picked up the review. "Hamlet finally meets up with his daddy's ghost and that's where he learns about the murder. He's really upset and vows revenge because he thinks he's the one who has to set things right."

"Thank you," Miss Brannigan said. "That was a fine summary."

"I still don't think it's proper," Mr. Harper said.

"And they talked about other ghosts, too," Mamie said. "Not just ones in the play."

"You did?" asked Mr. Darley.

"I said my daddy once seen a ghost in a tree when he was coon-hunting," Kenny said. "I didn't ask nobody to believe it. But I believe it. And if you got a problem with that, you ought to talk to my daddy."

"And a few of us told about stories we've head that have been passed around for a long time," Susan said. "Some folks believe 'em, and some don't. But Miss Brannigan never once said we had to believe. She even let us know right off that the whole play was made up."

Mr. Harper didn't say a word. But his hands were clenched into fists and his face was getting red. "And another thing," he said. "That story with the ghosts is wrote the same way God talks in the Bible. It's like it's making fun of God hisself."

There was a moment of silence. Mr. Darley looked puzzled.

"I don't understand how you think that Shakespeare's play is making fun of God, Mr. Harper," Miss Brannigan finally said. "Could you explain?"

"All them times *thou* and *thee* is used," Mr. Harper said, "and *doth* and *art*. They's God's words. They ort not to be made fun of in a ghost story."

"Oh," Miss Brannigan said. "You must mean the language of King James's time."

"I mean the language in the *King James Bible*," Mr. Harper said. "How God talked."

Bert, who no doubt couldn't wait to show he knew the answer, stood up and broke in. "That particular translation of the Bible was commissioned by King James the First of England and was finally completed in 1611. At that time in England, everyone talked that way."

Mr. Harper looked skeptical. Bert continued. "William Shakespeare wrote *Hamlet* at least a decade before the *King James Bible* was published. *Hamlet* was first performed in 1602 and published in 1603."

Mr. Harper glared at Bert. Several of the kids applauded until

Mr. Darley gave them one of his principal looks. Bert took a bow and then took his seat.

"Y'all think you're so smart, but I think you're all going to hell!" Mamie yelled. "You're going to burn in hell!"

"Mamie," said Mr. Darley. "That is not appropriate."

"You can go to hell, too!" she said. Her parents looked embarrassed, but they didn't correct her.

"What you've said is a suspension offense," Mr. Darley said. "You are hereby suspended for the next five school days. Since you'll miss the class assignment, I suggest you read a lengthy book and do a two-thousand word report on it."

"Will the *New Testament* do?" Mr. Harper asked.

"It'll do fine," Mr. Darley said.

After they'd gone, Miss Brannigan thanked the class for backing her up.

"Maybe we were born to set it right," Bert said. Some of the kids laughed.

"And if you'd got fired," Larry added, "we might end up getting Mrs. Southwark back. That would be worse than hell."

"Let's begin Act II," said Miss Brannigan, and everyone opened their books.

CHAPTER 9: PERCHANCE TO DREAM

The first week of November passed without anything unusual happening at school. We continued to read *Hamlet*, we continued to work on quilts, Mr. Wardell continued to try to get us interested in the election, and Loniss continued to be missing. The police continued their investigation but had no new leads. I continued to spend my evenings with Aint Lulie, and Mama continued to miss Scott. And I continued to ignore my gift. It was nice to be normal.

The weekend was a lot colder than usual, with wind that whipped down the mountain, so I brought in more wood for Aint Lulie. With the leaves gone from the trees, it was easier to see any deadfall in the woods. It was quiet in the woods, too, except for the wind. Most birds had gone south, most critters had denned up. There were none close by to talk to, even if I'd wanted—which I didn't. Once in a while I could hear a distant shot up the mountain, since deer season had begun.

I didn't use the slide since Aint Lulie didn't feel up to coming out in the cold. I walked back and forth I don't know how many times dragging the limbs back to her cabin. Some were so dry that they were easy to chop or break up. The ones that I couldn't chop easily, I left in a pile near the shed. By noon, I was glad to go into the cabin where the fire burned bright and Aint Lulie had soup on the stove.

Because the cold spell was likely to continue, one of Daddy's cousins sent word to him that there'd be a hog-killing come Monday. Daddy hadn't kept hogs himself for over ten years, but he got our supply of ham and sausage and bacon and lard by helping others with their own hogs. When I told Aint Lulie that we'd be getting some fresh hog meat before long, she pointed out that we were in the dark of the moon. "Likely we'll git a good supply of lard. Hogs killed in the dark of the moon make a heap more lard than usual."

On Monday, Daddy went off before daylight. Although Mama's help would have been welcomed by the women folk who'd be grinding sausage and making lard, she didn't go with him. I went off to school and endured math and science until I got to English where we read about Hamlet acting so strange Ophelia was frightened and how Claudius had noticed Hamlet's strange behavior himself. After what happened last week, nobody was complaining about having to read *Hamlet* and everyone wondered what would happen next. There was a lot of plotting in Act II. It seemed like everybody was plotting against somebody else, and some thought Hamlet was crazy. The class even got into a dispute about whether he was really crazy or just pretending to be crazy. I think Miss Brannigan was happy that we wanted to discuss what was happening and that Bert wasn't the only one to volunteer answers.

Mr. Wardell spent most of 5th period going over the election and urging us to make sure our parents got out and voted. Nobody told him that a lot of women in the county didn't bother to vote, and some men didn't either. I don't know if Daddy ever voted or not. He'd likely be too embarrassed to admit that he couldn't read the ballot.

In home ec, the group finished stitching my quilt. All I had to do was put the edging on it. Mrs. Carlton had several colors of wide bias tape that she said she'd give me. I decided on dark blue, and the other girls helped me pin it on. I decided to stitch the binding on the sewing machine because it'd be stronger and take less time to finish.

On Tuesday in English class, we read the part where Hamlet decided to have some players perform a play that would "catch the conscience of the king" and we began Act III. Several of the boys wanted to read Hamlet's "To be or not to be" speech, but Miss Brannigan picked Bert to read it. I guess it was his reward for standing up against Mr. Harper.

Mr. Wardell bragged that he'd been first in line when the polls opened at seven. You could tell that he was anticipating a big win for McGovern. And I finished my quilt. Mrs. Carlton had the four of us who worked on it stand behind it and hold it up while she took a picture with a little camera she had. Then the other girls spread out all the scrap bags and started picking through them to get the colors they wanted. Things were going pretty well, and I didn't mind ignoring my gift at all. I liked to be normal and not to be an outcast.

When I got home, I showed Mama my quilt. She fingered the material, looked at the stitching, and said it was real nice. I carried it with me to show Aint Lulie, who had heard my daily reports of how it was coming along. She looked it over carefully. "As fine a first quilt as ever I seen," she said.

That night I spread the quilt on my bed. Its brightness covered my old gray-beige quilt and, even by candlelight, it seemed to brighten up the whole room. After I'd snuggled under it and settled into its warmth, I thought back on how school was going and how much I enjoyed what we were doing in home ec and English. A line from the play popped into my mind—"To sleep, perchance to dream"—and I remembered what Aint Lulie had said about a dream you'd have the first time you slept under a new quilt. But I was too tired to take the quilt off the bed.

* * *

The next morning, I woke up shivering and shaking with the dream still fresh in my mind. I'd dreamed I'd been walking through the woods about twilight when a cold wind shook the trees and left them bare. I kept trying to get wherever I was going, but the wind got stronger and blew me sideways and turned me around. It was so dark I couldn't see where I was going, but I kept fighting the wind and trying to go somewhere. I think something I couldn't see—something behind me, maybe—reached out but couldn't take hold of me. I fought the wind and kept going. But the wind grew worse, and I looked for a place to take shelter but couldn't find any. In a strange dim light, I could see that uprooted trees surrounded me, and I wasn't where I thought I was going. I wanted to go ask Aint Lulie what my dream meant, but I had to get dressed and catch the bus.

In third period, we continued *Hamlet* with the scene where the players enact a murder of the old king. Claudius is naturally upset about the play and stops it.

"Hamlet got him good!" Kenny said, and everyone agreed. Then we read the scene about Polonius giving a message to Hamlet's friends to send him off to England. Hamlet has an opportunity to kill Claudius but decides to wait until later. When Hamlet confronts his mother, he hears a noise behind the curtain where Polonius is hiding and stabs him, thinking he is Claudius. Then he goes back to telling his mother, who pretty much thinks her son is crazy, how evil Claudius is. Hamlet's father's ghost appears again and reminds Hamlet to kill Claudius.

"It's a good thing that Mamie's still suspended," Larry said, "on account she'd have pitched a fit at this part." Everyone agreed. We discussed how complicated the play was getting.

In government, Mr. Wardell looked awful. He'd stayed up most of the night watching the election results on TV, and he couldn't understand how Nixon had won by such a landslide.

"McGovern only won electoral votes in Massachusetts and DC!" Mr. Wardell lamented. "And Nixon got eighteen million more popular votes than he did! That sets a new record! What is wrong with this country?"

Nobody answered him. Mr. Wardell had brought a radio to class so we could listen to coverage, so we did. Or pretended to. Mr. Wardell looked like he might cry any minute. After a day filled with complications, murder, and disappointment, it was good to go to home ec.

While I helped the others cut some squares from material they had gotten from the scrap bags, I noticed that lots of small pieces were left over. Aint Lulie's "Waste not, want not" popped into my mind. I decided I'd cut some tiny squares—maybe two and a half inches or so—for myself and sew them together to make a small quilt. Before long I had several dozen little squares. I asked Mrs. Carlton if I could borrow some pins to take home to pin my squares together, and she lent me some. The four of us quilters packed our squares into bags to take with us.

* * *

After I'd shown my little squares to Aint Lulie, and she'd told me what a good idea I had to use up the leftover material, I told her my dream.

She rocked by the fire and studied on it for a while. Finally she spoke. "Well, could be I'm wrong, but from what I recollect from Granny, a storm might stand for a right perplexing situation or it might be a sign of trouble coming or it might mean that a big change is coming. It might even mean progress is being made for something or other. Sometimes a storm dream means you got a lot of things on your mind that's been bothersome to you. Now if you'uz to dream of taking shelter from the storm, that means your troubles will soon pass. But if you won't able to escape the storm, it means you ort could use help from somebody else to fix that what troubles you."

Her explanation didn't really help. It went in too many directions. She rocked a little more before she asked me, "What you reckon it means?"

"A big change is coming when I graduate," I said. "I'll have to find a job. So I'll probably need help from somebody in getting the job. I've been making progress on quilt-making and in making a few friends. Maybe that's the meaning."

Mebbe so," she said. "Mebbe so."

* * *

I thought about what Aint Lulie said all the next day. Well, except for third period when Hamlet's problems were coming to a head in Act Four. He's hid Polonius's body and his mama thinks he's insane. Claudius wants to send Hamlet to England, and Hamlet agrees to go. When Hamlet is on the beach, he sees Fortinbras and his forces who want permission to go through Denmark to attack Poland. Hamlet decides he's got to kill Claudius when he gets back home. Meanwhile Ophelia goes crazy, and her brother comes back and he's mad.

We didn't get to finish Act IV, but it gave us something to talk about. Miss Brannigan said we would finish the play next week. Mamie would be back from suspension then, so there was no telling what trouble she might cause.

Compared to Hamlet's problems, my troubles didn't seem so bad after all.

* * *

On Saturday, Aint Lulie reckoned she'd go to church with us the next day—"Iff'n it's all right with your mama and daddy. I been thinking about what Pearl said about gitting out, and I ort to do it before the weather gits real wintry."

I told her I thought it would be fine, but she shouldn't say anything to Mama about Pearl's visit. "'Course tomorry's the Feast of St. Martin, and it's bad luck to go on a trip on that day. But I reckon going to church ain't like a real trip."

"I don't think church counts as a real trip either," I said. "We won't even be leaving the county."

When I got home, I told Mama what Aint Lulie wanted to do, and she thought that would be a fine thing. "'Bout time," Mama said. "'Bout time."

On Sunday morning, Daddy drove his truck through the path to Aint Lulie's cabin. Mama and I got out and helped her get in. It was a tight fit with all four of us in the truck's cab, but we made do.

"First time I've been off'n the farm in a coon's age," Aint Lulie said.

I could remember exactly the last time she'd left the farm. It was right after we'd gotten word about Scott, and there was a service for him at church. Not a funeral, since there wasn't a body to bury. But a service for him nonetheless.

Daddy pulled his truck up almost to the church door. We managed to get Aint Lulie unloaded without much problem, and then Daddy drove to the far side of the parking lot where he usually waited.

A lot of people seemed glad to see her. At least, they came by and welcomed her back: "Right nice to see you, Miz Caldwell," "Glad you decided to join us today," "Miz Caldwell, I been wondering how you was doing."

Elder Stoutmire already had a good fire going, so at least the church was warm when we took our usual place on our usual pew. Aint Lulie took the seat on the end nearest the window. I sat between her and Mama. When everyone was seated, he began the service with the usual announcements, including another thank-you to the unknown person who had donated and stacked the firewood. He ended his announcements with, "It pleases the Lord to see lost sheep return to the fold," and looked right at Aint Lulie. Then he began a prayer for the return of the Hathaways' "little lost gal" that she might be returned to her family.

He was maybe three or four minutes into his sermon, when Aint Lulie sat up straighter than she had for a long time, kind of like she had snapped to attention. But she wasn't paying attention to the sermon. Instead, she stared out the window and seemed to see something that I couldn't see. All I saw was the big pile of stacked firewood. She put her hand on my shoulder and pulled herself up so she was standing. Elder Stoutmire glared at her, and preached a little louder.

"The woodpile!" she yelled. All eyes turned away from Elder Stoutmire and toward Aint Lulie. She pointed at the window. "That missing gal!"

Elder Stoutmire stopped his sermon mid-sentence and ordered her to be quiet and sit down for it wasn't a woman's place to speak out in church. She paid him no mind and kept pointing.

"The gal is in the woodpile!" she hollered. "Look in the woodpile!" She clutched at her throat and made choking sounds like she was having trouble getting her breath.

Several of the men left their seats and raced outside to the woodpile. A few women came over to see to Aint Lulie. I watched through the window as the men started slinging logs off the pile. It didn't take long for them to uncover a pale white hand with a ring on one finger. One man yelled they ought to stop and call the state police. "Best not tamper with the evidence," he said. They came back in and reported what they were going to do. Elder Stoutmire didn't say a word.

"Law—law—gal says—law—" Aint Lulie collapsed back onto the pew.

"See?" said a man sitting across from us. "She's saying git the law!"

"Naw," said another. She's trying to say that Lawson boy did it."

Aint Lulie continued to gasp for breath. "Somebody go get a doctor!" I yelled.

A couple of men ran to their trucks and sped away to where they might find a telephone. In the meantime, Mama and I got Aint Lulie lying down on the pew and Mama bunched up her coat and put it under Aint Lulie's head for a pillow. Some women hovered around us, but there wasn't much they could do.

Elder Stoutmire looked lost. I guess he realized there was no point in continuing his sermon. "We ort to pray," he finally said, and some of his flock bowed their heads. Mama and I didn't. We kept our eyes on Aint Lulie, and I held onto her hand. For a second, I let my eyes wander to the window, and I caught sight of the pale hand dangling from between the logs. The sun glinted from the ring's white stone, and a shiver ran through me. I felt Aint Lulie shiver, too.

Don't die, I prayed silently. *Don't let her die.* Aint Lulie kept breathing. And Daddy came in and stood behind us.

Finally we heard sirens blaring in the distance, then closer and closer. An ambulance and a couple of state police cars sped up the church hill. The ambulance pulled up close to the church door and the medics came into the church and carried Aint Lulie out to the ambulance where they gave her oxygen. They'd told Mama and me to stay back while they worked with her. By this time, Elder Stoutmire had sat down and was praying silently.

I watched the policemen fling more logs from the woodpile. One of them took pictures every so often. Before long, I caught a glimpse of a red dress. Another policemen went back to his squad car and got on his radio—I guess to get more help. After he finished talking on the radio, he took a blanket from the car's trunk and placed it over what they'd uncovered.

One of the medics told us that Aint Lulie was coming around, but it was possible that she'd had a mild stroke and did we want them to take her to the hospital.

"No," Daddy said, "We'll take her on home where she belongs. She won't be satisfied anywhere but home."

He got his truck and pulled it up to the ambulance, and the medics helped get Aint Lulie in. Mama and I squeezed in, and Daddy drove off. I looked back to see the ambulance backing up to the woodpile. I guess it would take Loniss to the funeral home in town. We were almost down the hill when Wiley Shortridge came speeding up with his siren going. I wondered why he didn't get there when the state policemen did.

"Sure is a heap a' noise out in the world," Aint Lulie said. "What're we doing out in it?"

"We've been to church," I said.

"Well, don't that beat all," she said. "I don't recollect none of it. Was it a good sermon?"

Mama and Daddy didn't say a word.

"I'll tell you about it later," I told her.

Daddy pulled the truck up near the cabin door. We helped Aint Lulie inside, and I persuaded her to lie down for a while. I told her not to bother trying to cook, that I'd be back later with her dinner. An hour later, when I took her some chicken and dumplings, Aint Lulie still had no recollection of what happened at church. "But whatever 'twas going on, it plumb wore me out. I reckon I'll take me a nap jist as soon as I eat."

I built up her fire which had almost gone out, got her a bucket of fresh water, and told her I'd be back to help her get her night-work done up. When I returned a few hours later, she told me she'd just eaten and that she was going to bed early. I guess she was still worn out from what had happened at church. By the time I'd finished her chores and added more logs to the fire, she was sound asleep. I said, "You better come go with me," but there was no answer. I guess seeing the dead must be hard on a person.

* * *

No sooner had I gotten on the school bus the next morning, Clovis said, "'Pears to me your old aunt is still witching. Least that's what I heard."

"She had a feeling come over her," I said, "and the feeling turned out to be true." I took a seat in the middle of the bus and was glad when Cheryl got on and sat with me. I could tell she'd been crying.

"They found Loniss," Cheryl said. "And she's been murdered."

"I know," I said. "I was in the church when they found her." I didn't mention what I'd seen, and I didn't mention Aint Lulie. Clovis didn't say a word.

The bus ride was pretty quiet, maybe because Loniss rode this bus and had a couple of good friends who did, too. Likely it was taking a while for them to realize that Loniss would never again be riding it.

At school, though, it seemed like everybody was talking about what they'd heard. The police hadn't released much information— only that Loniss's body had been found buried in a woodpile beside one of the mountain churches. At least the police didn't say that an old woman's hunch led them to find a body. According to some who'd listened to the story on the radio, the police had received a tip where to look for the body. They weren't saying how they got the tip. But anybody who was at the church knew it was Aint Lulie. And there's no telling how many they told. Somebody had to have told Clovis.

Mr. Darley asked the teachers to bring their first period classes to the gym, so I got to miss algebra. When everyone had assembled, he basically told us what we already knew. But we were all wondering, *Did Lucas really kill Loniss? How? Why?*

After we'd returned to classes, teachers didn't get much done because everyone was so distracted. Loniss's cheerleader friends cried off and on all morning. Wiley Shortridge stopped by the school and popped into a few classes during second period to see if anyone wanted to tell him anything. No one did. Someone heard that a reporter from the Bristol paper had stopped by to see if he could talk to kids who knew Loniss, but Mr. Darley sent him away. Someone else had heard that state police and detectives were going back to the church today to look for clues. Another said a TV news team all the way from Roanoke was going to the church to do a story. But nobody really knew anything—only that Loniss had been murdered.

Miss Brannigan tried to get us back to reading *Hamlet*, but events in the play only reminded everyone of Loniss. Polonius's body had been hidden under the stairs. Loniss's body had been hidden in a woodpile. Hamlet hasn't yet realized that Claudius is plotting to have him killed. *Did someone plot to kill Loniss? When did she realize she'd be killed?* We didn't dare ask the questions aloud in class, but they hung silent in the air like circling buzzards.

Miss Brannigan asked us questions about the tragedy of *Hamlet*, and we did our best to answer them. But our minds were on the tragedy much closer to us.

At lunch, Bert wanted to talk about Loniss being found, but I told them I didn't want to. "You were at the church," Bert said. "You had to have seen something."

"I saw her hand," I said. "They uncovered her hand but didn't uncover anything more before the police came. That's all I'm going to say."

Then our talk turned to Mamie Harper, and how she hadn't said a word in class today.

* * *

Mamie didn't say a word most of the next day either. We read the parts about Gertrude and Horatio discussing Ophelia's insanity and Laertes wanting to be king as well as avenge his father's death. We read about Horatio receiving a letter from Hamlet saying he was taken by pirates and returned to Denmark. We read about Claudius telling Laertes he can have his revenge on Hamlet by challenging him to a sword fight. When we read about Gertrude telling them that Ophelia has drowned, I thought about the girl in the millpond Aint Lulie had told me about. I pictured Ophelia in a blue dress like that girl's. We talked for a bit about whether Ophelia accidentally drowned or if she committed suicide because Hamlet didn't love her. That's when Mamie spoke.

"Ain't no sense killing yourself about a man," Mamie said. "If you take your own life, you'll go to hell and burn for all eternity."

"But if you're crazy, you're not responsible for what you do," Bert said. "Ophelia was crazy. Anybody with any sense could see that." That shut Mamie up.

The bell rang, and we left class quietly. Thoughts of death still hung heavy around us.

Even home ec was quieter than usual. Most of us worked alone, either pinning patches together, or sewing what we'd pinned. It was good routine work, and for a while it kept us from having to think much about a world filled with craziness and death and revenge.

The rest of the week passed in the same strange quietness. By Friday, all the major characters in *Hamlet* were dead, and there was no chance of a happy ending. Even though the characters in the play were made up, their ghosts would haunt us for a long time.

Loniss's body, we heard, was at the state medical examiner's office for an autopsy. Nobody knew yet when the funeral would be, but there'd been a story in some of the papers saying that the Hathaways wished Loniss's story had a happier ending, but they were relieved that her body had been found. While they had offered a reward for her safe return, they were now going to use that money as a reward for information leading to the arrest and conviction of her murderer.

Lucas had already been arrested, but no one knew how he could have done it. Or even if he did it. Did the murderer still walk among us and we didn't know?

CHAPTER 10: TO THINE OWN SELF
BE TRUE

On Saturday, while Aint Lulie was taking her afternoon nap, I was in Mama's kitchen helping her make cornbread. I figured I'd make an extra batch to take to Aint Lulie since she liked it so much. I was just getting ready to pour the batter into a greased skillet when I heard the sound of cars. I peeked through the window and saw Wiley Shortridge drive up, followed by a state police car. I put down the bowl of batter and waited to see what would happen next. Daddy had been in the barn, but he must have seen them coming because he hurried in the back door before the police knocked on the front.

Daddy opened the front door a crack. "Can I he'p you gents?"

"These lawmen would like to get some information." Wiley Shortridge's voice sounded strained. Maybe his job was on the line because he hadn't solved the case. Maybe it was something else. Daddy stepped out onto the porch but he left the door open.

Aint Lulie's words flashed across my mind: "There's a lot to hear if we only listen." I tried to listen to what they were saying to Daddy, but they spoke low. From where I stood in the kitchen, I couldn't make it all out.

After a minute or two, Daddy hollered, "Annie! You best come out on the porch and talk to these lawmen."

I knew he wouldn't invite them in. I knew Mama wouldn't want him to. Mama said she'd see to the cornbread and for me to go on out, so I slipped on a sweater and went to the porch. Besides Wiley, there were two state policemen in uniforms and one man who wore a suit. Each one introduced himself to me. The man in the suit was a special investigator, Detective Adams.

Daddy and I sat in the swing, the state men took the three porch chairs, and Wiley sat on the porch steps.

"We thought maybe you could help us help with the investigation," the detective said.

"I don't think I can help you," I said. "I told Wiley—Deputy Shortridge—all I know back in October."

"You were at the dance the night she disappeared?" one of the state men asked me.

I told him how I was helping serve refreshments and didn't really see much—the same thing I'd told Wiley back in October. Daddy broke in and said he'd seen Loniss come out, then Alvin come out and go back in, then Loniss and Alvin left, and Lucas came out and left. He'd told it so many times he had it down pat.

"We know all that," Detective Adams said. "We've talked to a lot of people that Deputy Shortridge has already questioned. But we've reached an impasse, Annie, and we heard something about you that made us think you might be able to help us."

I felt caught. "What did you hear?" I said.

"Word is, at least according to a few older folks, that you, uh, know things," said the taller policeman.

"I don't know what you mean," I said. "I don't know anymore about what happened to Loniss than what I've already told."

"Some of the old timers said both you and your aunt had some kind of special ways of—well, after what happened with your aunt in church, a few people there remembered you could talk to animals."

"Likely they remember about the chickens," said Daddy. "I might've bragged about it some when you were little."

"So can you help us?" the detective asked. All of them looked at me. And waited.

I felt my face burning with shame. I could lie or pretend I couldn't do it. "Sometimes I can," I said. I thought about telling them what I'd learned from Precious and Ranger, even though it likely wouldn't be of any help. Then Bruno stood up and stuck his head out Wiley's patrol car window.

Listen to me! Bruno said. *I didn't want to get my master in trouble, but I can no longer keep his secret. He is the one who did bad things to the girl. He is the one who put her in the trunk of this car and took her to the church at night. Tell them to look in the trunk.*

Bruno showed me what he'd seen that night after the dance. I felt sick and thought I might vomit, and I guess the policemen could tell something was bothering me by the look on my face. "Oh, that I was born to set it right!" popped into my mind. Was that why I had a gift—to set things right? But trying to set things right didn't work out for Hamlet. What would it do to me?

Wiley stood up, although I hadn't yet said a word, and started to his car.

"Stop him!" I yelled with a voice I didn't know I had. "He had her in his car!"

Wiley spun around and reached for his gun, but the detective was faster and grabbed Wiley's wrist. The gun tumbled to the ground, and Daddy grabbed it. For an instant, I thought he would shoot Wiley. The two state men wrestled Wiley to the ground, and one of them managed to handcuff him.

"Look in the trunk," I said. "His dog tells me you'll find something." But I wasn't sure what they'd find. Only that Bruno thought they should look. While the taller man held Wiley, the shorter one opened the trunk, and he and the detective looked in.

"Well, well," said Detective Adams. "This is certainly interesting."

Daddy and I walked over to look in. A few red sequins glinted in the afternoon sun.

Tell them to look behind the tire.

"Bruno says you'll find something behind the tire," I said. Bruno hung his head and slumped down on the seat. You are a good police dog, I told him. You have solved a crime and brought honor to yourself.

Thank you for the cookie you gave me at the dance, he said.

When I disconnected from Bruno, the tall policeman was telling Wiley he had the right to remain silent. Detective Adams leaned into the trunk and looked. "Looks like a red shoe is wedged back there," he said. I remembered that Loniss had worn shoes that matched her dress.

The officers discussed the situation for a bit, and decided not to remove the tire to look just yet—something about corrupting the evidence—but would take the car to let some others investigate.

They radioed for back-up to take Wiley in. The shorter man took the gun from Daddy and thanked him for his help. I went back inside to see how the cornbread was doing. When Aint Lulie woke from her nap, she'd have fresh cornbread and good news waiting for her.

* * *

News of Wiley's arrest spread fast. We started to church as usual on Sunday, but we never got there. A sign on the road leading to the church said services had been cancelled until the investigation was complete. But folks coming to service pulled over and talked among themselves, and some prayed. Daddy talked to a few of the men to find out what they knew, and then we turned around and came home. From what Daddy had heard, no one had mentioned me. Daddy said he hadn't mentioned me either.

On Monday when I got on the bus, Clovis asked, "You hear anything about Wiley Shortridge being arrested for killing Loniss?"

"We'd tried to go to church yesterday, but it was closed. Folks gathered along the road and talked about Wiley, but nobody knew much except he'd been arrested." That much was true. I just didn't tell him about Saturday. Clovis stared at me for a few seconds while I took my seat. He didn't ask any others, though, but he heard Kenny and Larry talking to some of the other boys about Wiley's arrest and Lucas's release. Maybe what they said was enough for him.

Before the first class started, it seemed like everyone at school knew that Wiley Shortridge had been arrested and Lucas had been released. Some kids said that the TV news mentioned that a local deputy had been arrested for murder based on certain evidence that investigators had found. They weren't allowed to give details yet, so no one knew what the evidence was or how they got it. But I knew. At least the news people hadn't given out any details about me, and for that I was grateful. Mr. Darley came around to classes and told us that Wiley had been arrested and Lucas was free, but he didn't tell us anything that we didn't already know.

Lucas didn't come back to school, though. According to Kenny, Lucas was thinking about joining the army. He'd missed too many days and would never catch up. He couldn't see himself repeating a year. He'd turned eighteen while he was in jail. Lucas told Kenny that the jailer came to his cell on Saturday and said he was free to go. Lucas went.

"But he told me something else," Kenny said. "Lucas said he stopped by Loniss's house after Alvin took her home and got her to come out and talk to him. She got in his truck and they rode for a little piece. Then she got mad at something he said and got out. He got out to go after her, and somebody come up behind him and hit him in the back of the head. He said when he come to, it was almost dawn and he couldn't find Loniss anywhere, so he figured he'd better hide out for a while before whoever hit him came after him again."

I think all of us figured out pretty quick that Wiley Shortridge was the one who hit Lucas. It made sense to us that Loniss would get in the car with a deputy. Deputies were supposed to protect you and keep you safe. Everybody knew that.

* * *

I no sooner got to Aint Lulie's cabin after school than she wanted to hear what folks were saying. "I been studying on it most'a last night and all day today. And I been trying to recollect what happened at church, but it plumb left my mind."

"You said 'law, law' a couple of times, and folks thought you were trying to say 'Lawson,' but you must have meant it was a lawman that killed her."

"That could be it," she said. "You know, I been thinking about your storm dream. Maybe you taking up your gift agin is the big change that storm meant."

"Maybe so," I said. I didn't tell Aint Lulie that I still wanted my gift to stay a secret, and I was afraid that my secret couldn't be kept much longer.

* * *

Tuesday after school, I hadn't even had time to get to Aint Lulie's when the state police car pulled up in front of our house. I thought they wanted to talk to me, but this time it was Daddy they came to see. I asked them to wait on the porch while I ran to his shop to get him.

"What could they be wanting with me?" he wondered as we walked back to the house.

"Good afternoon, gents," he said to the three men. "Something I can he'p you with?"

"Mr. Caldwell," said Detective Adams, " We need to ask you a few questions about Elder Stoutmire."

"Well, all right," Daddy said. "But you got to know that I don't attend that church. My wife does. And Annie."

"Oh, this is about Stoutmire's other job," the detective said.

"His other job?" Daddy was starting to sweat even though it was chilly outside.

"We went up to the church this morning to ask him a few questions," the tall policeman said. "He wasn't there, so we walked up the path to his house. Turns out he's got quite a liquor business going, and we just happened to catch him at it. You wouldn't know anything about that, would you?"

Daddy didn't answer right away, so the shorter policeman jumped in with a question: "What we want to know is, did you ever buy any liquor from him?"

"I might've," Daddy said. "A time or two."

"Did you leave money in one place, and then pick up the liquor from another place—say, in the woods on the far side of the church parking area?" the detective asked.

Daddy hung his head. "Yeah," he said, "that's the way he works it."

"And there's more," the detective said. "Looks like he had a marijuana operation going, too. You know anything about that?"

"No," Daddy said. "I don't know nothing about that. Never have used that stuff."

"From what we can figure, it looks like Shortridge might have known about it and kind of looked the other way. You know anything about that?"

Daddy said he didn't.

The policemen said their good-byes. "If you hear of anything, or if you need help, you give us a call." Detective Adams gave a card with his phone number to Daddy and another one to me. Neither of us told him we didn't have a phone.

As they drove away, Daddy said he reckoned he'd better be getting inside. "And I reckon there won't be no church service again come Sunday."

I followed him in. While I was putting away my books in the hall, I heard him tell Mama in the kitchen what the lawmen said and why he wouldn't be taking her to church come Sunday.

"But he's a man of God!" I heard Mama say. "He knows the Bible!"

"He might know it," Daddy replied, "but he don't live it."

I hurried to Aint Lulie's to tell her the latest news. "I ain't a bit surprised," she said. "I never did think that preacher'uz a man to be trusted."

* * *

Next morning when I started out the door, I saw a bloody deer head on the front steps. I went back in to tell Mama so she wouldn't happen upon it and so she'd get Daddy to get rid of it. I also told her to check on Aint Lulie when she got a chance.

I was late getting to the bus stop, and Clovis was already there gunning the engine. "You having some kind of problem?" he asked. "Ain't like you to ever be late."

"No problem," I said. "Just running late."

He didn't ask if I'd heard about the preacher. I didn't volunteer any information. I was glad when Cheryl got on the bus. We'd been sitting together for a while now. We usually talked about quilts, and she'd tell me about her grandma and the old-timey things she'd learned from her. I'd tell her about Aint Lulie and some of the things I've learned from her. But I never mentioned Aint Lulie's gift. Or mine.

Because the next day was Thanksgiving, school was dismissed a half-day early. Most of the teachers used the shortened class time to give quizzes or tests. Before long, we were back on the bus again. The boys were all excited about having time off to do some deer hunting before dark as well as through the weekend. A lot of mountain families that didn't have much to eat would now have a chance for a feast. To be able to put meat on the table was the mark of manhood as far as the boys were concerned.

Cheryl and I had both brought bags of scraps home with us. We hoped to work on our quilts over the holiday.

Clovis had another milk can with him, but no one asked him if he was coming or going to the antique dealer. Clovis didn't have much to say at all.

After he stopped to let me off, he sped away without so much as a good-bye. I ran to see Aint Lulie without even going to the house. If someone would leave a deer head on the steps, there's no telling what they might do next—and maybe to Aint Lulie. To my relief, she was rocking by the fire and seemed fine. But still I was worried.

"What are you in such an all-fired hurry for, child?" she said when I burst in.

"I brought some quilt patches." I set the bag on the table. "I wanted to see if you'd help me with them."

"You know I would," she said. "I look forward to doing things like that."

"Would you mind if I stayed with you tonight?" I said. "I could sleep on a pallet by the fire."

"I'd be right glad of your company," she said. I was glad she hadn't asked why I wanted to stay.

I promised her I'd be back soon, and took off for home to tell Mama and Daddy what I planned to do. We never made much of the Thanksgiving holiday, so there wouldn't be any special things I had to do at home. Daddy might slip off during the day to see if he could get himself a deer, too. We could always use extra meat. Mama wouldn't mind being by herself. She'd pray and watch for Scott the way she always did.

"It's good you're staying with her," Mama said. "Aint Lulie needs looking after."

I put some clothes and nightclothes into a sack and headed back to Aint Lulie's. After we ate supper and did up the night work, I spread my quilt patches on the table. Under the glow of her kerosene lamp, we spent a while moving them around to see what color went best with what other color. Finally we were satisfied, and I started pinning. When I finished, I rolled up what I'd pinned while Aint Lulie got some quilts and a pillow to make my pallet by the fire. I lit Aint Lulie's old lantern and made a trip to the outhouse. On the way back, I held the lantern in different directions to see if I saw anything moving. But nothing was there, and only the bare branches moved lightly in the cold wind. If I'd seen or heard a critter I might have asked it if anyone was in the woods, but no critters appeared. I was alone in the cold and dark.

By the time I got back inside, Aint Lulie was already in bed. I built up the fire for the night, blew out the lantern and lamp, and snuggled into my pallet. When her clock chimed two, I thought I heard something outside, but I wasn't sure. Maybe I was just letting my mind get the best of me. But I didn't want to light the lantern to go out to see. If anybody drove in, they'd have to go by the house and Daddy would get up. If they walked in, they might be able to see where they were going by the waning gibbous moon, but there'd been clouds blowing across the sky earlier, so they couldn't have depended on moonlight. Aint Lulie's snoring told me that she hadn't awakened. I decided I was being foolish and finally went back to sleep.

At daylight, I put on my coat and went to the outhouse. When I came back toward the cabin, I realized we did have a visitor in the night. The remains of a headless deer carcass hung by a hind foot from a rope that had been slung over a limb. The deer had been gutted and skinned. It looked like the tenderloin had been removed. Leaning against the tree-trunk was a big wooden sign with "2 DOWN WHOZE NEXT?" painted in orange letters. I jerked loose the rope where it had been tied to the tree trunk and dropped the carcass to the ground, and I flipped the sign face down. If Aint Lulie looked out, she'd only see a hump in the leaves where the deer lay. She wasn't likely to go out in this direction, so I figured she wouldn't see anything amiss. And there was no reason for me to mention that we'd had a night visitor.

She was awake but still in bed when I got back in. I told her I was going to run home for a few minutes to see if Mama needed anything done today, but I'd be back in time for breakfast. It was unlikely Mama would need me to do anything, but maybe I could tell Daddy about the deer. He was headed to his truck when I approached the house. I told him what I'd heard in the night and what I'd found this morning. He said he'd take care of it before he went to the woods himself.

"Do you think we should call the detective?" I asked.

"Naw," Daddy said. "Likely he wants to enjoy Thanksgiving with his family. Ain't no use in having him leave home on account somebody is jist trying to scare us."

I went in to see if Mama wanted anything, so what I told Aint Lulie wouldn't be a lie. Mama gave me some eggs and some fresh-baked biscuits to take back with me. When I returned to the cabin, Aint Lulie was up and slicing some strips of bacon from off the slab. She brightened up when she saw what I carried.

"Well, ain't that nice'a your mama to give us that. I'll fry up some'a them eggs in the bacon grease, and I got a jar of apple butter that Maribelle Lewis sent me that'll go real good with them biscuits. We'll see if her apple butter tastes as good as what you and me made back in September."

After breakfast—when we decided that Maribelle's apple butter was real good but not as good as ours on account hers is a mite too spicy—Aint Lulie washed the dishes and put on a pot of soup to simmer. I rolled up my pallet, emptied the slop jar, toted in a few buckets of water, chopped some kindling, and hauled in a few logs. When our morning work was done and the table was cleared, we started on my quilt. We worked most of the morning.

"I been thinking," Aint Lulie said, "You got plenty more scraps left to make another quilt or two. I reckon I'll cut out some pieces to git you started on a log cabin quilt. But first, I'm fixing to put some sweet taters in the coals to cook up for our Thanksgiving dinner. Reckon you could go up to the loft and git four or five nice ones?"

I was ready to take a break from sitting for so long. I climbed up the steep steps and brought down some sweet potatoes. Aint Lulie arranged them in the ashes. "That ort to make a real nice feast, what with the soup and left-over biscuits. Maybe I ort to make a cobbler pie to go with 'em."

She sent me to the dogtrot to dip some flour from out of the barrel and to fetch a jar of blackberries she'd canned last summer. I moved my quilt work to one side of the table, so she'd have the other side to do her fixing.

While I went back to my basting, she mixed up some pie dough, rolled it out, and spread it in an oblong pan. She poured the blackberries on top of the crust and folded the edges over to form sort of a top crust. Then she put it into the oven. "Don't let me lose track of the time," she said. "I recollect it'll be done when the clock strikes eleven."

"Did folks used to have big Thanksgiving dinners when you were a girl?" I asked while we were eating.

"I cain't think of any that did," she said. "We et when we had food, and sometimes we had more'n other times. If harvest was good, we'uz pretty well fixed. Ma and Granny always had a big garden and what they put by got us through the winter. But we use'ta have all manner of celebrations. For one thing, lot of folks done their hog-killing about this time of year. It'uz cold enough so the meat would keep, and folks would go to help others git the job done. I helped grind many a sausage when I'uz your age because that'uz women's work. And we'd have us tenderloin for breakfast ever morning." She smiled, remembering. "And the chaps too little to be of any help would play ball with pig bladders. Somebody'd blow 'em up and tie 'em off, and the chaps would have the biggest time kicking 'em and tossing 'em. And it kept them chaps out of the way, too.

"And corn shuckings. Everbody needed their corn shucked for their winter feed, so we'd go to first one's house and then anothern's. It'uz like a big party in the barn. We might sing while we shucked or somebody might have brung a fiddle, and men might pass the bottle or jug around. If a young man shucked out a red ear, he got to kiss the gal of his choice."

"Did you ever get kissed?"

"I reckon I did. First time Sparrell Hobson ever kissed me, he'd done found hisself a red ear."

I helped her clear the table and went out to get a few buckets of water and bring in some more firewood. While Aint Lulie washed the dishes, I started working on my quilt again. After I'd stitched all the patches together and pulled out the pins, Aint Lulie heated up her flatirons so we could press what was becoming my quilt top. I pressed one end while she pressed the other.

"Now, you'uz asking about Thanksgiving," she said while we worked. "What we mainly had was a program at school the day before. The teacher'ud read us a piece or two about the first Thanksgiving and how Squanto helped the pilgrims. Each grade would recite something they put to memory about Thanksgiving or harvest or some such.

"There won't a set day for Thanksgiving when I'uz a chap, neither. If I recollect, it'uz the President that decided. Generally, it'uz last Thursday in November, but President Roosevelt come along in 19 and 39 and changed it to third Thursday. I don't know why he done that."

After we finished pressing the quilt top, I said, "If I just had some material to back the quilt with and some batting, I could finish it next week at school."

"You got that twenty dollars the teacher give you," Aint Lulie said. "You ort to be able to git what you need in town and still have some money left over."

"Problem is, I don't know how I'd get to town. It's too far to walk." I carefully folded my quilt top so it wouldn't get wrinkled.

"Well, might be you could ask your daddy to take you."

"But Daddy isn't likely to make a special trip to town for me."

"You got to wait for him to have a reason to go on his own," she said. "Then ask if you might ride along."

"I might do that," I said.

"When opportunity comes knocking, you got to open the

door," she said.

The opportunity came sooner than I expected.

* * *

Late that night when the clock chimed midnight, I woke up. I thought I'd heard something else besides the clock—the sound of a motor, the sound of tires on the frozen ground. Or maybe I was skittish because of the last time and just thought I'd heard something. I saw a light pass over the wall. I got up and looked out the window. Sure enough, somebody was driving up the path toward the cabin. It couldn't be Daddy because this vehicle was a lot quieter than his truck. The headlights were on low, like the driver wanted to be able to see but didn't want to attract any attention.

I could hear Aint Lulie snoring softly, so I knew she was asleep. There was no point in waking her. I didn't know what to do, so I put on my shoes and coat and grabbed the fireplace poker. If somebody got out and came toward the house, maybe I could surprise him.

When the truck had cleared the trees and was in the open space, a BOOM! sounded from the far end of the porch. The driver spun around and I could hear the sound of metal scraping against a tree while he sped away. Aint Lulie still slept. I stayed as still as I could by the door. Then someone knocked.

"Annie? Y'all all right in there?" It was Daddy's voice, so I opened the door. "I couldn't sleep on account I was skeert something might happen, so I come out and set on the porch. I don't reckon whoever that was'll be coming back tonight. We'll git the law tomorrow. I'd best go home afore your mama has time to get worried."

Daddy shouldered his shotgun and started down the path. All was quiet except for the clock ticking and Aint Lulie snoring. And maybe my heart pounding.

* * *

Early Friday morning, Daddy came by and looked at the blue paint where the truck had scraped the tree. "I b'lieve I know who done that," he said. "You still got that card with the lawman's number on it. I might could drive you to a telephone to call him."

"I've got it," I said. "It's in my room." Then opportunity knocked and I answered. "While we're out, could you take me to a store where I can buy some quilt supplies? Some material and stuff."

"Now whatcha wanta waste your money for on stuff like that?"

I didn't tell him that every bottle of liquor he bought was a waste. Instead, I said, "I've been piecing some quilts, and I think I might be able to sell some. I could maybe turn a little money into more money."

"Oh, well then. I reckon I can go ahead and run you to the store while we're out."

I told Aint Lulie that Daddy was going to take me to town and then went home to get the card and the money from under my mattress. Daddy was waiting in his truck when I came downstairs.

He didn't say much on the ride to town, but I didn't expect him to. We stopped first at the barbershop where he asked if we could use the phone. I dialed the number and Detective Adams answered. I told him what had been going on the last few nights, and then Daddy took the phone and added a few details. Detective Adams told Daddy he had some other business to take care of first but could probably get to us in two or three hours.

Daddy took me on to the Ben Franklin Store and waited out front while I went in and bought a few yards of plaid material that I thought would look pretty as a quilt backing, a half-yard each of a couple other fabrics for more patches, and two rolls of batting. I saw a small flashlight and bought that along with some batteries. I figured it would come in handy on the dark nights. I had about six dollars left after I paid. That was the first time I ever went into a store and bought something for myself.

Once we'd gotten back, I showed Aint Lulie what I'd bought. She fingered the material and pronounced it fine for what we wanted to do with it. "I cain't git used to that man-made batting, though. We generally used cotton."

We measured out the plaid material and cut it to make the backing. Then I started basting the three big strips of backing together. On Monday, I'd sew them on the machine. While I was basting, Aint Lulie fixed up our dinner.

We'd just finished eating leftover cobbler for our dessert when I heard some vehicles coming toward the cabin. I looked out to see Daddy walking along the path. He was followed by the state police car and a county car driven by a deputy I didn't know. Aint Lulie saw me looking out the window.

"What's all that commotion out yonder?" she asked, and I told her about the night visitor and the police who'd investigate. "That don't make no sense a'tall for somebody to slip around here at night. Ain't like I got anything for 'em to steal. Reckon you ort to ask 'em in?"

"I think they want to look around outside." I put on my coat and went out to join them.

Daddy was showing them where the truck had scraped the tree, and one of the state men scraped off some of the paint and put it in a plastic bag. The other took some pictures. The deputy mostly watched.

"Annie, this is Arlis Woodson," Detective Adams said when I walked up to the group. "He used to patrol the southern part of the county, but he's assigned to this district now."

The new deputy tipped his hat and smiled. Nobody had to tell me that he was Wiley's replacement, even though Bruno wasn't with him.

The lawmen looked around in the woods for a while. Daddy showed them where he had dumped the deer and the sign. They dusted the sign to see if they could get prints. Since Daddy had worn gloves when he moved it and I had only touched the edge, they were hopeful they might get some evidence.

"We're pretty sure that Shortridge and Stoutmire had at least one accomplice," Detective Adams said. "From what you've told me, I think whoever is harassing you might be the one."

"I been thinking," Daddy said, "and I b'lieve I know who it might be. Clovis Wilbur bought hisself a new truck not long ago, and it might be that it's the color of this paint. If you'uz to check his'n, might be it'd have some scrapes and mebbe some buckshot dents."

"Clovis Wilbur?" the tall policeman asked? "The school bus driver?"

"He drives the bus I ride," I said. "So he'd know about the path and the cabin."

"I guess we should pay him a visit," Detective Adams said. "Is he the owner of Wilbur's Dairy Farm?"

"His family owns it," Daddy said. "He lives there."

While the lawmen jotted down some notes, I sent my mind to the cows at the Wilbur farm. I connected with Number 62. *The truck? Woke us up in the dark way before milking time this morning when it come speeding home from somewhere. He drove it way out in the pasture and*

left it in that grove of pines where some of us take shelter. Walked back cussing
a blue streak! And he was late milking us. My udder was about to bust!

"Maybe I can help," I said. "One of his cows says you'll find his truck in a grove of pines in the pasture."

"That helps a lot," said Detective Adams. "Looks like we'll be paying him a visit."

The look on Deputy Woodson's face was pure puzzlement. I guess they hadn't yet told him about my gift.

* * *

I stayed with Aint Lulie the rest of the weekend, but no one bothered us anymore. We did a lot of work on my quilts. By Saturday evening, I had both tops and bottoms for the full-sized quilt and two baby quilts. One of the baby quilts was in the log cabin pattern, which was easier than I thought it would be. I folded everything up and put them in a bag to take to school on Monday. I figured I could get the basted seams sewn on the sewing machine in one day. Then I'd be ready to put the batting in.

I thought we could get another small quilt pieced on Sunday, but Aint Lulie was having none of that. "When I'uz a gal, Ma always said iff'n you sew on Sunday, you got to rip all them stitches out with your teeth when you get to heaven. Granny always said it was bad luck to sew on Sunday unless you finished the job. Ain't sure I believe either of 'em, but it don't pay to take no chances."

* * *

On Monday morning, a woman was driving the bus. She looked at a list when I got on. "You must be Annie," she said. "I'm Jerleen, and I'll be driving this route from now on."

I said I was glad to meet her. I didn't ask why Clovis wouldn't be driving. I pretty much knew. Other kids asked though, and she said the folks at the bus barn hadn't told her why. She did say that she'd been a substitute driver on an elementary bus on the other side of the county and she was glad to get on full time.

When Cheryl got on, she had a bag of quilt pieces, too. "My grandma helped me a lot," she said. "She even gave me some old clothes to cut up, and that's what we did." I told her about buying fabric in town and making my tops and bottoms.

At school, some had heard Clovis had been arrested, but they didn't know why. By the afternoon, nobody even bothered to mention it. School went on as before. Science and math continued to be boring, in English we started studying Chaucer's *Canterbury*

Tales, I took a long shower during 4th period, lunch was no different than usual, in government we studied the judicial branch of the government, and home ec was like a quilting bee. Mrs. Carlton said she was so pleased with our enthusiasm. And I did get the tops and the large bottom stitched on the machine. I carried them home with me so Aint Lulie and I could work on putting them together.

The next day was about the same, but Wednesday brought some news. Some kids said that it was on TV that the autopsy had been completed on Loniss Hathaway, and the results were that she'd been strangled. Her windpipe was crushed, and she had other injuries. The news didn't say what those injuries were. But it did say that her alleged murderer, former county deputy Wiley Shortridge, had previously worked in two other counties where young blonde girls had died in a similar manner and their murders had never been solved. One was the year before Wiley Shortridge came to our county, and the other was three years before that. That news was the talk of the school. I think every girl was wondering, *Could it have been me?*

When I got home, I told Aint Lulie right away. "It's good you went to church that day," I told her. "There's no telling how many girls you saved."

"It'uz you who saved them gals," she said. "If you hadn't a'talked to that dog, I don't know what might'a happened."

I didn't know either. And it worried me that folks might find out what I did, what I could do. I had gotten used to being normal. I didn't want to be an outcast again.

At lunch the next day, Bert started up. "What I can't understand," he said, "is how they knew it was Wiley. There's something they're not telling."

"They probably have a good reason for not telling," Sarenda said. "Maybe there's more to the story they can't tell yet. There's always more to a story."

But Bert was like a hound running hot on a rabbit's trail. "And is Wiley somehow connected to that bus driver? If so, how?" Then he looked at me. "Annie, you ride that bus. Do you know anything about it?"

"Maybe I do," I said, "and maybe I don't. If maybe I do, maybe I can't say. And if maybe I don't, I can't say either." I gave him what I hoped was a mysterious smile.

Sarenda laughed out loud. "You're too serious, Bert," she said. "Like *Hamlet*. 'But that I am forbid to tell the secrets of my prison-house, I could a tale unfold whose lightest word would harrow up thy soul, freeze thy young blood, make thy two eyes, like stars, start from their spheres.'" She winked at me, curtsied deeply, grabbed up her tray, and waltzed it around to the clean-up area.

What did Sarenda mean by the wink? Did she know what tales I could unfold? I hoped she was just being dramatic.

When I got off the bus that afternoon, Daddy was waiting at the house for me. "That detective stopped by today. He says before long they're gonna convene a grand jury to see if they got enough evidence to send Wiley Shortridge to trial. He says they reckon they do."

"Do I have to go to the hearing?" If I did, then everyone would know.

"He says you don't. But he says likely you'd be gitting one'a them orders to go to court when Wiley's trial comes up."

So, everyone would eventually know. "Did he say when the trial might be?"

"He ain't for sure, but he reckons it'll be sometime early in the new year. At least, that's when the county prosecutor hopes it'll be."

When I told Aint Lulie, she said, "If they summon you, you gotta go. Ain't no gitting around it."

* * *

The next couple weeks passed peacefully enough. There was some talk of enough evidence found to send Wiley to trial, but nobody was surprised about it. On the ride to school, Larry said, "I hope they give him the electric chair," and everybody on the bus agreed. I kept quiet. But with nothing new announced about the case, the talk about Wiley soon died down.

In English class, even though the *Canterbury Tales* was hard to understand, I liked the idea of folks telling stories to each other as they traveled. In home ec, I finished the baby quilts and was able to sell both of them. Miss Brannigan bought one as a Christmas present for her new niece, and Mrs. Watson bought the other for her daughter who was expecting. While I thought about what kind of quilt I'd make next as soon as I could get Daddy to take me to town for more supplies, I helped the others in class with their own quilts.

The Hathaways finally had a funeral for Loniss, but I didn't go. I had no way to get there, and Loniss and I had never been friends. A few girls on the bus talked about it. Cheryl said it was a closed coffin ceremony, and it was very sad. I figured it would be. Funerals always are.

The weather got colder and colder, and a few days brought snow. It was all I could do to keep Aint Lulie supplied with wood and water. With the days so short, it was nearly dark by the time I got off the bus. I was glad I kept my flashlight in my coat pocket. It came in handy when I had to be out at night, and I felt safer with it in the cabin. Pushing its button was a lot easier than trying to light a lantern or candle. I spent all weekends with Aint Lulie as well as a couple of school-nights during the week.

I got to like sleeping in the cabin. On windy nights, the cabin was a lot quieter than the house. The house creaks and groans and sighs as it settles down for the night. Its sawed boards expand and contract. Its windows rattle with the wind and let the outside sounds leak in. But the cabin's heavy logs hunker down, resist wind and weather, and muffle any outside sounds. If there's an outside noise, it's likely a branch brushing across the tin roof. I sleep sounder in the cabin.

A couple of days before school dismissed for Christmas vacation, Sarenda announced at lunch that her family was moving, so she wouldn't be back after Christmas.

"Where are you going?" Bert asked.

"I'm not sure," she said. "Out west somewhere. My parents want to experience different places."

I thought it was odd that they were just taking off with no specific place to go, but I didn't say anything except, "We'll miss you."

CHAPTER 11: WINTER TALES

When Christmas vacation came, I planned to spend most of it with Aint Lulie. She seemed to get a little frailer every day and could use my help. And I could use her help in cutting quilt patches. I planned to make as many quilt tops as I could while school was out. Mama and Daddy thought my staying with her was a good idea.

We never did much at home to celebrate anyhow—presents were whatever came in the order from Sears-Roebuck. We haven't had a Christmas tree since Scott left. He was always the one to go up the mountain and bring down a cedar that we'd make decorations for. Sometimes he'd bring some running cedar and some holly, too, and once he shot some mistletoe out of a big oak tree. But those days are gone.

The first night of Christmas vacation, I built a big fire and we sat in front of it before we went to bed. "What all you been studying at school lately?" she wanted to know.

"In English class, we're reading *The Canterbury Tales*," I said. "They were written hundreds of years ago in England. A group of people on a pilgrimage take turns telling each other stories every night while they travel. One of them, the Wife of Bath, rode an ambler and that put me in mind of your horse, Finn."

"Finn had such a smooth amble," she said. "You could ride him for miles and never bounce once. What kind of story did this bath wife tell?"

"She told a story about a knight who'd done something bad to a

135

woman," I began, while Aint Lulie rocked back and forth. "The queen gave him a year to find out what women really wanted or else he'd be beheaded. When his time was nearly up, an old woman said she'd tell him the secret, but he'd have to marry her. He figured he didn't have anything to lose, so he agreed. In front of the queen and all the ladies, the old woman said that what women really want is to have control over their husbands. All the ladies agreed."

"I reckon I'd agree, too," Aint Lulie said. "But from what I seen, it ain't easy to do. It's a man's world."

"But then he tried to get out of marrying her, but the queen said he had to. The old woman gave him a choice. She told him that she could be old and faithful, or she could be young and unfaithful. The knight couldn't decide, so he told her she could go ahead and choose. She chose to be young and faithful."

"Well, I reckon that story had a happy ending," Aint Lulie said.

"I reckon it did," I said. "They both got what they wanted."

Aint Lulie eased herself out of her rocker and got ready for bed. I unrolled my pallet and snuggled into the quilts.

* * *

The next night I wanted to hear stories of the old days. "What was Christmas like when you were a girl?" I asked her after we'd gotten the night work done. The wind was up—it rattled though the trees and whistled down the chimney. But the fire was warm, and I'd brought in plenty of wood.

"Oh, we had us a big time then," she said. "All the heavy work was done for the season, so folks could come and go. Folks done a lot of visiting up and down the ridges and hollers. Lotta young couples got married around Christmas time when their family could be there. Even if it'uz snowing, Daddy had a sleigh he'd hitch to Finn, and off we'd go. Like that old song, 'The horse knows the way to carry the sleigh.' Kinda like them tales you're reading at school, folks told stories to pass the time."

"Do you remember any?"

"I long forgot most of 'em, but sometimes part'a one'll come to my mind," she said. "But looking at the fire makes me recollect one fairy story Granny told that had fire in it. It's a right scary one, though. You real sure you wanna hear it?"

"Sure," I said. "I don't mind scary."

"Well, this story come from Ireland a long time ago," Aint Lulie began. "It come with Granny's granny, I reckon. A lotta the stories she knowed had fairies in 'em. Back in the old times in the old country, it'uz said fairies liked to steal babies from outten the cradle. Sometimes they'd change one'a their babies for a mortal one, and the real baby's mama mought not know right off what had been done. There'uz one woman whose red-haired blue-eyed babe was so fair she purely doted on him. Them fairies got wind of that baby, and one vowed to have him. While the babe and his mama slept, the fairy crept in and left a shriveled-up ugly squawling thing in the cradle and took away the mortal baby.

"Well, all the squawling and bawling woke up the woman who suspected right off that her baby had been changed for another, but she won't for sure. Could be her child had jist took sick in the night. Word got round the town that mought be fairies had been up to mischief, and other women commenced stopping by to see for theirself. Most told her the only way to see if it was a fairy child was to either roast it alive in the fire or throw it out in the snow or burn off its nose, but the woman couldn't bring herself to do any of them things. Then one old woman, what had the gifts of talking to the dead and charming off warts and other such things, come to see her and said she was moght nigh sure the fairies had made a swap.

"The old woman commenced telling the woman what she had to do. 'Git yourself a dozen eggs and crack 'em open' she said. 'Do with the yolks and whites as ye please, but bile the shells in a big pot of water hot as ye can git it. When the shells be biling, ye'll know soon enough iff'n the child is yourn or a fairy. If 'tis a fairy, you must take a red hot poker and ram it down that fairy-child's throat.'

"'Will I get my own babe back, then?' asked the woman. 'Likely as not ye will,' the old woman told her."

Aint Lulie rocked for a moment. "This part of the story used to skeer me nigh to death when I'uz a chap. When Granny told it, none of us chaps would say a word, but we'd all skootch up closer together."

"What happened next?" I asked.

"Well, as the egg-shells biled, the baby in the cradle quieted down and watched. Then it riz up and said, 'I ain't never before seen a body bile egg-shells.' The woman knowed then that the baby was a fairy, for a mortal baby would not suddenly be talking, and she put the poker against the hot coals to git it hot.

"Then the baby said, 'What now you fixing to do?' and the woman started towards it with the hot poker. But she tripped and the poker rolled to the other side of the room, and she fairly scrambled to get it. When she got holt of that poker, she started to the cradle agin, only instead of the ugly fairy child was her own baby sleeping peaceful as could be."

"That is scary," I said. "But at least it had a happy ending."

"I reckon so," she said. "I recollect Granny telling us that story showed sometimes we had to seek out truth in ways we mought not understand. And I reckon how it showed how a person with a gift could use it to do somebody good."

* * *

We passed the week in quilt patches, stories, and chores. Lots of chores. I missed taking a hot shower at school, but I got used to hauling in water and heating it to wash in. Sometimes I'd wash clothes first and, after I'd hung them on the porch line to dry, I'd add more hot water to the tub and wash myself in it. Then I had to dip the wash water into a bucket and pour the buckets off the side of the porch. Of course, it required extra stove wood to get the stove hot enough to heat the water. And before that, I'd have to fill a lot of buckets at the pump to have enough water. Washing towels in the automatic washer in the locker room was so much easier than washing towels, sheets, clothes, and dishrags by hand.

Meanwhile, something had to be on the stove to cook for dinner or supper. And the ashes in the fireplace had to be taken out, logs had to be brought in, the slop jar had to be emptied and cleaned, the floor had to be swept, dishes had to be washed. So much work was required just to keep living that I don't know how women managed in the old days. Aint Lulie said that when her granny was my age, she'd already been married a year and had a baby to look after.

Aint Lulie taught me how to cook a few things on the stove the way she'd done since she was young. Using her mama's "receipts," we made light bread one day and, on another day, apple cobbler from the apples we'd picked and canned months earlier. Most mornings, we made biscuits, and a few times we made cornbread. I asked Aint Lulie if any of the recipes had been written down. "Not that I know of," she said. "They jist got passed down from mama to daughter or daughter-in-law."

Everyday I walked to the house to see what was new, but nothing ever was. I brought back some notebook paper and a pen so I could write down all the recipes that Aint Lulie had in her head. Some nights, instead of us telling stories, she'd tell me how to make something or another. On Christmas eve, I asked her to tell me about Christmas when she was young.

"Well, I already done told you that a lot of visiting back and forth got done." She rocked for a minute, remembering. "There was some folks said Christmas was December twenty-five, and other'n—mainly older folks—said it was January six. Granny used to say iff'n you'd go to the barn at midnight on January six, you'd hear the critters talking. I never could stay up that long, though. But a lotta men would shoot their guns off at midnight on Christmas eve, though, no matter if it was New Christmas or Old Christmas."

"Did you decorate for Christmas?"

"Not right much. Folks had plenty enough to do without that. But Pearl always liked to go off in the woods and bring home running cedar and holly and put it all around inside. Sometimes Papa would bring home a little cedar tree he cut, and we'd make decorations for it. Ain't nothing smells as good as a cedar tree in the house." She smiled and rocked a little more. "Sometimes there'd be a to-do at church and we'd git a little something from under the church Christmas tree. One time I got a carnation vase as a Christmas tree present at church. That'uz a long thin fancy vase. Mine was the prettiest shade of blue."

"Do you still have it?"

"It'uz up in the loft somewheres last time I seen it. Reckon it mought still be there in one'a them cubbyholes under the eaves. No telling what all's up under the eaves."

"If you used to go to church a lot when you were young, why didn't you go much when you got older?"

"You full'a questions tonight, ain't you?" Aint Lulie thought for a moment. "Well, I reckon I had my reasons. Back then church'uz where boys and gals could see each other. Won't no dating back then. If a boy walked a gal home from church, that meant things'uz gitting serious. They'd soon go to courting. So, church was where young folks could see their friends and mebbe catch a sweetheart. Pearl always liked going to church, but after she died I fell outta the habit. Didn't seem much like God was in the church anymore."

"Oh." I got up and added a log to the fire. "Anything else folks did at Christmas?"

"Well, without a lot of farm work to do, Christmas was a good time for folks to get married, so they'd be some serenades or chivarees."

"What are those?"

"Well, after a new-married couple had gone home and commenced to settle down, some'a their friends would creep up in the dark and serenade 'em by banging on pots and pans and raise cane being rowdy. They might ring cowbells. They might even fire guns. Well, iff'n the new couple didn't invite 'em in for a drink or something good to eat, they might break in. Sometimes they'd grab the new bride and ride her around the house in a wheelbarrow. There'uz a lot of drinking and carrying on. Finally, they'd go off and let the couple alone to git on with their marriage."

"But times'uz different back then. You don't hear of such now."

Later, when I'd settled into my pallet, I watched the fire and thought what a different time it was back when Aint Lulie was my age.

On Christmas morning, Mama and Daddy walked to the cabin with a box of Sears-Roebuck things for me and Aint Lulie—mainly socks and underwear and gloves and scarves. Practical things. But I did get a new pair of winter shoes and a cardigan sweater. They also brought Aint Lulie some groceries from town, and—in with the usual things—was a sack of oranges. Mama brought a plate of ham biscuits, so we sat by the fire and ate those for breakfast. Then we shared an orange, and Mama and Daddy went back home. That was Christmas.

I know Mama would have liked to go to church, but a replacement for Elder Stoutmire hadn't yet been found, and other churches were a lot farther away. She would likely spend the day reading her Bible and watching for Scott.

Meanwhile, the necessities of life had to be dealt with. After I did the morning chores, I brought in more water and more wood. There'd always be a need for it, so I tried to stockpile it while the weather cooperated. While Aint Lulie napped in the early afternoon, I went for a walk into the woods where I knew sassafras trees grew. I picked a dozen or so twigs so Aint Lulie and I would have a fresh supply of toothbrushes.

140

After Christmas, Aint Lulie wasn't doing well, so I stayed close by her most of the day. Of course I stayed the night, too. It was hard to tell when she might need my help. I was doing all the cooking now, but I'd gotten used to it.

Early on the morning of December 28th, she announced, "I heard a horse last night. Circled the house and then went on off. I wonder who it is that's riding a horse around here."

"I didn't hear a horse," I said. "But the wind was blowing pretty steady. Maybe you heard a limb or something blow against the house."

"Mebbe you can look for tracks when you fetch the water. See which way they come from and which way they went."

There were no tracks on the frost-covered ground. When I brought the water in, I told her I didn't see any.

"Likely the ground is froze too hard for tracks," she said. "It'uz so awful cold today."

I noticed her rocking chair was pulled a little closer to the fire than usual. But the day was warmer than it had been for the last week—at least it was above freezing and the wind had calmed. Three black crows had flown over the cabin and cawed to me while I was pumping water, but I didn't connect with them. Some other birds had flittered through the bare trees. It wasn't a cold enough day for birds to seek shelter.

Aint Lulie got up and hobbled toward her bed. I noticed her rocking chair was still rocking. She'd always stopped it when she got up. It was still rocking when she returned with her quilt wrapped around her. I remember her once telling me to not ever leave a rocking chair rocking by itself.

After I'd done the night work and built up the fire, we went to bed. It was barely 6 p.m., but dark came so early and there was no reason to stay up. I don't know how long I slept, but Aint Lulie woke me up in the middle of the night.

"Annie!" she called. "Annie! Listen! Hear them hoofbeats? Sounds like a horse circling the house again, and it's stopping out front!"

In the firelight's dimness, I could see her raise up a little in bed. Aint Lulie was usually a sound sleeper. Maybe she did hear something, just not a horse. I got up from my pallet, pulled open the door, and was met with a blast of cold wind from the dark. "There's no horse. Just the wind in the trees."

"But I heard a horse. Ain't nothing sounds like hoofbeats but hoofbeats."

"Maybe you were dreaming about horses." I poked up the fire and threw on another log. Then I snuggled back into the quilts on my pallet while the flames danced around. I was just dozing off when Aint Lulie called out again.

"Oh, my lord!" Aint Lulie's voice was so raspy it didn't sound like her. "He's done come back!"

"Who has?" I said from under my pile of quilts. It was pretty clear to me that Aint Lulie and I were the only ones in the room.

"Didn't you see him come in when you opened the door? It's Sparrell! Sparrell Hobson!"

I didn't know what to say. But Aint Lulie went on like I wasn't here at all.

"Sparrell, I always knowed you'd be back! They said you won't coming back, but I knowed better. Ever night I been listening for your mare. I been waiting and waiting for you to come back. I kept the place for you. Kept it jist like we talked about.

"We ain't staying here? We got to go? Don't know how it'll set with Papa if I'uz to run off and marry you. But you come for me, so I reckon I'll go."

It was quiet for a minute or two. Then I could hear her singing, "The needle's eye that doth supply the thread that runs so true. Many a beau have I let go, because I wanted you."

Aint Lulie gasped, and then she was quiet. Her body lay still in her bed, but I knew that who she was—her soul, her spirit, her essence maybe—had gone and was never coming back. I got up and pulled up the sheet to cover her face. I thought about running to the house to tell Mama and Daddy, but it was too late for them to do anything to help and to early to make burial plans. I'd wait until morning to tell them that Aint Lulie was gone. I must have fallen back asleep because I think I dreamed about a man singing, "Many a lass have I let pass, because I wanted you."

At first light, I made my way to the house. Mama was already in the kitchen, so I told her first. She called for Daddy to come downstairs, and I told him the same words I'd told Mama: "Aint Lulie passed away last night."

Daddy got in his truck and went to the store where there was a phone. Somebody there likely helped him make the call to the undertaker in town because a black van came within a couple of hours. I waited on the cabin porch while two men went in and got her. I told them to wait a minute while I went to the dogtrot and got the bag with the clothes that Aint Lulie wanted to be buried in. One of them put the bag in back with her. They drove off and Daddy followed them. I didn't watch them go.

Instead, I went back inside and banked the fire and took the bedclothes off her bed and piled them up so Mama could wash them next time she did laundry. I folded up her quilt and laid it at the bottom of her bed. I took her black shawl from its peg and hung it over the mirror. Then I stopped her clock, locked the cabin's door, and went back to the house where Mama had my breakfast waiting for me.

Aint Lulie had told Mama and Daddy years ago when her time came that she wanted a simple funeral. She didn't want to be embalmed and she didn't want a fancy casket and she didn't want a visitation at the funeral parlor. That afternoon a man Daddy knew came with his backhoe, and Daddy went with him up the hill to where the cemetery was. Aint Lulie had once told Daddy she'd like to be put next to Pearl, and that's where he told the man to dig. By evening, her grave was open and waiting for her.

Next morning, folks started coming from all around the hills and hollers. Most of them were distant kin—some I hadn't seen since I was little—and most brought food. When the van came with Aint Lulie, some folks walked ahead of it to the hill and some followed it. I was glad the day was sunny and warmer that it had been for over a week. The sky was bright blue and, with leaves gone from the trees, we could see for miles and miles. A wind was blowing, though, and that brought an uncomfortable chill to the graveyard.

The funeral home men unloaded the casket, which was about as plain as you could get, and some of Aint Lulie's distant kinfolk helped lower it into the hole. One of the men from the funeral home said a few words over her—how she'd lived a long life and how she'd seen the world change from horse and buggy to cars and modern things and even a man on the moon—probably the same thing he said over any elderly person. But Aint Lulie hadn't seen all that. She'd likely never gone farther than fifty miles from home and didn't even know some modern things existed. If I'd ever told her about the moon landing, she wouldn't have believed me.

Some folks prayed, some cried, and Daddy and a few other men began shoveling earth into the hole. The women walked back down the hill to get the food ready, but I stayed up on the hill while the men worked. I noticed a cardinal perched on a bare branch overhead. As soon as the grave was covered, he flew away.

It was awkward for Mama to suddenly have a few dozen people in the house and it likely reminded her of when Scott was killed, but she did the best she could. She mainly stayed in the kitchen and dished out food and washed plates while most folks gathered in the front room—the room we rarely used unless there was a death or illness. While a few women from her prayer circle went in from time to time to keep her company, Daddy and I talked to the people who sat there eating deviled eggs and fried chicken or maybe macaroni and cheese—the kind of food that usually appears after a funeral. A lot of the older folks remembered Aint Lulie when she was young. A few remembered going to the Duff School with her, some remembered how sad she was when she got word of Sparrell Hobson's death.

Maribelle Lewis's daughter, balancing a piece of coconut cake and a sliver of sweet potato pie on her plate, edged her way over to me to pay her respects and say how sorry she was about Aint Lulie.

"How is your mama doing?" I asked. "I hope she's well. Aint Lulie always thought so much of her."

An odd look came over her face. "Mama died about two years ago," she said. "I just couldn't bring myself to tell Lulie. She always set such a store by any news I brought from Mama, so I just kept on pretending. You know how it is."

I nodded as if I knew, but I didn't. I really didn't. Maribelle's daughter edged away and was soon talking to someone else.

When everyone had gone, I moved back into my old room—the room Aint Lulie had slept in when she was about my age. Before she moved to the cabin. There was no longer a reason for me to stay in the cabin during the coldest part of the year. It would take all my time and energy just to keep the fire going, and the fire would likely go out while I was at school. Besides, staying in the cabin without Aint Lulie wouldn't be the same. I could be lonely at home.

CHAPTER 12: THE TRUTH WILL OUT

The first week of January was bitter cold. School should have started back on January 2nd, but we had spells of sleet and snow that left the roads treacherous, so we had no school for a week. I spent that first week of 1973 cutting and stitching quilt pieces. I was determined to "waste not, want not," whether it was my time or my quilt-making. By the time Old Christmas—January 6th—rolled around, I had a lot to show for my efforts.

I was just lying down for a nap when the cardinal, maybe the one I'd seen earlier, fluttered past my window. But it kept flying and didn't seem like it had a message for me.

When school finally started again, those who had heard about Aint Lulie dying told me how sorry they were about my aunt. At lunch, the table seemed empty without Sarenda.

"Have you heard anything from her?" Bert asked, and I said I hadn't. He hadn't either. After that, we didn't have a lot to say to each other. I was surprised then, when Cheryl asked if she could sit with us. Without Loniss at the cheerleaders' table—and with cheerleading over for the season—I guess those girls didn't have a lot in common. Plus Susan was eating at the table with Larry now. Before long, Mary Rose asked if she could eat with us, so we scooted over and made room. Bert didn't talk much except when one of us asked him about something we'd learned in class. Then he was happy to give his opinion.

It was good to be back in the school routine and to be able to take a hot shower most days. It was good to be a regular person.

But that didn't last long.

In mid-January, at nearly dark on a bitter cold evening when snow was beginning to fall, I saw headlights coming toward the house. Daddy reached for his shotgun. Since what happened in November, he was a little skittish of cars coming toward the house in the dark. The car pulled up to the front and Deputy Arlis Woodson got out and walked up to the house. Daddy put his gun aside and jerked the door open. By the light of the single bulb, I could see the deputy had something in his hand.

"I got this subpoena for Annie," Woodson said.

"What'uz this mean?" Daddy asked.

"It means Annie has got to go to Shortridge's trial in February and testify against him," he said. "But Claymore Phelps—the county attorney—needs to talk with Annie. Detective Adams would like to talk to her too."

I stepped up and took the envelope. Woodson left and Daddy closed the door, but the coldness had already blown into the house. I opened the envelope and read what was inside to Daddy.

"If you got to go, then you got to go," he said. I nodded, and wished that I didn't have to go to set it right.

The next morning the snow hadn't stuck to the roads, so school was on time. I told no one about getting the subpoena. It had been in the papers when the trial was going to be and that the county had a pretty good case against Wiley, and a few kids talked about it on the bus and in the halls. But I didn't. I was thankful that the papers still hadn't mentioned how the state police found the evidence in Wiley's squad car.

Instead, the papers that Mr. Wardell brought to class each day were full of news about Nixon's second inauguration, and that pushed the local news into the background. On January 19th, Mr. Wardell told us we ought to watch the event on TV the next day so we could see big historical events happening before our eyes. While Mr. Wardell wasn't happy about Nixon being re-elected, he thought it was important that we see history in the making. No one reminded him that a lot of us didn't have TVs. Plus semester exams began on Monday, and some needed to study rather than watch TV.

I was glad for exams because that gave the kids something else to think about than Wiley's trial. Two days after Nixon took office, former President Johnson died. The papers were so full of stories about Johnson, it seemed like they forgot about Bosworth County news.

A few days later, when school was on semester break and he probably knew I'd be home, Detective Adams came to the house to talk to me. It was so cold and windy out that we couldn't stand on the porch to talk, so Daddy invited him into the front room. Mama stayed in the kitchen, but I had no doubt that she could hear everything. The three of us sat stiffly on the chairs where nobody had sat since the day of Aint Lulie's funeral. Detective Adams told me what he'd learned.

"You might have heard that Wiley Shortridge has been linked to two other girls' deaths in other counties where he worked as a deputy. But he'll be tried here first," Detective Adams said. "Your testimony at his trial is going to be important. You're the key witness."

I nodded.

"But Clovis Wilbur and Elder Stoutmire won't be going to trial, so you won't have to testify against them. They realized that a jury might put them away for longer than a judge would, so they'll likely plea bargain or else ask for a bench trial. Stoutmire will likely serve several years since he's been both making liquor and growing marijuana. Clovis'll likely get a few years, too. He'd been transporting marijuana on the school bus. He'd put it in an old milk can."

"I've seen the can," I said. "He said he was trying to sell it to an antique dealer."

"Stoutmire had another accomplice, too. But I've recently gotten word that the accomplice has moved out of the area. When he pulled his daughter out of school, he didn't tell the school where they were going."

"Sarenda Lovejoy is his daughter, isn't she?" I asked. "She said she was moving out west, but she didn't know where."

"Yes, but Lovejoy isn't their real name."

So, I thought, *Sarenda had been hiding something too.*

"But what I need you to do," Detective Adams said, "is to go talk to Claymore Phelps down at the courthouse. He's the county attorney who'll be prosecuting the case. He can see you tomorrow at 2 p.m. Could you be there?"

Before I could answer, Daddy spoke up. "I'll git her there by then."

And he did. Mr. Phelps talked to me for nearly an hour and explained what we'd be doing. He told me some of the questions he'd likely be asking and how Jabez Randleman, Wiley's lawyer, would also question me.

"Randleman will try to make you look bad," Mr. Phelps said. "He might try to get you to contradict yourself. It's important that you stay calm and tell the truth."

I said I would. Because no court was in session, he took me down to the courtroom and showed where I'd be testifying in two weeks.

"If people ask you about the up-coming trial, I'd appreciate it if you didn't say anything," he said. "It's not a good idea to discuss it with your friends."

"I haven't even told anyone at school that I've been subpoenaed," I said. "I don't go around telling people about my gift. I haven't told anyone but the police—and now you—what all I know."

He thanked me for coming to see him, and he thanked Daddy for bringing me. By the time Daddy and I got home, it was almost twilight. I was dreading going to school on Monday. What if someone found out? I couldn't help but worry.

I needn't have, though. There was more big news happening and it wasn't because of me. On Saturday—January 27th—a ceasefire in the war had been announced. On Monday, news spread through the school, and Mr. Wardell spent all period talking about the ceasefire and its implications. Even though he didn't like Nixon, he quoted the part from Nixon's speech that went, "we stand on the threshold of a new era of peace in the world." It looked like the war would end soon, and everybody's friends or kin would come home. Well, not everyone. Scott wouldn't.

For a while, the news gave everybody something else to talk about than Wiley's trial, and for that I was grateful.

* * *

The afternoon before the trial, I'd told Jerleen I wouldn't be riding the bus to school next day, so there was no need for her to drive up the holler. She didn't ask me why, and I didn't volunteer any reason. I hadn't told anybody at school except for Mr. Darley. He seemed a little surprised that I'd been subpoenaed, but he said my absence would be excused and he'd let the teachers know.

Daddy and I left for town right after breakfast. Since we didn't know how early I'd testify and when I'd be able to leave, Daddy planned to stay for the whole day. He'd even shaved and put on a tie, something he didn't normally do. I guess watching the trial was a big thing for him. Mama had packed us a lunch just in case the trial did take all day. We were as ready as we'd ever be.

We didn't say much on the way in. Daddy did give me some advice, though. "When they ask, jist tell 'em what ya know and how ya know it. And don't let Wiley's fancy lawyer git the best a'ya."

The roads were icy and the truck slid once or twice, but we made it to the courthouse on time.

Outside the courthouse a big crowd had gathered. I heard folks saying TV people had been sent from Bristol, Johnson City, and Roanoke. I saw TV cameras with the letters WDBJ, WSLS, WJHL, and WCBY on them. Some people with microphones were there, too, and they were running around and talking to folks in the crowd. But none came up to me. I guess Daddy and I didn't look like anybody important, so we got inside easy enough.

Inside, the courtroom was packed. I guess everybody wanted to see the trial. I hoped I'd be able to watch the trial, too, but it turns out the witnesses had to be *excluded*—kept in separate little rooms until our turn came. There weren't many witnesses—Detective Adams, the two state policemen, the coroner, me, and Lucas Lawson. I guess maybe the lawmen and coroner testified before me. At least it took a long time for a county deputy to come get me. When I went into the courtroom, I saw it was almost eleven o'clock. I was glad that the TV cameras weren't allowed inside, but there were a lot of folks who looked like they might be reporters. Loniss's parents were on the front row. I caught a glimpse of Daddy sitting way in the back.

Claymore Phelps had already told me what questions he'd be asking, so I wasn't surprised. But answering the questions in his office was a lot different from answering them in a packed courtroom.

Mr. Phelps asked me how long I'd known Wiley Shortridge, and I told him a couple of years. He asked how I knew him, so I told about Wiley bringing news of my brother's death, about Wiley being at the school dance, and Wiley coming to the house with Detective Adams and the state policemen. Then he asked how I knew that Wiley was the one who'd killed Loniss.

"His dog Bruno told me." I barely spoke above a whisper, but I could feel everyone's eyes on me. I could see the reporters writing fast in their notebooks.

"How was the dog able to tell you?"

"I—uh—I have a kind of gift that lets me talk to animals—that lets me know what animals are thinking."

"And how does this work?" he asked.

"Objection!" yelled Jabez Randleman, the defense attorney. "I don't see how any of this hocus-pocus is relevant. Or probative."

"Your honor," Mr. Phelps said, "we're getting to how it's relevant and probative both."

"Objection overruled," the judge said. "I'm kind of curious how it works myself. You may proceed, Mr. Phelps."

"Now, Annie," said Mr. Phelps, "can you tell us how you do this?"

I nodded. "My mind kind of connects with an animal's mind, and the animal sends pictures into my mind of what the animal is thinking. It's like I can sort of see through the animal's eyes."

"So you talked to Deputy Shortridge's police dog on the day Shortridge was arrested?

I nodded. My hands began to shake. I gripped the chair's arms to steady myself.

"Was that the first time you talked to the German shepherd?"

"No, I'd talked to Bruno when Deputy Shortridge brought the news of my brother's death."

"What did Bruno tell you on the day Shortridge was arrested."

"I didn't mean to talk to Bruno, but he connected with me first. He said he didn't want to get his master in trouble but he couldn't keep the secret. He told me that his master—uh—did bad things to Loniss and put her in the trunk of the police car and then took her to the church." I was starting to sweat, and I hoped that Mr. Phelps was done questioning me. But he wasn't.

"What did the dog mean by 'bad things'? Can you tell us?"

I could, but I didn't want to. I was sweating and shaking. I didn't want to say what I had to say in front of Loniss's mother. But I had to say it. "He got her to get into the car. He said he'd take her home. But he didn't. He drove off the road and across a field into some woods or brush or something. Loniss was yelling, so he grabbed her by the neck. Then he—" I didn't know how to say it, couldn't find words, saw the reporters writing faster, saw Mrs. Hathaway crying, started to cry myself.

Mr. Phelps handed me his handkerchief. It took a minute or two for me to get myself together. "He dragged her out of the car and—and—pushed her against the hood where he—he forced himself on her. He had one hand on her neck pinning her against the hood. When he was done, he put her in the trunk." I sobbed and couldn't help myself. I heard someone else sobbing not far away and knew it was Mrs. Hathaway.

"Where was the dog during this? Was he in the back seat?"

I nodded.

"Objection!" yelled Mr. Randleman. "He's leading the witness."

"Overruled," the judge said. "I think it's obvious that the witness is upset about what the dog told her."

"Then did he take her to the church?" Mr. Phelps asked.

"Same objection." This time Mr. Randleman didn't yell.

The judge just looked at him without saying anything. So I nodded again and whispered, "Yes."

"I know this is difficult for you," Mr. Phelps said, "but you need to tell us what the dog showed you that Deputy Shortridge did next."

"He drove to where the wood for the church stove had been dumped. There was a lot of wood scattered around. He pulled her out of the trunk and put both hands around her neck and squeezed hard. Then he laid her on some of the logs. She didn't move. He started stacking the wood on top of her and around her. He spent a long time stacking the wood. Then he drove back to town."

"Thank you, Annie," Mr. Phelps said. "I have no more questions."

I was worn out and wanted to leave, but it was Mr. Randleman's turn to question me. "You say you can talk to dogs, Miss Caldwell? Is that right?"

I nodded.

"Speak up, Miss Caldwell. We can't hear you."

"Yes."

"That's certainly an interesting talent you have. How can we be sure you haven't made this story up just to get attention for yourself? Or maybe you have a grudge against Deputy Shortridge and thought this was a good way to get back at him. That's it, isn't it?"

At first, I didn't know what to say. I shook my head. "No," I whispered.

"Do you know any other people who can talk to dogs?" He asked.

I was pretty sure there must be others, but I didn't know any. "No," I said.

"Can you talk to any dog, not just Deputy Shortridge's dog?"

"Yes."

"How can we be sure you can really do that? Could you, for instance, talk to my wife's dog?"

"Yes," I said louder than I'd answered before. "At least I think I can."

"Think? Think! You don't know for sure?"

"I need to know the dog's name and what the dog looks like. Then I'm pretty sure I can talk to your wife's dog."

"Ah, now you're pretty sure!" He turned to the judge. "Your honor, if it please the court, will you permit me to conduct a brief experiment that I think will prove the witness cannot do what she says she can."

"At your peril, Mr. Randleman," the judge said.

"My wife has a miniature poodle, Foofie," he said. "Can you talk to Foofie even though he isn't here? Or would you like someone to go get Foofie so you can have a little chat with him in front of the court?"

I didn't like the way he smirked at me. "I can do it from here," I said. "Do you have a picture of him?"

"As a matter of fact, I do," Mr. Randleman said. "If it please the court, may I show the picture of my wife's dog to the witness?"

"You may," the judge said. Mr. Randleman flipped through his wallet and pulled out a picture of a white poodle in the arms of a woman. His wife, I figured.

"Well," said Mr. Randleman, "what does Foofie have to say? Did he enjoy his morning walk? What's he up to?"

I connected with the little white poodle who was pacing back and forth in front of a closed door. The dog wasn't happy. What he told me was very interesting.

"Foofie wants his teddy bear," I said. "He loves that teddy bear."

Mr. Randleman smirked even more. "Lots of dogs have toys. Often teddy bears. That was merely a lucky guess, wasn't it?"

"Foofie is outside a door upstairs and he's not happy," I said. "His mistress and her friend closed him out. He wants in. He left his teddy bear under the bed, and he wants to get it."

Mr. Randleman stopped smirking. "A friend? My wife is playing bridge now at the club. Like she does every week."

"Foofie is showing me a little car parked out front. A convertible but the top is up. Foofie says that's what Ronnie drives every time he comes to see your wife. Foofie says your wife got very mad at you when she found a stack of magazines in the back of your closet, and she said she'd get even——"

"That'll do!" said Mr. Randleman. "No more questions." His face was beet red and he wasn't smirking anymore. Some of the spectators looked like they were trying not to laugh. The judge looked like he was trying not to laugh, too. The reporters were writing like crazy.

Anyhow, the judge said I could step down now, and he called for a recess for lunch. I was glad my testimony was over. Mr. Phelps walked me out of the courtroom and thanked me for my testimony. "Randleman's law partner, Ron Vaden, drives a little sports car that's a convertible," he said. "Since you were the next-to-last witness and you aren't likely to be called back, the trial should be over before long. You can go home, or you can come back after lunch and watch the outcome."

"I'll see what Daddy says," I told him.

* * *

I saw Daddy gesture toward the door, so it looked like he'd wait for me on the courthouse steps. I figured we'd go to the truck and eat the lunch Mama had made and maybe come back to watch the end if Daddy wanted to stay for it. But I didn't figure that, as soon as we went out, a bunch of reporters would come running at me and sticking microphones toward my face. A couple of TV cameras followed them.

"This is the girl who talked to Wiley Shortridge's police dog," a blonde lady said toward the camera. Then to me, "Tell us how you talked to the dog."

I wanted to run, but they surrounded me. Daddy pushed through, grabbed me by the arm, and hurried me away. "She ain't got no comment," he said over his shoulder. We walked fast toward the truck and locked the doors once we were inside.

"You seen enough for the day, or you wanna go back?" he asked. "From what I heard this morning, looks like the jury gonna find ol' Wiley guilty."

"I'd like to see it," I said. "But I hate having to walk back through those reporters."

Daddy decided to move the truck. He drove past the front of the courthouse, so they would think we were leaving. Then he went down a side street and ended up behind the courthouse. There was a parking lot across from the back door and there were a few empty spaces. He pulled into one. "I b'lieve we can git through the back door without them news folks seeing us," he said.

We managed to get in without any problems. I sat in back with Daddy. After the trial resumed, Lucas Lawson was called to testify, but he didn't look like himself. He was leaner and his hair was short. He wore an army uniform. His face was blank and showed no emotion. When Mr. Phelps asked him what happened the night Loniss disappeared, he told about going to her house, persuading her to come out and talk to him, and then driving around. But Loniss got mad at him and told him to pull over. She got out of his truck and walked along the road. He got out and went after her. A vehicle pulled up behind him, but he was more concerned about finding Loniss than seeing who it was. Then someone hit him over the head, and that was the last he remembered. He woke up in his truck at dawn. He didn't know how he'd gotten in his truck, but he figured he'd better lay low for a few days.

"But you didn't know what became of Loniss?" Mr. Phelps asked.

"No sir," Lucas said."

"No more questions," Mr. Phelps said.

Then it was Mr. Randleman's turn. His questions came fast. "You were jealous that Alvin Bosworth had stole your girl, weren't you?"

"Yes, sir."

"You even fought with Alvin after the dance, didn't you?"

"Yes, sir."

"And then you figured that if you couldn't have Loniss Hathaway, no one else would either. Am I right?"

"No, sir."

"You killed Loniss Hathaway, didn't you?"

"No, sir." Then he added, "I loved her. I asked her to marry me."

Mr. Randleman looked over the crowd. He looked like he was going to ask one more question, but he must have seen me sitting toward the back. "No more questions, your honor," he said.

Both lawyers made closing arguments. Mr. Phelps went through all the steps of what had happened that night. He explained how all the signs pointed to Wiley, especially Loniss's shoe and earring in the squad car's trunk. He said that the coroner's report about the cause of death and what I had learned from Bruno were too similar to be just a coincidence. He asked the jury to find Wiley Shortridge guilty of first-degree murder.

Mr. Randleman only spoke for a minute or two. He tried to shift the blame to Lucas. He wouldn't look my way.

Wiley looked my way, though. The way he glared at me, if looks could kill I'd be dead.

While we waited for the verdict, I thought about Bruno and wondered what had become of him. I sent my thoughts in search of him, and he soon got back to me. *I am working in Charlottesville in central Virginia*, Bruno told me. *I have a good master now, and I do good work.*

You did good work here, Bruno, when you told me what you did.

The jury was out for less than ten minutes. Their verdict: *Guilty*. I don't think anyone was surprised. Wiley Shortridge would spend the rest of his life in prison. As he was led away, I expected him to glare at me again, but he didn't look my way.

Daddy and I thought we could slip out the back way with no one noticing us, but we were wrong. There were a couple of reporters there blocking the way. One had a TV cameraman with her.

"There's the star witness," she said into a microphone. Then she pushed it toward me and asked, "Annie Caldwell, how does it feel to be the one who identified Wiley Shortridge as the murderer and to see him convicted?"

"I did what I thought was right," I said. "What I had to do. That's about it."

But she wasn't going to turn me loose. "What about your ability to talk to animals? How long have you been able to do that?"

"All my life, I guess." I said. A couple of photographers snapped my picture.

Daddy grabbed my arm and pulled me away. "I thank y'all for taking an interest in my gal," he said, "but we need to git going."

The two of us walked away fast toward the truck while the

reporters descended on the next person who came out of the door. Daddy sped away and didn't slow down until we'd reached the town limits.

"You did real good in there," he said when we were nearly home.

I left it to Daddy to tell Mama what happened. I ate a quick supper and went to bed exhausted. I slept sound all night—the soundest I'd slept for weeks, I reckon.

* * *

No sooner I got on the bus, Jerleen mentioned she'd seen me on the news last night. "This was a Roanoke station, too," she said. "One of the big ones. Looks like you put Bosworth County on the map."

As others got on, they mentioned the same thing. Some said they saw me on a Bristol station, some on a Knoxville station. Apparently I was the closest Bosworth County ever came to having a celebrity. Everybody on the bus had a lot of questions, but I said I was too tired to answer them yet. And I was.

Before classes started, kids—some who'd never before spoke to me—kept stopping me in the hall and telling me they'd heard about me on the news. Kids in my math and science classes did the same thing. I was nearly late to English because so many stopped me in the hall, but I made it just before the tardy bell rang. Mamie Harper was waiting to confront me. "What you do is witchcraft!" she said. She put her face close to mine. "Thou shalt not suffer a witch to live!"

I stood there, not knowing at first what to say and waiting for her to get out of my way. "I'm not a witch," I finally said. "I have a gift. That's all."

Bert got out of his seat and stood beside me. He looked down at Mamie. "There are more things in heaven and earth, Mamie, than have been dreamt of in your philosophy," he said.

Kenny Ketchum came up and stood by my other side. "But this is wondrous strange," he said to Mamie. "And you'd best not mess with Annie or you'll have to mess with all of us."

Mamie backed up a step or two and sputtered. "Say what you want, but that strange stuff she does is evil."

Then everyone else in the class got up and formed a half circle around me. "Just because you think it's evil, Mamie, doesn't make it so," Cheryl said. "Without Annie, Loniss's killer would still be loose."

Miss Brannigan called the class to order, and we took our seats. Mamie kept glaring at me, her eyes burning like hot coals.

"Well," Miss Brannigan said, "it looks as if I'll get little teaching done today. Since so many of you seem to be interested in Annie's experience in court yesterday, perhaps she could give us a report on what happened. Would that be all right with you, Annie?"

I was surprised to hear myself say yes. I didn't want to, but I figured this would be a chance to tell once and for all. Then I wouldn't have to keep repeating myself. Miss Brannigan let me have her chair in the front of the room. I was glad I didn't have to stand.

I started with how I'd always had a gift, but I'd kept it to myself because it made me different. I told about Aint Lulie and how she had a different gift, and it was her gift that let her know that Loniss's body had been in the church woodpile. I told about talking to Wiley Shortridge's dog and what he told me and how the police found the evidence. I told about testifying in court and how the defense attorney tried to make me out a liar. When I finished, everyone applauded. Except for Mamie.

"So you can talk to any animal?" Lizzie Cleveland asked. I nodded. "Can you tell me where my little sister's kitten is?" She asked. "He's been missing two days. His name is Sooty and he's black. My sister is really upset."

I sent my mind out and connected with a frightened kitten. *I don't like it here*, he said. *The dog was after me and this looked safe. But it's scary and I don't like the smells. I'm so hungry!*

"He's in the garage," I said, "hiding behind a toolbox. A neighbor's dog chased him, and he hid in there. Then somebody closed the door. He's all right, but he's scared and hungry."

"Sorcery," mumbled Mamie. "Sorcerers will burn forever on the lake of brimstone."

Then I felt another connection, and I saw a box of writhing snakes. A large rattler coiled up. I could feel his anger. "Mamie," I said, "you should stay away from rattlesnakes." I wanted to add that one was likely to strike her if she got too close, but I decided I shouldn't.

"You're just trying to scare me," she said. "But it won't work."

When class ended, Miss Brannigan thanked me for my report. Kids gathered around me asking questions on the way out. I was glad to get to fourth period where the class taking physical fitness tests meant I'd have plenty of time for a long hot shower. As I scrubbed myself, I thought how odd it was that my gift which had set me apart from others for so long now seemed to connect me to them.

At lunch, Bert and Cheryl had plenty of questions. "Why didn't you tell us about what you knew about Wiley and all?"

"I couldn't." I let Bert think that I wasn't supposed to talk about the trial, instead of the real reason why I couldn't.

But Cheryl guessed it. "Your special ability is why you always kept to yourself, isn't it? You were always so quiet."

I admitted it was.

As the day wore on, kids kept asking me questions, and I answered as best I could. In government class, Mr. Wardell had a newspaper with a story about the trial. My picture was on the front page. He asked me to tell the class about the trial so I did, even though many had already heard my report in Miss Brannigan's class. This time I explained how I didn't get to see much of the trial until I testified. Mr. Wardell talked some about how trials generally work. I was glad when the bell rang and I could go to home ec.

The four of us in the quilting group were each close to finishing a quilt. It felt good to be back in the routine of stitching away and watching our efforts take shape. I liked the routine and the predictability of quilting. While I hoped to sell some of the quilts I made, the work was kind of its own reward.

I was in a good mood when I got home. But Daddy was standing by the door as if he'd been waiting for me. He had some official-looking envelopes in his hand and a worried look on his face.

"These come today," he said. "Might be you could take a look at 'em and see if you can figger what we ort to do."

One was a tax ticket from the county. While Daddy had paid a little whenever he could, he still owed close to a thousand dollars. The other was a bill from the funeral home for Aint Lulie's casket and expenses—six hundred dollars.

"I reckon we could let the funeral home slide for awhile," he said. "But the county'll put us off our land fer sure if we don't pay. With the sawmill pretty much shut down for the winter—"

"Maybe something will turn up," I said. "Maybe the sawmill will start up again before long."

But I didn't have any idea how we would get out of this. I thought about it off and on all night. It looked like we might soon have to be among them that go.

But where would we go?

CHAPTER 13: REWARDS

As I walked to the bus next morning, the cardinal flitted past. *Do not worry*, he said. *You will be provided for.*

I wanted to ask him how, but I heard Jerleen coming and hurried to get to the clearing so she wouldn't have to wait.

I was in first period algebra less than ten minutes when Mr. Darley appeared and told me to come with him. I wondered if something I said had gotten me into trouble. Maybe Mamie's parents were angry because of my report in Miss Brannigan's class or what I'd said to Mamie. But the person waiting in the office was not Mr. Harper. It was Mr. Hathaway.

"Hello, Annie." He held out his hand, and I shook it.

"Have a seat, Annie," Mr. Darley told me and I did. "Mr. Hathaway has a matter of some importance to discuss with you."

"Annie, as you probably know, my wife and I had offered a reward for information leading to the arrest and conviction of our daughter's killer. Since you were the one who provided the information that resulted in Wiley Shortridge's arrest, you've earned the reward. I'd like to give you this." He handed me an envelope. I stared at it.

"Open it," he said.

I did. Inside was a check for five thousand dollars. More money than I ever before imagined.

"Thank you," I said. I didn't know what else to say.

"You shouldn't have to carry the check around all day," Mr. Hathaway said. "If it's all right with you and Mr. Darley, I could drive you to the bank this morning so you can put it in your account."

"I don't have a bank account."

"Well, then," he said. "I'll take you to the bank, and we'll open one for you."

"I'll tell your teachers to excuse you," Mr. Darley said. "You go on with Mr. Hathaway."

And I did. His Buick was parked out front, and he held open the door for me. It was a short drive to the bank, so we didn't have to talk much. When we got there, Mr. Bosworth himself helped me open a checking account. I asked if I could write checks right away, and Mr. Bosworth assured me I could.

I asked Mr. Hathaway if he wouldn't mind taking me to two other places before we went back to school. He said he'd be glad to. We went first to the funeral home, which was right down the street. I paid up what we owed for Aint Lulie, and the lady at the desk wrote me a receipt. I tucked the receipt into my new checkbook.

Next we went to the courthouse, which was in the next block. Mr. Hathaway helped me find the County Treasurer's office, and I paid off our taxes to a gray-haired lady who gave me a receipt with "Paid in Full" stamped on it.

"Did you want to pay the tax on your other property while you're here?" she asked. "I was going to send out your tax ticket today, but this'll save you another trip to town."

"Other property?" I said. "I don't understand."

She rummaged through a pile of envelopes in a basket marked out-going mail. "Here it is." She handed it to me. "Since your aunt's deed had you listed as co-owner with right of survivorship, I assumed the tax bill would go to you now."

I was puzzled. "You mean that Aint Lulie's cabin is mine?"

"The cabin and the five acres surrounding it," she said. "I remember when she put your name on the deed—about a week after you were born. Not many folks share their property rights with a baby. But Miss Lulie said back then that she reckoned you were gonna turn out to be real special."

I wrote another check, this time for only thirty-five dollars, and I put another receipt in my checkbook. Then Mr. Hathaway drove me the three blocks back to school. When he let me out, I thanked him again.

"I'm the one who should thank you," he said. "If you ever need anything, you get in touch with me."

When I went back into school, I'd missed the rest of algebra and most of science. English class was pretty much back to normal, but Mamie was absent. And Lizzie Cleveland announced that the kitten was just where I said he'd be. "My sister was so happy," she said.

All day, I kept checking my pocket to make sure my checkbook was there. And, in between classes and at lunch, I kept answering questions about animals. It seemed like everybody knew who I was now, and everybody was glad to speak to me. At lunch Bert asked me where I'd gone in the morning, and I told him I had some business at the courthouse. I didn't tell him or anyone else about the check.

When I got home, I waited until supper before I mentioned it. When Daddy sat down to eat, he looked more worried than he had the day before.

"I been studying all day about what we can do about them taxes," he said, "and I cain't think of nothing except we sell off most of our land and live on the little bit that's left."

"We don't have to sell anything." I reached in my pocket, pulled out my checkbook, and took out the receipts. I handed him the ones for his tax bill and Aint Lulie's burial expenses.

"What's this?" he said. I knew he could make out the numbers even if he couldn't read what was written.

"It's the receipt for the taxes and funeral home. They're paid in full." I traced my finger along the words "Paid in Full."

Mama left what she was tending on the stove and came over to look. "Praise the lord!" she said. "It's a miracle!"

"It's no miracle," I said. "Mr. Hathaway stopped by school to give me the reward for my part in getting Wiley arrested and convicted. He took me to the bank and helped me get a checking account." I showed them my checkbook. "Then he took me to pay the bills. We don't owe anybody any money now."

"I still count it as a miracle," Mama said. She set our plates in front of us. "The lord works in mysterious ways." She bowed her head and prayed over our supper.

"What's that other little slip a' paper?" Daddy asked.

"That's the receipt for my taxes," I said. "Turns out I own Aint Lulie's five acres."

"Don't that beat all," Daddy said. He sat for a moment staring at the receipts. "I thank you for what you done, Annie."

Mama stared at my checkbook. I guess she could see that I still had money left after subtracting for payments. "You didn't spend it all?" she asked.

"No," I said. "Likely I'll have some other expenses. The rest of the money is safe in the bank." My parents nodded and said no more about the matter. We ate for a few minutes in silence.

But it popped into my mind that there was something I really wanted. I figured now was as good a time as any to mention it. "What I'd like to do," I said, "is use the rest of the money to build us a bathroom with running water."

"Why'd you want sich as that?" Daddy asked.

"If I get a job in town after I graduate, I'd need to go to work clean. I won't be able to take a shower at school like I've been doing, and I'd have to carry in enough water to wash in a tub every day."

"That's so," Daddy said. "But it'ud take a heap a' work. And I 'spect a good bit a' money."

But did I have enough money left? I had no idea how much building a bathroom would cost. I asked Daddy if he knew. While Mama cleared the table, he started to figure.

"Well, we'd need us a room built onto the side of the house. I reckon where part of the back porch is now might work. I still got some sawed planks in the barn that Scott was gonna use for something or another. They might do. If you don't mind a tin roof, I got some leftover tin, too. But we'd need a 'lectric pump to git the water in, a septic tank for the waste to go, and one a' them hot water heaters. That'ud take big money. Plus fixtures. I reckon they'd want a pretty penny for 'em."

It seemed to me like a bathroom was way beyond our means, that I'd been foolish to want one. But then Daddy added, "It'd be good to have us one'a them indoor bathrooms, though, for when your mama and me git older. Might make the difference in us being able to stay here instead a'having to go off someplace when we cain't git around so good."

I nodded. I knew it would fall to me to look after them in their old age. Toting water for Aint Lulie and myself had been hard enough. Toting for three when I was getting old myself would be even harder.

"I tell you what," Daddy said. "They's a builder usta come to the sawmill right often to get boards. Next time I run into him, I don't reckon it'd hurt to ask him how much something like that costs and what all's involved."

A few days passed, and Daddy didn't mention it again, so it was likely the builder wasn't interested.

* * *

School went on as usual, and most kids stopped asking me about my gift. But Mamie Harper hadn't been to school for a week, and some were beginning to wonder why. We'd had a light snow, so maybe she couldn't get out of her holler. Or maybe her daddy took her out so she wouldn't learn things that didn't agree with their beliefs. But Miss Brannigan told us otherwise.

"I thought you might like to know why Mamie isn't attending class," she said after she checked the roll. "Her parents decided she might as well drop out of school. She was bitten in the face by a rattlesnake, and it's going to take her some time to recover."

All eyes turned to me. I guess everyone remembered my warning to Mamie.

Kenny spoke up. "The church her family goes to has snake-handling as part of the service. They believe if you got faith you can take up serpents and nothing'll happen to you. My uncle went there a time or two, and he got a look at the snakes and said their fangs had been pulled out. Somebody must've forgot to pull out the fangs on the one that got Mamie."

There were murmurs from others in the class. Apparently some others had heard the same thing. But no one said anything else aloud about it, and Miss Brannigan went ahead and began the lesson on Greek mythology. If Mamie had been here, she'd surely have objected.

That evening, when Daddy came back from the hardware store, he said he'd run across the builder and asked him. "He sez it wouldn't hurt none for him to come out and give us some idee of how much we're looking at. Sez he might could make it tomorry sometime on account he don't have any big projects underway and can spare some time."

The next afternoon, when I got off the bus, I saw a truck parked in front of our house. I hurried up the drive to see what was going on. A sign on the side of the truck said Roberts Construction. I heard voices around back, so that's where I headed.

A man was writing something down on a clipboard while Daddy watched. "Annie," Daddy said, "This is Lem Roberts, the man I told you about. He's done some figuring."

"Nice to meet you, Annie." Mr. Roberts held out his hand to shake mine. "It looks like you gonna need several things done before a bathroom can be built."

"What kind of things?" I had an awful feeling they'd cost way too much.

"Well, you need an electrical line coming in to support a hot water heater and a pump, plus you need a septic tank for all the waste to drain. And, of course, the pipes and fixtures."

How much?" I said.

"We're looking at about six thousand dollars," he said, "give or take a little."

"Oh," I said. "I don't even have half that. I thank you for your time, Mr. Roberts, but it looks like a bathroom is way out of my price range."

He sat down on the edge of the porch and wrote a few more things down on his clipboard. "Let's not be too hasty. I think I might be able to get the price down a mite."

I felt like whatever he came up with wouldn't be enough. Still, he was here, so I might as well listen to what he had to say. "What do you mean?" I asked.

"I'm kind of obligated to you for being the one that got Wiley Shortridge locked up. I'm pretty sure he was stealing building materials from several of my jobs when he was supposed to be patrolling to keep thieves away. At least, since he was arrested, I haven't had any more thefts. And something else, I've got a ten-year-old daughter. I'd hate to think of someone like Shortridge— well, I'm glad he's been put away for the rest of his life." He looked at his clipboard again. "I've just about finished remodeling a house that has some perfectly good fixtures that the woman wants replaced and hauled off. If you'd accept used fixtures, that'd save you nearly a thousand. And, if I'm not mistaken, the hot water heater she thinks is too small for her needs would likely do just fine. That'd save you more."

"But we still cain't afford it," Daddy said. "I'm real sorry I wasted your time, Lem."

"It wasn't a waste," he said. "Where there's a will, there's a way. You let me talk to some folks I know, and I'll see if they can give me a few more discounts. Then I'll come see you again."

I thanked Mr. Roberts for his time and trouble. I felt foolish that I'd wasted his time and gotten my hopes up.

* * *

The following Monday morning, the cardinal flew along as I walked to the clearing. *I told you*, he said. *And more good is coming to you. Be of good cheer, cheer, cheer.* Then the March wind carried him above the trees and out of my sight.

I did have a good day at school. Most of my days were good days, now. Somehow, despite my gift or maybe because of it, I'd become accepted as a regular person. Perhaps that was the good that came to me.

At lunch, the talk turned to what we'd be doing next year. Bert planned to go away to Bluefield College, Cheryl had just learned she'd been accepted at Virginia Intermont, and a few others were still waiting to hear. A lot of Bosworth County High students, however, would just go looking for work. Some of the boys who couldn't find work would go into service. Some of the girls would go looking for husbands who had jobs that would support them. A few—the youngest in the family—would stay home to look after their parents who would be getting older and not able to do for themselves much longer. When Bert asked what I was going to do, I told him it was likely that I'd look for work in town, that I was hoping that I could get on regular at the mill. But all the rest of the day, I couldn't help but wonder what I'd do. Likely I would end up taking care of Mama and Daddy since they had no one else to do it.

* * *

That afternoon when Jerleen came to my stop, she said, "What all's going on at your place, Annie? Looks like a whole lotta commotion over something. All them trucks, and all."

"I don't know," I said. I hoped there hadn't been an accident. I ran all the way up the drive and saw that one of the trucks was from Roberts Construction. Another was from a plumbing contractor, and another pulled a flatbed that must have had something big on it. I heard noise from around the back and ran to see what was happening.

A big hole had been dug in the back yard and a big cement box was in it. Some trenches had been dug, too. On the porch—I guess where the bathroom would be—Daddy was nailing some framing up. A pile of boards lay on the other end of the porch next to a yellow sink, toilet, and tub. Mr. Roberts saw me and waved me over and introduced me to his friends. One was a plumber, another was an electrician, another operated heavy equipment, and others worked for Mr. Roberts in one way or another.

"But I can't afford—" I tried to say, and he waved my words away.

"Every man here is glad to see Wiley Shortridge go. So they all feel obligated to you. And this is the way they can thank you. March is a slow time for most of us, so it ain't like you're keeping us from business. You pay what you can, and we'll take care of the rest."

A little over a week later, we had a bathroom. I still had a little money left that I decided I ought to save to put toward the electric bill, which would likely go up because of the pump and the water heater. When that money ran out, I hoped my quilts could bring in a little more. I was selling a few of the ones I'd made in school to some teachers and their friends, but I had to keep buying more fabric so that took a lot of my profit.

CHAPTER 14: CHANGES

I missed Aint Lulie something awful during the winter. I missed hearing her stories and sitting in the welcomeness and warmth of her cabin. Mid-March was still frosty, but it wouldn't be long until spring. If Aint Lulie had been here, she would say, "Change is in the air. I feel it in my bones." The first buds on the oaks were faint green, and that was a promise good enough for me after the snows of winter. Soon the dogwoods and apple trees would bloom, and the world would be filled with color.

That was when I made up my mind to move into Aint Lulie's cabin—*my cabin*—on the weekends. After school was out, after Mama had got used to me living there on weekends, I figured I might move to the cabin full time. But I could wait 'til summer to tell her that.

Even if we had us a spring snow or two, there was enough firewood left that I could keep the fireplace and cookstove going, enough canned goods to see me through the summer until my garden came in. I figured I could make do on my own, at least for a while. Plus I'd go back to the house to take a shower, and I'd eat some meals there, too. It wasn't like I was going far away.

I told Daddy I'd like to get Aint Lulie's garden spot plowed and try to have a garden of my own this year, and he said he'd see to it. I was glad that Aint Lulie always saved seeds. It saved me having to buy any. I needed to get myself an almanac, though. Aint Lulie always set great store by hers. Maybe it wouldn't hurt for me to try the old ways myself.

A week later, I came home to find my spot had been plowed along with one near the house for Mama. I started planning what I'd plant where.

Besides my decision to move to the cabin, something else happened in late March. Something big. On March 29, the war officially ended. When she heard the news, Mama got her hopes up again that somehow, some way, Scott would be coming home. There was no point in telling her he wouldn't. Hope was what she lived on.

On the last day of March, I opened the cabin, built a fire to take out the chill, and started working to get it "redd up" as Aint Lulie would have said. I wondered if what I was doing was like how Aint Lulie fixed up the cabin when she thought she and Sparrell Hobson would live there together. I wouldn't move in today, though. Aint Lulie had warned me many times that Saturday was an unlucky day to move into a house or take a journey or even get married. Well, I had no plans to get married and the journey from home to cabin was less than a quarter mile, but still I'd not take the risk of moving. I figured I could move a little at a time, using the wheelbarrow to move my things after school during the next week. But I could at least clean the cabin and have it ready.

I swept and cleared cobwebs and dusted until my nose started itching and I started sneezing. In my head, I could hear Aint Lulie saying, "Your nose itching is a sure sign of company coming." But no company was likely to visit me here. When I'd cleaned enough to make the place livable, I went home to get my things together and to tell Mama that I'd decided to stay in the cabin on weekends.

"If that's what you want to do," Mama said. She went to the kitchen to start fixing Daddy's supper. He'd been working at the sawmill today. With winter mostly gone, he was getting regular work now.

* * *

On the first Saturday in April, we had a warm spell so I thought it would be a good time to move a few more things to the cabin. Now that the days were longer, I'd had some time to work in the afternoon. I'd already laid off a few rows in my garden and had gotten some peas and mustard greens planted, so now I wanted to concentrate on moving in. I was up in my room going through what clothes I wanted to take when I heard Mama yell from downstairs, "Praise the lord! Scott's come home! My boy's home!"

I looked out my window and saw the cardinal fly past. Through the trees, I could make out the figure of a man in a uniform walking up our driveway. I knew it couldn't be Scott, but I ran down the steps two at a time and caught up with Mama who'd opened the front door to go onto the porch. She was wringing her apron in anticipation, and a smile played around the corners of her mouth. For a moment I thought she might forget herself and run to whoever it was.

When he came out of the woods and saw us watching, Mama's smile vanished.

"Is this the Caldwell place?" he asked. "Where Scott Caldwell once lived?"

Mama nodded woodenly, and I told him Scott had been my brother.

"You must be Annie," he said, walking closer. "Scott told me about you. I'm Carl Irwin. Scott and I served together."

"You knew Scott?" Mama asked, finding her voice. "You knew my boy?"

The soldier nodded. "I would have driven up here to the house, but Scott had told me how your road might be a little hard to navigate after I turned off the main road. So I left my car down there." He pointed in the direction of the main road.

"Well, come on in, I reckon," Mama said. "Ain't no use to be standing out here."

This was the first time I could remember that Mama asked a stranger inside. When we were seated in the front room, Carl Irwin told us why he'd come.

"Scott made me promise if he didn't make it back for me to visit you and give you a message from him. I was discharged last week, and I finally made it here."

"Scott's not coming back then?" Mama asked.

"No ma'am." I guess he thought she meant his body and not him in person. "We tried to recover his body," Carl Irwin continued, "but it just wasn't possible. The fire, and all."

A tear rolled down Mama's cheek and she dabbed it away with her apron. She'd never cry full-out in front of a stranger.

"The message," I said. "You said Scott had a message?"

"Oh. Yeah. That. Well, Scott wanted me to tell you that he'd gotten married several weeks before we shipped out."

"Married?" Mama's face froze in disbelief. "But he never wrote us such."

"No, ma'am. He was hoping to bring her here and surprise you when he got out. But then, well—"

"Her name is?" I said. Mama still sat frozen, and I didn't want Carl Irwin to keep groping for words.

"Lorraina," he said. "But she goes by Raina. She's real nice. I stopped by to see her the other day."

"How—how did Scott meet her?" Mama found words to ask.

"She was a waitress in Newport News. Some of us would eat at the place where she worked when we got tired of eating in the mess hall at Fort Eustis. Scott liked to hear her talk because he said she sounded like home. It wasn't long until they hit it off."

"Sounded like home?" Mama asked.

"Raina's from up around the Gate City area. She was living in Newport News with her sister. She couldn't find much work at home, but there were plenty of jobs on the peninsula. But she's been back for a while now. I had a heckuva time tracking her down."

I guess he expected Mama to question him some more, but she didn't. That Scott had married without telling her only put more distance between her and him. I guess she thought even if he came back now, it wouldn't be to us. It'd be to his wife.

"Why'd she come back?" I asked.

"She was expecting."

Mama's eyes got wide. "Expecting? A baby?"

"Yes, ma'am. She wanted to raise the baby at home and her mama was having some kind of health problems, so that's why Raina came back. She's fallen on some hard times lately though."

"Boy or girl?" Mama wanted to know.

"Boy. Scott Junior. She calls him Scotty."

"Scott Junior," Mama said. "Scotty."

"It's a shame that Scott didn't know he was going to be a daddy." Carl Irwin looked at his wristwatch. "Well, I've kept my promise to him and delivered his message, and I've got to be going. I've still got a couple hundred miles to go to get home."

"How can we get in touch with Raina?" I asked.

He took a scrap of paper from his pocket. "This is her address," he said, and handed it to me. I noticed a part of a map had been drawn on the back.

I thanked him and showed him out. Mama just sat there. She

was still sitting in the front room when Daddy came home an hour later.

"Supper ready?" he asked.

"You ain't gonna believe why I ain't started it yet," she told him. "I don't quite believe it myself." Then she hurried to the kitchen to start frying the chicken.

I was the one who told Daddy about our visitor and about Scott being married. And about the baby.

"So I got me a grandson," he said. "Don't that beat all."

I told him about where Scott's wife and baby were. "Ain't nothing to do but go see 'em," Daddy said. "I reckon the truck'll make it that far. But maybe I ort to go check it over."

He returned a half hour later with a map that he usually keeps in the glove compartment. "I added a quart of oil and checked the tire pressure. Truck ort to do fine. But can you make heads or tails outta how to git there?"

Daddy handed me a map, which looked like it had never before been unfolded. I studied it a bit, and traced a line with my finger. "I at least can get us close," I said. I figured maybe if we got close enough we'd run across somebody who could tell us how to get all the way. Between the regular map and the one Carl Irvin gave me, we ought to get pretty close.

We sat down late to supper, and Daddy told Mama what he aimed for us to do.

We left early the next morning. Despite the morning's chill, the day looked to be sunny and warm, and Daddy proclaimed it good traveling weather. Mama packed what was left of the fried chicken so we'd have something to eat. It didn't matter that it was Sunday morning, since Mama no longer had a church to attend. The women she met with for Bible study could make do without her, and she had herself a grandson to go see. The cardinal flitted behind the truck until Daddy turned onto the main road.

It was maybe 9:30 when we got to Gate City. We weren't sure how to get to the trailer park where Raina and the baby lived, but the second person we asked was able to point us on the right way. Daddy drove into the park slowly. I guess he was trying to figure out which trailer was hers.

When we turned into the second row of trailers, I saw a toddler playing with a toy truck in the dirt in front of some steps where a young woman sat. The toddler had the same reddish-blonde hair like Scott did.

Mama gasped and pointed. "There he is!" she yelled. "I'd know him anywhere!" She was out of the truck and running toward him and yelling "Scotty! Scotty!" before Daddy even had the truck fully stopped. The woman rushed up and grabbed the child.

"Who are you?" the woman asked. "How do you know my son's name?"

No sooner than Daddy had come to a full stop, I jumped out and hurried to explain. "I'm Annie Caldwell," I said. "Scott's sister. This is my mama and daddy."

"Oh," she said. "I reckon Carl musta told you. He said he was gonna."

Mama nodded, but she never took her eyes off the little boy. "He's the image of Scott," she said. "The spitten image."

Raina put the boy down and he stood looking up at us. Mama knelt down and said, "Scotty, come see your granny."

The boy toddled toward her and she grabbed him in a hug. Raina didn't object this time. He didn't struggle but settled against her. Her face was hidden against his shoulder, but I'm pretty certain she was crying. Daddy just stood back, watching.

"Where are my manners?" said Raina. "Y'all come on in. It's real nice to finally meet Scott's people."

With Mama carrying Scotty, we climbed the steps and followed her inside. She gestured to a sofa and said, "Y'all set down and get comfortable."

The trailer wasn't fancy and was as sparsely furnished as our house. It was as chilly inside as it had been out. Toys were scattered around the floor. We sat on the sofa, and Scotty struggled to get loose from Mama and fussed to go toward his toys. She let him go, but I could tell she didn't want to.

For a minute or two we just looked at each other. Finally Daddy spoke. "It come as a surprise to learn about y'all. Scott never let on he had a wife. But welcome to the family." Mama nodded.

"Scott never was one to write much," I said. "Usually it was a postcard to tell us he was doing all right. His last one just said he was shipping out and he'd write more once he got settled."

"He told me about y'all, though," Raina said. "And about the farm. He said what a nice place it was, with the mountains so close by and all. He said the house had a big porch where one day we'd set and watch our kids play. He talked about how he was going to have a dairy farm there. He had such big plans. He said no sooner he got out, we'd head for home and he couldn't wait to see y'all's faces when he showed up with me."

"Why didn't you come find us?" Daddy asked. "After what happened."

"I was a couple months along then, so I come back home. "Mama'd just found out about her cancer, so she needed me here real bad. She died last year, and I had a year-old baby and lots of doctor bills to deal with. Once, when I was at the library where they had phone books from other places, I tried looking y'all up, but none of all those Caldwells were the right ones."

"I'm sorry about your mama," Mama said. She didn't mention we'd never had a phone. "Leastways, it's a blessing she got to see her grandbaby."

"I guess," said Raina. "But I still miss her, and it's been real hard providing for Scotty. Her doctor bills needed paying, so I had to sell her house. That left me with a little money to get by on. I've got a friend who looks after Scotty a couple days a week, so I can usually get enough waitressing work in town to pay the rent."

When he heard his name, Scotty got up and toddled to his mama. She stroked his hair and he leaned against her.

"Ain't right the baby's got no family to see to him while you work," Mama said. And what she said next took Daddy and me purely by surprise. "Why don't you and Scotty come go with us?"

Raina didn't say anything. Mama continued, "Seems like Scott was planning on having y'all live with us anyway. Seems right to honor his wishes."

"We got plenty a'room," Daddy said. I guess he was willing to go along with Mama's idea.

"I reckon I could give it a try," Raina said. "Is there somewhere nearby there I could get work?"

"There's a few places in town," I said.

"What'll I do about moving?" she said. "There's not room in my old car for all we've got."

"I got the truck," Daddy said. "I can take some stuff now. Then I can come back for the rest, now I know the way."

"I'll need a few days to get things closed up and packed," Raina said. "Maybe next Saturday?"

"It's bad luck to move of a Saturday," Pa said. "How about I fetch you on Friday? Likely I can get off work then."

I was surprised that Daddy knew the old superstition. Had he once heard Aint Lulie say it?

"Friday ought to be all right," Raina said. "I reckon I can get everything ready by then."

We talked a little more, and Mama picked up Scotty and held him until he drifted off to sleep. Daddy figured he might as well go ahead and put some of Raina's things she wouldn't be needing for a while into the truck. So while Mama rocked Scotty, Daddy and Raina and I gathered up some quilts, her sewing machine, a couple chairs, some clothes, a box full of dishes, and some of Scotty's toys and put them into the truck. By the time we finished putting everything in, we had a full load.

Back inside the trailer, we talked for a while about this and that until Daddy reckoned we ought to get going. While Mama and Daddy were saying good-bye to the sleeping Scotty, I wrote down directions on how Raina could find us if she needed to. I didn't tell her about my gift or about Loniss's murder or anything. Likely she'd find out soon enough. I just wanted her to like me as a regular person. As her sister-in-law.

As we were leaving, I said, "Well, you better come go with us," and Raina smiled and answered, "Cain't. You mought as well stay." I knew right then she was one of us. She closed her door before we were in the truck, and I was certain she didn't watch us 'til we were out of sight.

Before we left town, Daddy stopped at a gas station and filled up. There was a grassy area nearby with a picnic table, so we sat there and ate our fried chicken. Mama was happier than I'd seen her for years. She kept talking about the baby, and how she'd fix up Scott's room for him. I suggested I'd go ahead and move completely into the cabin by Friday, so Mama could give him my room and let Raina have Scott's room, which was bigger. She thought that was a fine idea.

When we were almost home, I remembered what Aint Lulie had said about her dream—that somebody's bad fortune would lead to another's good fortune. Mama had the bad fortune to lose Scott, but now she had his son. Raina had the bad fortune to lose her mama and husband, but now she had a new family. As far as I could tell, things were working out. When Daddy pulled the truck up to the house, the cardinal was perched on a limb. *Cheer, cheer, cheer,* he sang.

The week flew by. Every afternoon, I moved a little more to the cabin. I kept myself busy by working in the garden, working on quilts, and thinking about how much my life would change. I hoped it would be a change for the good.

On Thursday night, Mama decided she'd better stay home Friday and get things ready for Raina and Scotty. "I got to have supper ready for everybody, and I cain't do that if I go. How about if Annie takes a half-day off from school and goes instead of me. I could write her a note to give to her teachers."

I'd never before left school except for Wiley Shortridge's trial and when Mr. Hathaway took me to the bank. But Daddy thought Mama's idea was a good one. "I'll stop by school 'bout noon and pick you up," he said. "Your mama can fix you lunch so you can eat on the way."

And that's what we did. I gave the note to the guidance counselor and told my afternoon teachers that I had to go out of town with my daddy and I'd miss their class. At noon, the guidance counselor came to tell me Daddy was waiting for me out front.

"Here's your lunch," he said, handing me a sack. "I reckon we ort to git on the road." I figured he was looking forward to getting there.

I didn't have to give Daddy directions. He remembered all the places to turn, and he didn't have any trouble finding the trailer park. An old Chevy Impala—Raina's, I guess—was parked beside the trailer. Before I could knock on the door, she came out with Scotty.

"I've got our clothes and Scotty's toys in my car," she said. "We just need to put the beds and dresser and stuff in the truck."

It didn't take us long to pack the bed of the pick-up. When Daddy had looped the rope around Raina's furniture, we decided that I should ride with Raina in case she and Daddy got separated.

"I'll be glad for the company," she said. She fastened Scotty into a baby-seat in the back, and I sat in the front seat. Daddy pulled away, and we followed.

At first, I didn't know what to say. Finally, "We're glad to have you come live with us," I said.

"I don't know what I'd a'done if y'all hadn't showed up like you did," Raina said. "I was getting real low on money." She told me about some of the problems she'd been having. And I told her about how I'd be living in the cabin instead of the house so she and her son could have their own rooms.

Then she told me about Scott's death. "I'd just come back from the doctor that morning, and I was sure about the baby. First thing, I sat down and started writing a letter to Scott telling him he was gonna be a daddy. Then somebody knocked on the front door. I got up and through the window I seen two men in uniform. At first I didn't realize. By the time I opened the door and got a look at their faces, I knowed it was bad news." She wiped her hand across her eyes and changed the subject.

She asked what I did besides go to school, and I told her about the quilts I was making. And she suggested that maybe we should put her sewing machine in the cabin if I hadn't already done so. Before long we were talking like we'd known each other all our lives while Scotty slept in back. I asked if our talking would wake him, but she said he could sleep anywhere. After we'd been on the road about an hour, I told her about Aint Lulie and what all she'd taught me and how I was going to live in her cabin, but I never mentioned our gifts. Turns out, Raina already knew about mine.

"You're the girl on TV!" she said. "I figured you might be kin to Scott, but I wasn't for sure. Everybody in the diner watched the news about that deputy's trial. It was a fine thing you done getting him sent to prison. No telling who else he'd a'killed if you hadn't talked to his dog."

"So my gift doesn't bother you?" I didn't look at her to see how she'd react but kept my eyes on Daddy's truck ahead of us.

"I think it's great," she said, "that you can do that. If I'd knowed for sure that you was my sister-in-law, I'd a'bragged about it to everybody in that diner."

I went ahead and told her about Aint Lulie's gift, and how the first girl in every other generation is gifted in some way.

"So if Scotty has a daughter, she'll have a gift?" Raina asked. "That'll be cool!"

"I guess so," I said, "but it's hard to say what kind of gift it will be."

Our conversation turned back to us, though. She asked me what school was like, and I told her about what we studied in English class and about making quilts in home ec.

"I've made a quilt or two myself years ago," she said. "Nothing fancy. But I'd kinda like to take it up again."

She asked what kind of animals we had, and I told her we only had Mama's chickens.

"The way Scott talked about starting up a dairy, I figured you'd have a herd of cows," she said. "No dogs or cats or anything for you to talk to?"

"Nothing. Daddy doesn't want to feed anything that won't make us money, so he sold the two cows Scott owned when we got the news. I sometimes talk to wild critters, though." I changed the subject and told Raina about how I was planting a garden. She seemed eager to help. I told her what I'd already put in, what I planned to put in, and how Aint Lulie always went by the signs.

"My mama and grandma always planted by the signs, too," she said. "We got to get your potatoes and green beans planted on Good Friday," she said. "That's the way we always done it."

"Do you always press down the dirt with your foot when you plant a hill of beans?" I asked. "That's the way Aint Lulie always did it."

"Every time," she said. "I didn't know there was any other way to plant 'em."

"Then I bet you didn't put in your garden until oak leaves were the size—"

"Of mouse ears," she said. And we both laughed.

As she drove along behind Daddy's truck, we talked about all kinds of things, and I could see how Scott was attracted to Raina. She seemed like one of us.

When we were about a half hour from home, she asked, "Would you like to drive?"

"I never learned how," I admitted.

"I thought all country girls was born knowing how," she said. "Seems like I was. We'll have to do something about that once I get settled in. I'll teach you."

"You'd really teach me?"

"Sure," she said. "Why not?"

Before long we were home, and Mama was running out to see her grandson who'd slept most of the way. Raina let Mama take him while she, Daddy, and I carried her things to where they needed to be. Raina liked Scott's old room—"I can almost feel him here," she said—and she thought my room would do fine for Scotty's nursery. Then we ate the big dinner that Mama had fixed for us.

The sun was almost down when I walked alone down the path

to Aint Lulie's—to *my*—cabin. The spring leaves had greened out considerable on the trees and made a canopy over me. I couldn't see the cardinal, but I could hear *cheer, cheer, cheer* from somewhere among the leaves.

* * *

It didn't take Raina but a few days to find a job at the diner in town. Since she worked the breakfast and lunch shift, she didn't have to do the supper shift so she got off early. After she'd played with Scotty for a while and helped Mama out, she'd come out to the cabin and visit with me until suppertime.

She was a big help in getting the garden put in. And we got our green beans and potatoes planted on Good Friday. We took turns pressing the bean hills, but we worked opposite to each other hoeing the trenches for the potatoes. When our hoes clanked together, she laughed and said, "You know what that means? That we'll work the same field together this time next year."

"I reckon that'll be fine with me," I said.

The week after Easter was school's spring break. I made the most of my time off to work on some quilt orders I'd gotten. Using Raina's sewing machine, I was able to get two baby quilts done. I was glad she'd let me bring it to the cabin. It turned warm enough I could leave the cabin door open, and I could treadle the machine while looking at all the green.

With Easter being so late this year that left only five weeks between Easter break and graduation. As I sewed, I kept thinking of my problem—*what was I going to do?* Without Aint Lulie to look after, I didn't have much reason to stay at the cabin all day, so I could work in town if I could find a job. *If.*

At any rate, I'd need to have some money coming in regular. I didn't know if I could manage to look after myself by gardening and sewing. I was getting a little money now and then for my quilts, but I couldn't see how it would support me for the long run. I had no prospects of getting married like a lot of the girls did right after high school. Raina helped out by giving Mama a little money for watching Scotty, and sometimes Raina brought leftovers home from the diner.

But Daddy still had more mouths to feed than he'd got used to, and he wasn't working all that steady. He must have been thinking about the situation, too. On Easter Monday, while I was working on a drunkard's path pattern, I heard footsteps on the porch and then a knock. I looked toward the open door and saw Daddy standing there. It was the first time he'd been to the cabin since Aint Lulie died. I asked him to come in, and he pulled up a chair near to where I sat. It took him a minute to say anything.

"Annie," he finally said, "I been doing some figgering, and—well, you got to start looking for a job. For when you finish school. I'm headed to town tomorrow, and I could stop you off at the mill. Seems to me Mr. Hathaway ort to give you a job, after what you done and all." He cleared his throat. "Anyhow, I wanna get a early start."

I stopped stitching and left my needle marking my place. "All right," I said. "I'll be ready." Working at the mill seemed like as good a job as any. If I got a job on the morning shift, I could probably ride into town with Raina.

Tuesday morning, I put on my best skirt and blouse and made sure my shoes were polished. Daddy was waiting in his truck when I walked down the path. We got to the mill around eight, and Daddy let me off not far from the front door. He said he'd be at the hardware store and I could walk there to meet him when I finished. He drove off, and I walked up to the big glass door and opened it.

A woman—the receptionist or secretary, I guessed—sat at a typewriter. It took her a minute to finish what she was doing before she noticed me.

"May I help you?" she said.

"I'd like to see Mr. Hathaway," I said. "About a job."

"Usually the personnel office sees applicants," she said. She got out a little book and picked up a pen. "Now if you'll just give me your name, I'll make an appointment."

"Annie Caldwell," I said. She started to write and then stopped.

"Oh," she said. "You're the girl who—"

I didn't let her finish. "Yes," was all I said. All I needed to say.

She picked up the phone, and I figured she was calling Mr. Hathaway. When she hung up, she said for me to go down the hall and into the third door on the right.

Mr. Hathaway was standing at the door when I got there and told me to come right in.

"This is certainly a pleasant surprise, Annie," he said, gesturing to a chair for me to sit in. "Now what can I do for you today?"

"I need a job starting after school's out," I said. "I was thinking maybe you might have an opening on one of the assembly lines." I wasn't sure how to act at a job interview. Especially when the head of the company was interviewing me. Especially since everything that happened.

"We don't have any openings at the moment," he said. "But I believe I've heard of an opportunity you might be interested in. I wish I could tell you more about it now, but it's still in the works. Could I have your phone number?"

"I don't have a phone." I could feel my face getting red. "But you could write me a letter." I gave him our box number.

"No problem," he said. "You should hear from me in a week or two." He stood up and I did, too.

At the door he said, "Annie, thank you again for what you did. My wife and I—"

I could tell he couldn't find the right words. "I'm glad I could be of help," I said and hurried off. It was plain that he didn't have a job for me.

* * *

About two weeks later, mid-way through second period science, the school secretary came in and said I was to report immediately to the guidance office. I figured it was about graduation, since Mrs. Loomis, the counselor, had been calling seniors in to settle up their plans. Since I couldn't justify paying for the cap and gown, I meant to tell her that I wasn't planning to attend graduation and for the school to just mail me the diploma. Mrs. Loomis would surely understand. She was the one who fixed it so I could get free lunches, so she knew my situation.

Mrs. Loomis wasn't the only one in her little office, though. A couple more chairs had been pulled in, and the Hathaways were sitting in them. They smiled at me.

"Mr. and Mrs. Hathaway have something that might be of interest to you, Annie," Mrs. Loomis said. "I want you to listen carefully and consider what they have to say."

I was confused. If he was going to offer me some kind of a job, why was his wife with him? And why would he come to school to do it?

Then Mrs. Hathaway spoke up. "Annie, my husband and I have been thinking. You might not know that Loniss was accepted by Hollins College right before she—well, we never cancelled her space, and we'd like you to have it."

Before I could answer, Mrs. Loomis broke in and said that she'd already sent them my transcript and, since my grades were so good, the college would be glad to have me.

"I don't know what to say," I said. "I hadn't ever considered going off to college."

"We realize that money might be an issue," Mr. Hathaway said. "That's why we're offering you a full scholarship."

"I don't understand," I said. And I truly didn't.

Mrs. Hathaway explained. "Ever since Loniss was a baby, we'd been putting money into a college fund for her. We never ever dreamed she wouldn't be here to use it. So, we decided we'd like to use the money to send a deserving girl to college in her place. For all you did in getting her murderer convicted, well—you're the one we picked."

"We'll announce the winner of the Loniss Hathaway Memorial Scholarship at graduation," Mr. Hathaway said. "And you can accept it there."

"Mr. and Mrs. Hathaway," I said, "you've already done plenty for me with the reward money. And I don't plan to be at graduation."

"Why not?" Mrs. Hathaway said. "You certainly wouldn't want to miss a big event like graduation."

"My parents don't have money to rent the cap and gown," I said. "And I've already spent most of the money you gave me."

Mr. Hathaway pulled his checkbook from his jacket pocket. "How much is it?" he asked, and Mrs. Loomis told him. He handed her a check. To me he said, "Now you're going."

So. I could go to graduation. And now, if I wanted, I could go off to college. I realized this was a big, big thing happening to me. But I felt like the only world I ever knew was spinning me off it and onto a different world where I'd be a stranger.

"I don't know about college," I said. "I appreciate your offer, but nobody in my family ever went before. And I don't know what my parents would say. I'll have to talk to them about it."

"Understood," said Mr. Hathaway. "We'll check back with you in a few days."

I went back to class not knowing what to think—or what to do. I thought about their offer the rest of the day.

Mama and Daddy could hardly believe it when I told them at supper that I had a chance to go to college. To a place called

Hollins up near Roanoke.

"We don't take charity," Mama said. "It wouldn't be right."

"It ain't charity," Daddy said. "She earned it with her—well, whatever she did that got Wiley Shortridge sent to prison." He shoveled some mashed potatoes into his mouth, chewed, and added, "Still, I hate to see her go off."

"Scott went off," Mama said, "and he never come back."

It sounded like the matter was closed. Then Raina spoke up. "I went off," she said. "A lot farther than Annie will go. If I hadn't done it, I'd never have met Scott, and I'd never have had my son. And y'all wouldn't have a grandson."

"That's so," Mama said. "That's so." She got up and picked Scotty up from his highchair and hugged him close. "That's so."

"I haven't made up my mind yet," I said. "I'm still studying on whether or not I should go."

We ate for a while without saying anything. It occurred to me that this might be the meaning of my dream about the storm—if I took the Hathways' offer, I'd be up-rooted like the trees in my dream. And it was the meaning of Aint Lulie's dream, too, of someone's good fortune coming from another's misfortune. She must have dreamed that I would be the one with a chance to go away, and the chance would be the result of someone else's misfortune, but she hadn't wanted to come right out and tell me.

On my way back to the cabin, the cardinal flitted from limb to limb just ahead of me. For a moment, he'd vanish into the green leaves, then he'd reappear. I sent my thoughts to him: *What should I do, red bird?* He swooped in front of me and answered right away: *Be one of them that go.* Then he flew beyond the trees and out of my sight.

On Wednesday, I was called to the guidance office. I figured Mr. Hathaway would be there, and he was.

"Have you decided?" he asked.

"I have," I said. "I talked to my family, and we've decided I should accept your offer."

Mrs. Loomis gasped. I guess she thought I wouldn't.

"Very well," Mr. Hathaway said. "We'll make the scholarship announcement at graduation. My wife and I will see you then." He rose, shook my hand, and was out the door before I could say, "Thank you."

When I got back to class, I didn't tell anyone that I'd be going to college. I wanted to keep the idea close to myself for a while.

* * *

Two weeks before graduation came the second biggest event in the school year—the prom. Bert had offered to take me, but I had to tell him that Mama didn't want me dancing, so he asked Cheryl instead. I didn't want to have to spend money on a fancy dress anyway. I'd kind of hoped that Mrs. Carlton would hire me to help out, but the school had hired a catering company to provide refreshments.

So—on the Saturday that most of the other kids were getting ready to go to the prom, I had other plans. Raina and I climbed the hill to clean off the old family graveyard. Mama would have gone, but she stayed home to keep Scotty who would have gotten bored and cranky on the long climb up. I think Mama was happy to have Scotty to herself, even though she had to miss graveyard cleaning-off day. Aint Lulie had never missed a day that I could remember. Every time we went, she'd always told me who was buried where.

Carrying our rakes and cutters and a sack lunch, Raina and I followed the ruts from where the hearse had taken Aint Lulie up four months earlier. Since the graveyard can't be seen from below, it was the first time Raina had seen it. It took us a while to walk up there, and—when we reached the top—we were what Aint Lulie used to call "plumb tuckered."

"Law!" Raina said, looking around, "A body'd never know it was here. And you can see for miles! Is that a cabin up there?" She pointed midway up Byrne Mountain across from us.

I was glad I'd paid attention when Aint Lulie had told me who lived where.

"There's several old cabins still standing on the mountain. They belonged to Duffs and Byrnes that are kin to us. Caldwells mostly lived lower down. But they call this graveyard the Duff-Byrne-Caldwell cemetery."

"You ever climbed all the way to the top of the mountain?" Raina kept looking up at it. "I bet you could see for a hundred miles up there."

"I never did," I said. "If you're crazy enough to want to try, it'd be best to do it after the first hard frost when the rattlers and copperheads aren't around."

"Maybe one day we ought to do that, but for now I reckon we ought to get busy," Raina said. "No use wasting daylight."

It took at least an hour for us to rake off the leaves and pull the weeds and cut back little saplings that were trying hard to grow. Aint Lulie's grave was the cleanest one. Grass was just now barely starting to grow on it. I had a handful of the zinnia seeds that she'd saved, and I planted them on her grave. When Raina and I were done cleaning, I pointed to each stone and told her who was buried where. None of the stones were marked with names.

"This is where my grandpa James Caldwell is," I said. "He's Daddy's daddy, so he'd be Scotty's great-grandpa. He's named for his grandpa, James Elexander Caldwell, who didn't make it back from Cold Harbor in the Civil War, so we don't know where he's buried. Grandpa James's wife Eliza is there next to him. James Elexander's wife Mariah married again, so she's buried in the next row back beside her second husband, Jacob Caldwell, who was a third cousin to her first husband."

"This is getting awfully complicated," Raina said. "I can't keep track of who's who."

"One of these days I'll write it all down for you," I said. "But in the meantime, Mariah Caldwell is Daddy's great-grandma by her first husband and also Mama's great-grandma by her second husband. One of these days, you can explain to Scotty how he's kin to himself."

"I hope you write it all down by then," she said.

An over yonder's Daddy's grandpa Duffield Caldwell, who was known as Duffie. His wife Sarah Dempsey Caldwell is beside of him. Duffield is James Elexandar's son."

"You've got to write it all down soon," she said. "There's no way on this green earth I'll ever remember all this."

"I haven't even told you the most interesting part," I said. "There's a long tragic story about Aint Lulie's Aint Pearl. She's buried over yonder." I pointed to Pearl's grave on the other side of Aint Lulie. "I'll tell you about her while we eat our lunch." And that's what I did.

When we'd gathered up our tools and were ready to start back, Raina said, "So this is where Scott should have been buried? It's a shame there's not a marker for him."

"We could drag a rock from down below," I said. To mark the place for him."

"No," she said. "I want to buy a little stone with his name and the dates on it. Like a memorial for him."

"Wouldn't that cost a lot?" I asked.

"Probably not all that much," she said. "I can ask around. You want me to ask about a stone for your aunt while I'm at it?"

I thought about it for a few seconds. I had a little money left, but not much. I'd planned to use it for whatever expenses I'd have next year. "All right," I said. "It wouldn't hurt to ask."

Going down the mountain was a lot easier than going up. It took us about half the time to get back down. When Scotty saw us, he twisted out of Mama's arms and came running toward his own mama.

"You gonna help us weed the garden?" Raina asked him when she grabbed him into a hug. "Your Aint Annie and me are gonna do that directly."

"Yeth," he said. "Wee gar."

While Raina and I pulled weeds in my garden, I watched Scotty run about the yard, the late afternoon sunlight glinting off his hair, and realized my brother's shadow no longer hung over our house. I don't know when it left, but it was gone.

I was so tired that night that I slept good. I didn't miss going to the prom a bit. At lunch on Monday, Bert and Cheryl filled me in on what I'd missed. Voting for king and queen of the prom had been done that night instead of in advance. I guess Mr. Darley didn't want what happened at the harvest dance to happen again. Alvin Bosworth had been elected king, and his date—a girl who took all advanced college-track classes—was queen. Alvin was going to Duke, his date was going to UNC. Cheryl said everybody had a good time and nothing out of the ordinary happened, except that Susan was wearing what looked like an engagement ring with a little tiny diamond, and she and Larry danced every slow dance awfully close together. Bert said everybody mostly sat around and looked at each other because they didn't want to get their good clothes messed up. I still didn't tell them that I was going to college. Maybe it was because I didn't yet believe I would really go.

During home ec, I finished another quilt and got an idea for my next one. I needed some yellow material, though, and there wasn't much in the scrap bags. I decided I'd ask Raina if she'd get me some in town.

That evening, Raina was late getting home because she'd checked on the prices of stones. "I stopped by to see Mr. Slocum who does stonework and sometimes makes tombstones. He said he had some stones that were chipped, so he couldn't sell them for regular-size tombstones. But he said he could cut one down into two small stones and engrave them if we didn't want anything real fancy. He'd let us have them for ten dollars each."

"That seems kind of cheap," I said. "We could do that."

"That's what I thought," Raina said. "Normally, he'd get more, but he said he always thought a lot of Scott and it was a shame about what happened. And he was real pleased with what you done in getting Wiley put away. So he's only charging for the engraving. But he said it would take three or four weeks for him to get around to it."

That night, after we'd had supper and Scotty was asleep, Raina and I sat at the kitchen table with a piece of paper and figured out what we wanted on the stones. Scott's stone would say "In memory of Scott Duffield Caldwell" with the dates of his birth and death. Aint Lulie's would just have "Louisa Lee Caldwell" and her dates.

I took my envelope of money from my pocket and gave her the ten dollars for my part. Then I asked her about getting me some material and she said she would, so I counted out another five.

It was twilight when I walked back to the cabin. I'd nearly let my fire go out, but I built it up again to take out the night's chill.

I'd planted a lot of tomato seeds a few months earlier, and the plants were big enough now to put in the garden. I'd always heard that tomatoes ought to go in the garden on Memorial Day, which Aint Lulie had always called Decoration Day. I reckon folks figured that any chance of frost was gone by then. So, on the last Monday of May, I set my plants out. I figured that was the end of things I'd plant. If Raina wanted to plant any late crops, she was welcome to space in the garden. I figured she'd be the one to harvest what would ripen after I'd gone.

CHAPTER 15: SUMMER DAYS

On the evening of June 1st, all of us piled into Raina's car to go to my graduation. Mama had wanted to stay home with Scotty, but Raina convinced her to go.

"Well, if Scotty starts to fret, I reckon I take him out so he won't make a disturbance," she said.

"He'll be fine," Raina said.

Earlier that day, Raina had helped me get ready. After I'd washed my hair, she'd rolled it up on her curlers. When she took the curlers out and brushed my hair, I didn't look like myself. Mama had sucked in her breath like she didn't approve, but she didn't say a word.

"This'll look better with that flat hat y'all got to wear," Raina said.

It was hot and crowded in the school's gym. But this was what all the seniors and their families had been waiting for, so nobody complained. Before we went in, Raina took some bobby pins and pinned my hat on so it wouldn't fall off. Then she took the little Kodak Instamatic camera she'd bought a few days earlier out of her pocketbook and had us line up for a picture. Mama said she didn't want her picture taken, but Raina said she wanted a picture of Scotty with his grandparents and aunt, so she gave in.

Inside, I went down front and took my seat with the other graduates. Miss Brannigan was there making sure we were lined up in alphabetical order while Mr. Darley and Miss Filsten were on the platform checking over the diplomas. Mr. Darley had a clipboard he looked at every so often.

I looked back to see Mama sitting on an aisle toward the back with Scotty on her lap and Daddy beside her. Raina sat in front of Mama.

When the big clock on the wall said seven, Mr. Darley called everyone to order and began speaking about how this wasn't an end but a beginning and how some of those graduating today would go on to do big things and other stuff. Some of the boys did their best to suppress their yawns. Susan Collins, who was sitting on the same row I was, kept looking at her ring. Word was that she and Larry were getting married in a few weeks, so neither of them would likely go on to "big things." She'd likely be pregnant within a year, and he'd work at his daddy's garage. At least he'd have a job waiting for him. Some of the graduates wouldn't even have that.

Then the girl that Alvin Bosworth had taken to the prom gave a speech because she was valedictorian. Then Alvin, who'd come in second to her, also gave a speech. Both of them spoke about the challenges of the future. Nobody paid much attention but everyone applauded when they were done.

Mr. Darley began handing out awards. Several of the guys lettered in football, so they went first and stood awkwardly while their pictures were taken. Then some academic awards were handed out. Bert got the English award and the government award, but everyone figured he would. I was surprised to hear my name called for a home ec award. Finally, Mr. Darley moved to other awards. I kept waiting for him to call the Hathaways up to the platform to announce my scholarship, but he never did. I looked around, but I didn't see them. Maybe they had decided not to give it to me after all.

Then he started calling us to the platform to get our diplomas. Since my name started with C, I didn't have to wait long. When I went onto the platform, Raina stood in the aisle and took my picture. Since there were nearly a hundred graduates, the whole ceremony took a while.

After Mr. Darley had handed out all the diplomas, he announced, "The class of 1973 should have had another graduate, but her high school career was tragically cut short. However, we at Bosworth County High School would like to award a posthumous diploma to Loniss Dianne Hathaway. Will her parents please come forward to accept it?"

For a moment, no one moved. Then, from midway back on the far side, the Hathaways came forward and accepted Loniss's diploma. Everyone applauded politely. Mrs. Hathaway dabbed at her eyes with a tissue.

"Thank you for honoring our daughter," Mr. Hathaway said. "It means a lot to my wife and me that you have remembered her. Now we would like to honor Loniss's memory by awarding a college scholarship in her name to one of the graduates here tonight."

A hush fell over the gym. Graduates started looking around. No doubt many were wondering, *Is it me? The person next to me? Who?* Alvin Bosworth sat a little straighter and adjusted his tie.

Mr. Hathaway continued, "The winner of the Loniss Hathaway Memorial Scholarship is a good student who performed a valuable service—Annie Caldwell. Without what she did, Loniss's murderer might still be at large. Annie, will you come forward?"

I did. Mrs. Hathaway hugged me when I was on the platform. "This is a full four-year scholarship to Hollins College," she announced, "where Annie has already been accepted. And it includes a shopping spree before Annie leaves for college."

She handed me a certificate. I was the one crying now. "Thank you," I said, dabbing my eyes with the tissue Mrs. Hathaway handed me. "I'm honored to accept this."

And then everybody in the gym stood up and applauded. They applauded me and my gift.

Raina finally stopped applauding and started snapping pictures. Scotty started to cry, but Mama didn't take him out. She managed to hold him and applaud at the same time.

When everybody finally sat back down, Mr. Darley announced that commencement would be over as soon as the new graduates had marched out and that everyone else was to stay seated until the music stopped. Miss Filsten played *Pomp and Circumstance* on the piano as Miss Brannigan directed us which way to exit.

Once we were outside, kids swarmed around and congratulated me. I must have said "Thank you!" a hundred times. And I meant it every single time. Still I was glad to see my family come out so we could soon leave.

After Raina took one more picture of me holding my diploma, I joined the line to hand in graduation caps and gowns to Mrs. Loomis and Miss Filsten. I was glad the line moved fast. Before we got away, the Hathaways came over and introduced themselves to Mama and Daddy, and I introduced them to my sister-in-law and nephew.

"It's good to meet y'all," Daddy said, shaking Mr. Hathaway's hand. "We appreciate all y'all done for Annie." But I could tell Daddy felt awkward and trapped. Mama hid behind Scotty and murmured her thanks.

Miss Brannigan came over and told my parents how proud she was of me and what a good student I'd been. "I know you'll do well at Hollins," she said to me. "I was proud to write a letter of recommendation for you."

Finally we edged our way to the car, and my high-school life was officially over. On the way home, Scotty fell so sound asleep that Daddy had to carry him inside once we got home. Mama took my diploma and propped it up on the mantelpiece in the front room. I'd hoped she or Daddy would tell me how proud they were of me, but pride is a sin and is frowned upon in their world. When I got back to the cabin, I soon fell sound asleep, too.

* * *

I woke to the sound of someone pounding on the door. "It's unlocked!" I yelled, and Raina came in.

"Wake up, Sleepyhead," she said. "You're burning daylight. We got us a garden to work, and you're going to learn to drive today."

"Huh?" I slung my legs over the side and got out of bed.

"It's Saturday. I don't have to work. Figured this was as good a time as any to teach you to drive. You ain't in high school anymore, and you got to learn to do stuff. You got ten minutes to get to the house and eat breakfast with us." Then she took off toward the house. I got dressed as fast as I could and followed her.

After breakfast, we went to her 1964 Impala that was as big as a battleship. She made me get behind the wheel, showed me how to adjust the seat and mirrors, and handed me the key. "I figure it's like learning how to swim," she said. "I'll just throw you in, and we'll see how you do. We'll drive down to the road and you can turn around in the clearing."

Luckily the car was pointed in the direction I wanted to go, so I didn't have to back up. It took me a few fits and starts to get the hang of the accelerator, but it wasn't all that different from treadling on the sewing machine. After we'd gone up and down the drive five or six times and Raina was satisfied that I wasn't going to wreck, she had me back up. Then she taught me to park. "Looks like you know enough to get your learner's permit and go on the road," she said. She took a booklet out of the glove compartment and told me to study up on all the rules. When I knew them, we'd go to town and I could take the test for a learner's permit.

It was still early and some of the morning's coolness remained when we finished my driving lesson. Raina and I pulled a few weeds and picked peas for lunch and for canning. During the heat of the afternoon, we sat on the shady end of the porch and shelled peas. That evening, when it was cooler, we canned them.

Within a week, I had my learner's permit.

I developed a rhythm during the early summer days. I'd go to the house for breakfast, work in the garden while it was still cool, go to the house for a shower, fix myself lunch unless mama invited me to eat with her and Scotty, and come back to the cabin and work on quilts all afternoon, unless I had something that needed to be canned right away. After Raina got off and played with Scotty for a while, she'd help me with picking or canning.

The quilt I mostly worked on during June was a log cabin pattern for the Hathaways. I used Loniss's favorite colors—turquoise, yellow, and pink. I made a few baby quilts, too, because they sold well. Raina would take some to display at the diner and folks would buy them for their children or grandchildren. That gave me a little money coming in.

One afternoon in late June while Scotty was taking his nap and Mama was working in her own garden, Raina slipped in with a big bag of something.

"I didn't want your Mama to see what I was doing," she said. "It might upset her."

She carried her bag into the room on the other side of the dogtrot and dumped a pile of shirts onto the bed. I recognized them as Scott's.

"Your mama kept Scott's things in his chifferobe," she said. "Likely the way he left things on the day he went away. I sort of want to keep them because they're part of Scott. But they're taking up space, and I can't see giving them away. What if your mama saw another man dressed in Scott's clothes? She'd have a fit."

"Why are you giving them to me?" I asked.

"I ain't exactly giving them. I want to help cut them up and make quilts. A quilt for me and a quilt for Scotty. What do you

192

think?"

"I think it's a good idea. If you have any of Scotty's things that he's outgrown, we could add them too." I went to the chest and got the quilt that Aint Lulie had made years ago from the clothes Scott and I had worn when we were Scotty's age. I spread it out and pointed to each piece and told Raina about them—like Aint Lulie had done for me.

"That's beautiful," Raina said. "That's the kind of thing I want us to do."

I nodded. I folded up the quilt and started to put it away. But I was going away myself, and there was no point for the quilt to go unused. I handed it to Raina. "Here. This is for you," I said. "Or for Scotty. He ought to know what his daddy and his Aint Annie wore when they were little."

She put the quilt in her bag. "Now, let's get busy," she said. We spent the next half-hour cutting off buttons and adding them to Aint Lulie's button jar. *Waste not, want not.* Then we cut the shirts into pieces.

By the time we had a big pile of patches, it was nearly suppertime. We walked back to the house together and agreed that after supper, we'd pick the rest of the June apples.

"Scotty can come with us and pick up the ones from the ground," she said. "That'll tire him out so he can sleep good tonight."

And it did. Peeling and canning the apples a few days later wore Raina and me out, too. But at least there'd be a break between the June apples and the others. Raina would have to see to picking the winesaps and golden delicious herself because I'd be gone before they ripened.

* * *

I turned eighteen on July 9th. My family never did much for birthdays, but Raina brought half a cake home from the diner and stuck candles in it. I let Scotty help me blow out the candles.

Raina said now that I was of age, I ought to get my driver's license, so she got Daddy to promise to bring me into town the next day. The plan was he'd park his truck, and we'd take her car to the motor vehicle place. Her old Impala was a lot easier to drive than Daddy's truck.

When we returned her car to the diner, I flashed my new driver's license. On the way home, Daddy said I ought to learn to drive the truck in case of emergency or something, but I told him I needed to get used to driving the car before I attempted a stick shift.

The rest of the day I worked on the Hathaways' quilt and wondered what kind of car they would have bought Loniss for graduation. It would likely have been sporty. And yellow.

When Raina came to the cabin that afternoon, she said I needed a new look now that I'd come of age, so she was going to cut my hair. "I know long straight hair is in," she said, " but yours needs some shape, and it'll be a lot cooler and easier to take care of if I snip off three or four inches." She pulled out a pair of scissors from her pocket.

I was hesitant at first, but I let her do it. While I sat and watched hunks of my hair hit the floor, I wondered if the haircut had been a good idea. But then Raina told me to go look in the mirror. I liked what I saw.

"You look more grown-up," Raina said. "Now what are we going to do with all this cut-off hair?"

"I reckon we ought to bury it," I told her. "You know the old sayings about cut hair, don't you?"

"You mean the one about you should bury hair right after you cut it so the birds won't pick it up? 'Cause if they do you'll have headaches for months to come?" She got the broom and started sweeping my hair into a pile.

"And if the birds make a nest of your hair, you'll go crazy," I added. "And if your hair falls into the wrong hands, it could be used to witch you."

"Best get the shovel," she said, "so we can get this hair buried."

We buried my hair near the Madame Hardy rose bush Pearl had planted at the cabin's corner so many years ago.

* * *

A week later, while I was sitting on the porch and playing with Scotty, Raina drove up with the trunk of her Impala almost dragging the ground.

"What's wrong with your car?" I said.

She parked beside the house and opened the trunk lid. "Come take a look."

I picked up Scotty and walked over to see what she had. Scotty reached toward his mama and she took him and danced him around. In the trunk were Aint Lulie's and Scott's stones wrapped in burlap.

"Mr. Slocum come by the diner and told me they were ready, so I stopped by his place and he loaded them for me. Now the problem is, how do we get them out of the trunk and up to the graveyard? Ain't no way this car can make it up there."

"Daddy's truck sure couldn't make it either. I wonder if the two of us could pull them up on the old slide if we only took one at a time. And maybe Daddy could help us get them out of the trunk."

"Wouldn't hurt to ask him, would it?" She put Scotty down and chased him around one of the trees. He laughed and laughed. And then she let him chase her.

When Daddy came home from the sawmill, we asked him. He looked at the stones and studied over the matter. Mama came out, too, but she didn't say a word. We decided not to unwrap the stones so they wouldn't get scratched until we got them in the graveyard.

Finally, Daddy figured that Raina could drive the car as close to the graveyard path as she could get, then he could put a board from the trunk to the slide, and he'd help us get the stone onto the board. Then we'd slide it down to the middle of the old slide. "Seems like the three'a us ort to be able to move 'em."

That's what we did after we finished supper. Because the grass had grown longer on the graveyard path, it would likely now be crawling with bite-y bugs, so we took precautions. First, we rubbed our faces and arms with mashed peppermint leaves and stems to keep away the skeeters. Then we dusted our legs with powdered sulphur to keep away the chiggers. Aint Lulie had always sworn by both remedies. Then we loaded the slide into the back of Daddy's truck, and he followed Raina and me in her car. His plan worked just like he said it would.

It took a good bit of pulling through the high grass to get Aint Lulie's stone up to the graveyard, but we did it. We pushed the stone as close as we could get it to the head of Aint Lulie's grave. We knew we couldn't get Scott's stone up before dark, so—once we got the slide back down the hill—we just loaded his stone onto the slide and left it at the bottom of the hill. By lamplight, I picked off a few ticks that had hitched a ride on me. I reckon back at the house Raina was doing the same. I slept so sound that night I didn't even dream.

The next evening, we did the same with Scott's stone, only this time everybody went, even Scotty. Mama and Daddy had to take turns carrying him, though, while Raina and I pulled the slide. It was easier this time because the grass was mashed down from the day before. Daddy brought along a pry-bar to help move the stones where we wanted them. We set Aint Lulie's first, and I thought Raina would pick the place for Scott's but she surprised me.

"Miz Caldwell," Raina said. "Where do you reckon Scott would'a wanted his marker?"

Mama didn't say anything at first, but then she walked around a little and looked different ways. Finally she settled on a spot near the edge where the view was best. "I reckon he'd like right here," she said. "He always did like to look way into the distance."

And that's where we put it. When it was set, Mama knelt beside it and ran her fingers over the engraving. "In memoriam," she read aloud. "Scott Duffield Caldwell. Gone but not forgotten."

I thought she'd cry, but she didn't. She'd never forget him, that was sure, but now she could let go of the idea he would ever be back."

"Gamma, take me!" Scotty held up his arms, and Mama scooped him up. She held him close most of the way down.

CHAPTER 16: MOVING ON

In mid-August, I was going through my clothes, trying to decide if I had anything I wanted to take with me to Hollins. But I didn't have much that I thought college girls would likely wear. I figured I could leave most of my things to Raina. What didn't fit her, she could make over. Mrs. Hathaway said she'd take me clothes shopping in Bristol the week before she drove me up to Roanoke. Mama hadn't liked the idea of me taking charity, but I reminded her it was part of the scholarship. Mrs. Hathaway had told me how she'd looked forward to helping Loniss pick out her school clothes. I figured I'd let her buy me whatever she wanted, whether it fit my taste or not. I'd go along with whatever made her happy.

I knew I would take Aint Lulie's quilt. It was part of home that I wanted to keep with me. I had already folded it up tight in my suitcase—Scott's old suitcase. It took up half the space, but that was all right. Mrs. Hathaway would likely buy me some new luggage.

And she did. On the day of our shopping trip, I rode into town with Raina, and Mrs. Hathaway picked me up at the diner. Since Raina planned to work an extra shift, she'd still be there when Mrs. Hathaway and I got back.

As she drove along, Mrs. Hathaway mentioned several stores where she wanted us to go, but I hadn't heard of any of them. This was what she wanted to do, so I'd go along with whatever she said.

I noticed the ring on Mrs. Hathaway's right hand before we'd gotten very far. It was the same ring that I had seen on Loniss's hand. I think she saw me looking at it, so I said, "That's a pretty ring. Is it your birthstone?"

"Yes," she said. "It's an opal. I was born in October."

So, she was safe. But I knew Loniss had been born in the spring.

At a store called Leggett's, Mrs. Hathaway had me try on a lot of clothes and picked out several outfits that she thought would be suitable. "Pants with flared legs are so popular now," she said. "I think three or four would be about right. But you'll also wear a lot of skirts and blouses and sweaters to class. Do you want midiskirts or miniskirts?"

I figured Loniss would likely have wanted miniskirts, but I hated to think what Mama would say if I came home in one. "Midis," I said. "I think they'll be a lot more practical."

"You're probably right," Mrs. Hathaway said. She grabbed several off a rack and handed them to me.

It took me nearly an hour to try everything on. Mrs. Hathaway convinced me that I should get at least one miniskirt, so I tried on the one she handed me. She said it was perfect for me. She also had me try on some jeans, which looked so boyish that I knew Mama would never approve of, but Mrs. Hathaway said I'd wear them more than I thought I would and bought me a couple of pair.

But we weren't finished yet. At a fancy store called Sterling House, she bought me a winter coat and a couple of sweaters. At H.P. King, she bought me some blouses and another sweater.

Then we visited more stores where she bought me pajamas, socks, underwear, and several pairs of shoes. And pantyhose, something I'd never owned before. After we'd put all the bags into the Buick, she took me to a drugstore and bought what she called toiletries. She bought me some lipstick and nail polish, too. We ate lunch at a small restaurant—the first time I'd ever eaten in one. Our last stop was when she bought me a matched set of Lady Baltimore luggage—a large suitcase, a smaller suitcase, and what she called a train case.

As we started home, I thanked her but she said she was the one who should thank me—that she'd been looking forward to this shopping trip. I knew she meant she'd been looking forward to shopping with Loniss.

When she dropped me off at the diner late that afternoon, Mrs. Hathaway said she might as well take everything with her so she could go ahead and pack and have it ready for me. That way I wouldn't have to bother. I figured that's what she'd wanted to do for Loniss, so it was okay with me. Plus, Mama wouldn't have to see my clothes and be disappointed in my choices.

About a week before the time came to go to college, Mrs. Hathaway stopped by the diner and told Raina that maybe I should come spend the night at her house so we could leave earlier instead of her having to come pick me up at home. But Raina knew that would mean I'd have to sleep in Loniss's room, and she figured I didn't want to do that. Raina told her she had the early shift that day and could drive me into town easy enough, so Mrs. Hathaway agreed that might be best.

When Raina told me about her plan to drop me off, she added, "But it'd save us some time if you closed up the cabin a day early and spent your last night here in the house."

I thought that was a pretty good idea.

"But don't close it up too tight," she added. "If it's all right with you, I'd like to spend some time at the cabin while you're gone. I could work on my sewing and canning and keep the place from going down."

I told her I'd like that.

"I'll keep the home fires burning," she said, smiling. I knew she would.

* * *

On my last morning at home, Mama got up way before daylight and had breakfast ready for Raina and me when we came downstairs. Daddy came down to breakfast early, too. Only Scotty slept late. I'd told him good-by the night before.

"You take care, now, Annie," Mama said as Raina and I were leaving. "You study hard and do right."

Unlike Polonius's farewell to Laertes, Daddy gave me only a brief bit of advice. "Be cautious," was all he said.

"Well," I said, "you better come go with us."

"Cain't," Mama and Daddy said together. But they didn't add, "You mought as well stay." They stayed at the table and didn't get up to watch us go.

The sun was just rising when Raina dropped off me and my one suitcase and a grocery bag with the quilt in front of the Hathaways' house. "Have a good time and study hard!" she yelled as she drove off.

"Keep the home fires burning!" I yelled back. Then I carried my suitcase and bag to the Buick that was in the driveway.

The Hathaways came out, followed by Precious. *Well*, the little dog said, *at last we meet*. She danced around the yard while Mr. Hathaway put my suitcase in the backseat. "The trunk is already full," he said. Then Mrs. Hathaway and I got in, and he told me that going to college was a big adventure and I should enjoy it. Then he told us good-bye and to have a good trip.

Mrs. Hathaway piloted the Buick through town, which looked like it was still asleep. The diner was open though, and Raina was probably just now putting on her apron as we passed. Before long, the town would wake up, folks would come into the diner for breakfast, and we'd be long gone.

Mrs. Hathaway and I made small talk as we traveled. She told me about how she went away to Hollins herself, and how she was so homesick for the first few weeks she thought about quitting. "But I didn't quit," she said, "and that has made all the difference in my life." She told me about working for a few years after graduation, and getting married. And having Loniss. "She was the most beautiful baby. Her head was covered in golden curls."

Then she was quiet for a while. I guess she remembered that she really wanted to make this trip with Loniss and not with me. Anyhow, she didn't say anything more about Loniss. After a while, she asked me what I wanted to do in life, and I said, "Probably teach English, like Miss Brannigan." I figured that teaching had changed a lot since Jesse Stuart's time, and I wouldn't have all the problems he'd written about in his book. "Thank you again—you and Mr. Hathaway—for making it possible for me to do this," I added. "There's no way I could be going to college without your help."

"Again, you're welcome, Annie," she said. "You know, at Hollins, students don't know which others have financial aid or scholarships and which don't."

"So I'll be just like a regular student?"

"As regular as you want to be," she said. "You can be whatever you want."

"I'm going to need a job, though. Do you know where I can get work there?"

"As a matter of fact," she said, "a job is waiting for you if you want it. Hollins has a riding program, and I arranged for you to work part-time at the stable. But only if you want to."

Seemed like Mrs. Hathaway had thought of everything. "I think I'd like that," I said.

* * *

It took us a few hours on Interstate 81 to get to the college. I'd never seen so many other cars going so fast to so many places. When we were almost there, Mrs. Hathaway asked if my ancestors were Caldwells that came from Botetourt County. I told her that some of them did.

"Botetourt County is the next county north of where you'll be living. Did you know there's a Caldwell Mountain in Botetourt County?"

I knew my ancestors had always lived in the mountains, but I didn't know a mountain was named for the Caldwells. I made up my mind that someday I'd go see that mountain.

She pointed to a mountain to our left. "That's Tinker Mountain," she said. "Before long, you'll climb that one. Hollins has a Tinker Mountain Day every fall and students climb the mountain and have a picnic on top."

"Seems like a long way up there."

"Not as far as you'd think," she said. "And the dorm where you'll live is called Tinker."

Before long, we turned off the interstate, drove a little, and turned again. Soon we turned into the college driveway. I noticed that apples trees grew on the campus, and many apples littered the ground. Seeing them made me a little sad that this was the first fall I could remember that I wouldn't be making apple butter with Aint Lulie. When I was little, she had me pick up the apples because I was so close to the ground and it was easier for me to do it. I wondered if Raina would tell Scotty the same thing.

We found my dorm and went in to register and get my key. Then we started unloading the car. Mrs. Hathaway reached for the bag on the back seat, but I told her to leave it. "That's for you," I said, "But you mustn't open it until you get home."

"Sounds mysterious," she said, grabbing the suitcase instead. It took us two more trips to get everything into my room. All around us were girls and their parents carrying stuff, too.

After we'd gotten everything unpacked, I put Aint Lulie's quilt across my bed. Mrs. Hathaway hugged me good-bye, reminded me of an orientation meeting and pointed out where it was, told me she'd let me know about getting me home for Thanksgiving, and left. I watched her get into the Buick, but I didn't watch her drive away.

While I smoothed out the quilt, I could hear Aint Lulie's words inside my head just as plain as if she was beside me: "There's them that stay and them that go."

A year ago, I'd never have taken myself for one of them that go. But times change, people change, circumstances change, roads diverge. That's the way of things, I reckon.

CHAPTER 17: NOW

The steps to my second floor office seemed to get steeper every time I climbed them. *Seven months to retirement,* I told myself. *You can do this.* I plopped the stack of essays from my two o'clock class onto my desk and eased myself into my chair. Since grading thirty essays on stereotypes and archetypes in literature isn't a particularly enjoyable task, I decided to check my email first.

I logged onto my computer and noticed a plethora of messages, most—I figured—from students wanting to know (A) when the mid-term was, (B) if they could do anything for extra credit, (C) both of the above. I'd deal with them later. I scrolled down to a message from my nephew telling me his daughter had just told him and his wife that they were going to be grandparents, and he couldn't wait to share the joy. Only two years ago I'd been to the wedding, but it seemed like yesterday. *The older you get, the faster time flies.*

A gentle rapping at my door interrupted my composing of the congratulatory message. One of my freshman Grammar & Comp students stuck her head inside. Tess, I think her name was. Or Bess. One of those. My mind isn't as sharp as it used to be. But I invited her in.

"Professor Caldwell, I have to talk to you." She perched on the sofa that sat catty-corner to my desk. "About the midterm."

Oh no, I thought. *Another sad story about how—pick one—I forgot to study, I don't understand the material, I lost my notes, I have to work that day, my grandmother died.*

"Midterm schedule's on the door. My classes are highlighted in yellow." I turned my attention to the stack of essays that needed to be graded ASAP. "Noon Friday," I added since she hadn't gotten up to look. She dropped her backpack on the floor beside her, so it looked like she intended to set a spell. "Tomorrow," I added in case she didn't realize which Friday. I really needed to get to my emails and calls. The old-fashioned answering machine on my desk blinked like crazy. And no telling how many calls had gone to voicemail on my cell.

"I know when it is," she said. "The thing is, I need to go home. I won't be back in time. My sister. . . ."

Ah, it wasn't the dead grandmother. "Is your sister ill?" I asked. Usually students stalling for time on exams had a sick mother or father. A sister was a new one "Or getting married, maybe?" While I waited for her answer, I turned my attention back to my e-mail. At least a dozen were from students who demanded my immediate attention. I really didn't have time to deal with freshman woes.

"No. I just have a bad feeling. I can't explain it." She groped in her backpack and produced a phone in a shiny pink case.

Was she going to call her sister and have me talk to her? Sheesh. "Let me take a look at your records, Bess." I closed my e-mail and logged into the VCU gradebook. "Give me a moment."

"It's Tess," she said. "Tess Garrity. In your nine o'clock class."

"Right. Tess." I accessed her records. Only one absence. Mostly Bs. "Well, you're doing OK. But missing the midterm will drop you to a D."

"Yeah, I figured. But maybe I could take it—when I get back?" For a second, I thought she said *if* instead of *when*. She held out her phone so I could see a picture. "This is my sister. Terri. She's a senior this year. In high school."

The brown-haired, dark-eyed girl in the picture wore a cheerleader's outfit. She had her arm around a Jack Russell terrier that nuzzled her ear. She looked enough like Tess to be her twin. "Nice-looking girl," I said. "Cute dog. But why do you have to go home?"

"Yeah, that's Scrap." Tess nibbled her lip. "I can't explain it, Professor Caldwell. I just feel like something's wrong. Terri hasn't texted me or called since yesterday afternoon. She won't return my texts."

"Did you email her?"

"Yeah. Nothing."

"What about your parents? Did you call them?"

"They left two days ago to go on a week-long cruise. Their 25th anniversary. They're not into smart-phones and stuff, so I don't know how to reach them."

"They left your sister alone?" I was getting an uneasy feeling.

"She's almost eighteen. She's pretty responsible. And it's only for a few days."

"Give me a minute," I said. Tess slumped farther down on the sofa and tapped at her phone. I stared at my computer screen. I had the dog's name and knew what he looked like. "Where is it you're from, Tess?"

"Western Bedford County, near the county line. We sort of live in the country."

"By any chance is your high school's homecoming this weekend?" I pulled up Google Earth on the screen while my mind connected with the little terrier.

"Yeah—uh, yes ma'am. But that's not why I need to go home."

In an instant I knew why she wanted to go home, but I kept talking to her while Scrap showed me the bruises on Teri's arms. "Your sister will be cheering, of course?"

"I guess. She's co-captain."

I don't like him, Scrap told me. *I want to bite him.*

"I see," I said to Tess. "And you can't tell me anything specific about this feeling you have?"

For an instant, I saw something in her eyes. A knowingness, maybe? Then she looked away. "It's just a feeling," she said. "A dark feeling. I guess you think I'm crazy or something?"

"No," I said. "Not at all. Sometimes we have to go with our feelings." Then I had a feeling myself. "Let me see your sister's picture again."

This time she showed me a different one—her sister and a boy leaning on the hood of a jeep. The Jack Russell was in the picture, too, sitting beside the jeep's bumper and glaring at the boy. *Listen to me,* I could hear the dog telling me. I noticed the three letters of Jeep's license plate—*AWD.* I couldn't quite make out the numbers. *He's up to no good.*

"I called her school this morning," she said. "They said she'd emailed them last night that she was sick and wouldn't be in. But if she was sick, she would have told me. She'd answer her phone."

"What about her friends? Could they check on her?" I studied the picture, trying to memorize the details.

"We live in kind of a remote area. Her friends don't live close. But I called her best friend. The last time she heard anything was in school yesterday."

I handed her back the phone. "You can make up your mid-term on Tuesday at 8:00 a.m. Will that work?"

"Thanks, Professor Caldwell," she said. "That'll work." She picked up her backpack and headed out.

She's not sick, Scrap told me. *She's up in her room with him. They closed me out. But I took his keys from his coat pocket and ran out my dog door and buried them beside the porch.*

"Wait," I said. "Is the boy in this picture her boyfriend?"

Tess shrugged. "They've gone out a few times. He just moved into the county last month."

"Did you check if he was in school today?"

"He doesn't go to school. He's older. I think he works on a construction crew, but I don't know which one."

Listen to me! Scrap said. *He's bad. I want to bite him!*

An uneasy feeling crept over me. "Tell you what, Tess, make sure you keep your eye on your sister at the game tonight—if she feels well enough to cheer." I could see the puzzlement in Tess's eyes. I wanted to tell her why, I wanted to tell her what I knew and how I knew it, but I couldn't. At least not yet. She probably wouldn't believe me anyhow. "It's just a feeling I have," I added.

The look in her eye flashed again. Did she have the gift, too?

"I'll do it," she said. "I just hope she's okay."

"I do too."

From my window, I saw her hurry down Franklin Street. For a moment, I watched the gold and red leaves swirling over the cobblestones. But I had work I needed to do, papers to grade, calls to answer, miles to go before I slept. *An underage girl. An older guy.*

I phoned a buddy at the state police. After I'd told him my worries, given a description of the jeep and its partial license number, and told him the address, he said he'd notify someone in that district to drive out and check on the matter.

"How did you know this girl might be in trouble?" he asked.

"A little dog told me," I said.

-THE END-

ACKNOWLEDGEMENTS

Lots of folks helped me with *Them That Go*! Without their encouragement, input, and critiques, this book would have never happened. Here are a few to whom I owe special thanks:

- My FaceBook friends who offered help and guidance when I asked for information about what things were called, whether something worked or not, etc.
- Members of Botetourt County Virginia Genealogy group on FaceBook who offered helpful information.
- Appalachian author Sharyn McCrumb and Ferrum College Professor Tina Hanlon, who both suggested I use the Greenbrier ghost story.
- Sally Roseveare for Beta-reading, proof-reading, and editorial input.
- Eduardo Mitchell for cover design.
- Dorothy Hemenway Carter for invaluable editorial suggestions.
- Ibby Greer, Theresa Hartman, and Susie Reeser for Beta-reading parts of the work-in-progress and offering me input.
- Members of Lake Writers (my writing group) for numerous critiques and helpful suggestions.
- Karen Wrigley and Ginny Brock, two Lake Writers with "gifts."
- Chuck Lumpkin (president of Lake Writers) and Tom Howell for formatting advice and back cover assistance.

ABOUT THE AUTHOR

Becky Mushko is a three-time winner of the Sherwood Anderson Short Story Contest and a five-time winner of the Lonesome Pine Short Story Contest. Her work appears in in *A Cup of Comfort for Writers*, Vols. II & III of *Anthology of Appalachian Writers, It Was a Dark and Stormy Night, Voices From Smith Mountain Lake,* and many other publications.

Website: http://www.beckymushko.com
Blog: http://pevishpen.blogspot.com